Herne Bay Howlers

Steve Higgs

To Hermione Rose, my six-week-old daughter, who did her best to co-author this book by yelling at me for milk every time I tried to type. I was unable to translate her scornful looks and ear-splitting bleats, yet had I been able to do so, I have no doubt her social commentary would have added depths to the book which I could never manage with the viewpoint of someone her age.

Contents

Kraven Says. Friday, December 16th 1027hrs

I GOT THE CALL yesterday morning, but it took me twenty-fours hours to get to their house. The delay came about due to other work, a case I was working with Amanda Harper, my business partner and girlfriend.

My name is Tempest Michaels, I own and run a private investigation business which specialises in cases with a strange, unexplained, or paranormal element. You might think the number of cases available might be limited, but you would be wrong.

Very wrong.

Arriving in a career as a paranormal P.I. did not occur through choice, but as the result of poor luck. I have friends who call it fate or destiny though I believe in neither thing. It is true though that the success I enjoy through the paranormal speciality might not have been mine were my cases a little more ... vanilla.

I don't believe in the paranormal. Not one bit, so each case is approached with the same expectation that an ordinary criminal, or someone with ill-conceived intent, is behind the strangeness I am called upon to investigate.

Today was no different. The call yesterday morning came from Harry Burke, a postman living in Cranbrook with his wife Agatha and fourteen-year-old daughter Paige. He was fraught with concern, his tone, like so many of my clients, bordering on desperate when he called me and begged for my help.

As I parked my car and let my two dachshunds plop out and onto the pavement, I thought again about the precarious line I walk with my trade. I know with unshakeable conviction that all my clients are deluded. They approach me to solve mysteries that have obvious answers, or crimes which have ordinary explanations. The Burkes' case would be no different. However, the issue is that I often feel like I am taking money under false pretences. I know they have fooled themselves into thinking something supernatural is happening when, in fact, it isn't and sometimes, they genuinely do need rescuing. Not from a poltergeist, or monster, but from a person who has chosen to target them. Rescuing people from a crime is rare though. More normally, I have to politely point out that they are stupid, and it made me feel bad when they then paid me.

'Come along, chaps,' I coaxed, and tugged their lead to guide them in the direction of Mr Burke's garden path. As I passed the car on their driveway, I noted the scratches and dents all along the side facing me. The paintwork was ruined, but not as the result of a crash or collision, someone had attacked it.

Mr Burke has been suffering a series of hard luck events, or so he originally thought. There were several small fires, including his garden shed which burnt to the ground with his tools, bicycle, and secret stash of naughty magazines inside. He also had a pipe burst inexplicably, the cat got shaved, and then there was the damage to his car.

He'd called the police, but there wasn't much for them to investigate. On the face of it, someone was playing tricks on him or waging an annoying hate campaign. Or so he first thought.

Unable to explain what was happening, he asked his daughter if she knew about it. Typically for a teenager, she denied all knowledge but then the couple awoke in the early hours of the next morning to find her standing at the foot of their bed with a kitchen knife.

They were a little freaked out.

The incident with the knife was last night and he called me at 0900hrs when business hours started because Paige claimed to be receiving messages that told her what to do. All the evil acts had been perpetrated by her, which meant Mr Burke no longer wanted the police involved. And he called me specifically because Paige said the messages came from hell.

As so often happened, the front door of their house swung open before I could get to it. Not in a spooky, the-house-knows-you're-coming-and-plans-to-eat-you-way, but because Mrs Burke had been watching for me from her living room window.

She looked to be fretting.

'Mrs Burke?' I asked, extending my hand.

'Thank you for coming so swiftly, Mr Michaels. I'm Agatha,' she sobbed as she took my hand. 'Paige is in her room and refusing to come out. She knows we hired you. Do you think she is possessed?'

Mr Burke appeared at the end of the hallway that led around their stairs. I noticed his right hand was bandaged and greeted him verbally without offering a handshake. The Burkes lived in a small semi-detached place on the outskirts of the small town. The carpets, décor, and general condition of the house, built probably circa 1930, was above average. However, in stark contrast to the couple's style the hallway wallpaper to my right bore a large crayon drawing of a severed head dripping blood. It hung from the hand of a beast with yellow eyes.

Mr Burke saw me looking at it as he approached. 'This is new,' he explained. 'We woke up to it this morning.' He put a comforting arm around his wife's shoulders.

'Is this Paige's work?' I sought to confirm. I had a good idea what was going on but no idea why.

They both nodded, Mr Burke sounding sad when he said, 'She's so emotionless about it all. She just says it isn't her and that she knows she is doing it but cannot stop herself or Kraven will get her when she sleeps.'

3

'Kraven?'

'That's what she calls it. Did I not mention that?'

With a shake of my head, I said, 'No. Do you know who or what Kraven is?' by my feet the dogs were fussing. I have two miniature dachshunds, Bull and Dozer. They are brothers, though not litter mates, and have been with me for several years. I take them most places I go, unless it is going to be dangerous or I feel it likely I will need to employ stealth – they don't do stealth.

'Kraven is the being who has invaded one of her toys. It's a pink bear plushy that she's had since birth,' Mrs Burke explained. 'It used to be called Mr Huggins and it's supposed to talk,' she added. 'But it used to say, "I love you, Paige," and, "A hug is like a warm blanket from your best friend," plus other saccharine phrases. It broke five years ago, but she refused to let us throw it out or buy her a new one. Now it talks to her again, but with a different voice.'

I felt my right eyebrow twitch involuntarily. 'You've heard it?'

'Oh, lord, yes,' Mrs Burke replied, her voice betraying a sense of fear. 'It was awful. It's like a monster inhabits that little bear. Its eyes glow a dark red like the pits of hell and when it talks, it knows who it is talking to. It said my name,' she croaked, still horrified by the experience.

'Mine too,' admitted Mr Burke. 'It said if I tried to separate Paige and Kraven I would choke to death on my tea. I haven't been able to drink a cup since.'

It wasn't what I expected to hear, but it changed my theory not one little bit. 'Can you show me the other damage?'

With a wordless nod, Mr Burke led me back through the house and into their garden. 'I take it you saw my car in the street when you pulled up?' he asked as we walked.

'I glanced at it. When did the damage happen?'

'About a week ago,' he replied. 'It was one of the first *events*.' Whether deliberate or not, when he said the word 'events' he added a chilling tone to his voice. I noticed his wife shudder.

In the garden next door, their neighbour, a man in his fifties with pot belly and ill-fitting trousers, eyed them suspiciously.

'That's our neighbour, Mr Greys. His fish all died two nights ago. He says someone put bleach in his pond. We haven't asked Paige about that one yet, but I expect it was her.'

A charred pile in the corner, with several blackened shrubs around it, was the remains of the garden shed. They'd called the fire brigade but by the time they could get water onto it, there was nothing left to save.

'Is that how you injured your hand?' I asked, inclining my head toward the bandaged digits.

He smiled ruefully. 'Sort of. I didn't burn it trying to save my belongings if that is what you are asking. I ran to turn on the garden hose.'

'There was superglue all over the tap,' his wife explained. 'He couldn't get his hand free and when he tried to yank it away, he left his palm stuck to the handle.'

I had to grimace at the mental image, but also nod a salute of acknowledgement to the devious mind behind this spate of attacks. Set a fire and then booby trap the obvious garden tap – ingenious.

Sucking in a breath, I let it go slowly through my nose. The couple were looking at me expectantly. 'I think I ought to meet Paige.'

'She's in her room,' replied Mrs Burke. 'She won't come out and won't open the door.'

'Are you bothered if I force entry?'

Their eyes widened. 'Like break down the door?' Mr Burke asked, his voice almost a whisper as if we were talking about doing something illegal.

I frowned. 'Yes, Mr Burke. Most interior household doors are lightweight and very easily outwitted. They are also cheap, and likely to break before the frame which might require a carpenter to repair.' I was either going to kick the door in or go home. It was their choice.

Reluctantly, surprisingly so, in fact, they agreed that it was time to address the issue of the evil pink plushy bear toy. As we walked back to the house, I hit them with a few more questions: Had there been any trouble at school? Has she fallen out with her best friend or friends? Had they recently instigated any new rules?

I got it on the third attempt.

'Paige.' I knocked politely on her bedroom door. Thrash metal played on the other side at a volume one might expect of a deaf person or, since it was thrash metal, a person hoping to soon be dead. 'Paige, my name is Tempest Michaels. I'm a paranormal investigator here to deal with Kraven. Can you let me in please?'

Despite the deafening volume of the music, it increased in response to my question.

I knocked again and tried again and added that I would have to force entry if she didn't let me in.

'I think he means it sweetie,' shouted her mother in a soothing tone.

The response from Paige, verbal this time, was short, terse, and filled with the kind of language one might expect to hear in a dockworkers' bar.

I tested the door handle to make sure it wasn't open, then handed the dogs' lead to Mrs Burke. 'Could you hold the chaps for a moment, please?' I didn't wait for a reply. The moment her hand opened, her response automatic as I thrust the canvass strap in her direction, I swivelled from my left foot and drove out with my right. I wasn't wearing the right shoes for the job; leather oxford brogues because my army boots would not go with my casual outfit, but they did the trick, nevertheless.

My foot struck the door just beneath the lock, shattering the thin sheet particle board as it went right through. The impact jarred my leg and I got a small splinter in my ankle, but the door exploded inward leaving the lock mechanism in place for a second. Then it fell to the carpet with a clunk.

A surprised squeal of alarm came from within the room as the door slammed open but was cut off quickly as Paige remembered she was supposed to be in league with an evil toy. I strode into her bedroom with purpose, looked around for the device playing the music and yanked the power supply from it. Speakers might be wireless these days, but they still need electricity to work.

Immediately, the music switched to her phone which had been sending the music to her wireless device. In her pocket the noise came out tinny and quiet. I elected to ignore it, choosing instead to stare down at the moody-faced teenage girl.

'You have desecrated Kraven's sanctuary,' she growled in a deep voice. Paige Burke was really into the role she'd chosen. That was my first impression. She wore a pinafore dress and knee-high socks but the sock on her right leg had been allowed to slump down and it had several holes in it. Her face and hands were dirty, and her hair was a mess, hanging unkempt as if viciously backcombed. It partially covered her face where the girl employed makeup to make her eyes look sunken and dark.

I could understand how her appearance and behaviour were freaking her parents out. This was all new to them. For me it was just Friday.

'Is that Kraven?' I asked. From her left hand hung a pink bear. She held it by one paw, the smiley-faced animal dangling limply. 'I am here to commune with him.'

Nothing about her changed when I spoke. She didn't move, her eyes didn't even twitch. Until they did. A devilish smile parted her lips and her eyes twitched to look at her mother. Mrs Burke, peering around the doorframe to see her daughter, gasped when her evil-looking child made eye contact. The parents were half the problem in my opinion. Their reaction fuelled the girl's ridiculous act and made her want to do it all the more.

'Kraven will speak with you now,' Paige announced in a twisted sing-song voice.

I was about to speak myself when a dread voice emanated from the pink teddy. 'Who dares to desecrate my sanctuary?' the bear asked, its eyes flashing red each time it spoke. The voice was that of a man; a man with a very deep voice but hinting at the edges was a gravelly quality. As background to the voice were the sounds of beings in torment, wailing in the background as presumably they were tortured in hell.

Playing my part and trying to supress my smile as I dissected the voice, I replied, 'Tempest Michaels dares. I have come to cast you out, Kraven.

Kraven the pink teddy bear laughed in response to my statement, a deep booming roar of belly laughs that went on a little too long. I waited patiently for them to end, casting my eyes around the room in a search for something very specific.

Still on the right side of forty, my experience of teenage girls' bedrooms was nevertheless a long way behind me, but I figured the habits of teenagers were relatively universal and timeless. I spotted what I was looking for hanging over the back of a computer chair. Feeling no need to be polite or ask permission, I invaded the young girl's privacy by picking up what I took to be her school backpack.

My actions drew the first emotional response from her, as she said, 'Hey! That's mine. You can't touch that!'

With a ziiiip noise, the backpack was open. Upending it over her bed spilled the contents.

Paige yelled, 'Kraven, he is messing with my stuff!'

Once again, the deep, demented voice echoed out from the pink bear. 'You will suffer, Tempest Michaels. For your sins you will endure a plague of boils! Your life will be nothing but misery. Be gone from this place and leave my servant.'

'Why did you pick the name Kraven?' I asked conversationally as I picked through Paige's belongings. 'It's not a name I am familiar with. Is it from a game? I'm not much of a gamer myself. Or maybe you are better educated than I give you credit for and did some research to come up with the name,' I added, wondering if it came from a book. I could ask Frank, my local occult expert later. 'Either way, I think I'll use your real name ... Kyle.'

I let the name hang in the air for a moment, waiting to see whether it would be the person inside the bear or Paige who spoke first.

It was neither.

'Who's Kyle?' asked Mrs Burke.

Paige's cheeks flushed.

I pressed onward. Speaking to Kraven, I said, 'Hey, I'm just guessing that it's Kyle doing the voice of Kraven because that's the name all over her schoolbooks with pretty hearts drawn around it. Paige for Kyle; that sort of thing.'

Kraven broke first. 'You said you were finished with Kyle.' It was still the booming deep voice but now it sounded whiney and upset, the demonic edge forgotten for a moment.

'What going on?' asked Mrs Burke.

I held up a finger to beg a moment's grace, then quicker than the pouty teenage girl could react, I snatched Kraven from her hand and tore its head off.

A phone dropped out, one of the cheap ones a person can buy for a tenner anywhere.

Paige screamed in horror. 'Mr Huggins!'

White fluff tumbled to the carpet as I dug inside the head to get to the LEDs someone had installed. Ignoring the angry teenager trying to retrieve the phone from my hand, I turned around to show her parents. 'Someone took Mr Huggins apart and gave him some upgrades.'

There were tears running down Paige's face, but she was going on the offensive, rounding on her parents as they stared at her in disbelief. 'This is all your fault! You drove me to do this.'

'H – hello?' said Kraven.

I still had the phone in my hand. Lifting it to my face, I considered what I wanted to say. 'Would you like to give me your real name?'

After a beat of silence, which was only silence at his end; at my end it was bedlam as the angst-ridden teenager railed at her parents for cruel and unnecessary behaviour, Kraven said, 'Um, no. I don't think I should do that.'

I drew in a breath. I could just about remember being a horny teenage boy and getting suckered into doing things because a girl asked me to. Despite my feelings of empathy, the Burkes hired me to expose the truth behind their mystery so I pressed on. 'Young man, I'm afraid I'm going to have to insist. And here's the reason you should. If you don't, I'll just come and find you. How hard will it be for me? You'll be the one in her class looking guilty tomorrow when I turn up at the school. Would you rather avoid meeting me?'

'Daniel,' he blurted. 'It's Daniel Bennett. I didn't know she was going to start setting fires. She said she'd go to the Christmas dance with me if I helped her.'

Barely able to hear him with the ruckus going on four feet from me, I gave him a few words of advice, let him know he was being used and ended the call.

Paige was most certainly not the first teenage girl ever to revolt against her parents' strictures. When I asked earlier about trouble at school or any new rules, they told me she had a new boyfriend and wanted to be out later than they would allow. I didn't ask the name, I didn't need that information, and I knew all about it now because the tear-soaked girl was screaming her displeasure at the top of her lungs.

She ignored their instructions, came home after midnight and they stopped her going out the next day. That was more than a month ago, the young man, Kyle, was older and had less strict parents, I guess, but he dumped her to date a girl who could stay out late. Or had bigger boobs perhaps; young love was a fickle thing.

Whatever the case, I felt certain of two things: 1. Kraven was gone for good. 2. Paige was grounded until she turned thirty.

It took a few moments to get someone's attention because I was attempting to be polite. When finally, Mr and Mrs Burke stopped shouting at their daughter, I said, 'I believe we can close the case, yes?'

Mrs Burke had a vein visibly throbbing next to her temple and Mr Burke was red in the face, possibly from counting the cost to repair the damage wrought by his daughter.

'How did you know it was a boy's voice coming from Mr Huggins?' he asked.

I tilted my head in question and frowned when I asked a question in return, 'What made you think your daughter possessed an evil toy?' It was a rhetorical question; I didn't want to hear the answer. I met people every day who, for whatever reason, have convinced themselves a non-rational explanation is the one that fits. 'Did you notice that Kraven had a local accent?' I asked before he could attempt to answer.

His mouth opened and closed like a fish. 'No, I didn't notice that.'

I flipped my eyebrows and shot my cuff to check my watch: 1053hrs. 'I'll let myself out. My accountant will send over a final invoice before the end of the week.' Or I would probably do it myself, I thought, because the person who had been doing the accountancy work was now solving cases instead.

I collected Bull and Dozer from Mrs Burke. I'd thought they might come in handy; that was why I'd taken them with me and all the way up to her room. Cute sausage dogs who roll pathetically onto their backs at the first sign of any attention coming their way, are always a hit regardless of age, gender, or sexual orientation. Had I needed to win Paige over, they might have proved useful.

In the end, they were unnecessary, but I liked to take them places with me; it meant I never had to wonder where they were or if they were alright.

'Case solved before lunch,' I commented as I made my way back to the car. 'I think that calls for a treat, dogs. Don't you agree?'

I got no answer, of course, but vowed to stop off for some treats to put in the office. It wasn't something I did very often, but I felt buoyant and positive this morning. Little did I know the drama awaiting me.

Wolf Attack. Friday, December 16th 1147hrs

MY OFFICE SITS TOWARD the bridge end of Rochester High Street where it has an enviable amount of trade walking by it. I augment that by advertising in local magazines and newspapers with the combination delivering enough business to keep three detectives busy. Mostly we work our own cases, though sometimes it is necessary to draw in one or more of us to focus on a singular investigation. There can be many reasons for this but the usual two are that it looks likely to result in a violent altercation or there is a high bounty for reaching a solution.

We actively avoid the former and constantly seek the latter.

Rochester High Street is a wondrous place with quaint little shops which have stood for centuries. The businesses inside them may have changed many times over the years, but a few boasted signs to say established in 17somethingor other. One or two were even earlier than that.

Mr. Morello's Royal Cake Shoppe was at the Chatham end of Rochester High Street where it was sandwiched between a butcher's shop and a pub. The row of buildings was a later addition to the buildings nearer to the castle and cathedral which sat at opposite ends of the long, straight, cobbled road, but they were still more than two hundred years old.

I hadn't been in the confectioner's shop for years; sweet treats just didn't have a place in my diet. Telling myself I could relax for a day, I strode in to inspect their cabinet of cakes. Two minutes later, with my wallet twenty pounds lighter,

I left the shop holding a box of filled donuts. They were expensive, but also hand-crafted and unique: If one is going to buy a treat, one should indulge.

The box was getting a lot of attention from the dachshunds who could smell the sugar inside. I'd parked the car behind the office in my usual spot – the office had three reserved parking spaces – and walked along the High Street to the cake shop. This close to Christmas, the picturesque central business area of the town was filled with the smells of street sellers hawking bags of hot chestnuts or roast pork sandwiches. I counted no fewer than five mulled wine outlets and the mile-long street had been decorated elegantly to reflect the traditions of the season.

Walking back through it and soaking in the sights and sounds made me smile. I felt warm inside, buoyed by my relationship with Amanda and aware that, due to my flourishing business, I had no financial worries which meant I rarely worried about anything. The beautiful blonde woman who chose to lavish me with her affections did, however, present one minor hurdle – what to buy her for Christmas.

We were spending it together at my house. My parents were travelling to my sister's place in Hampshire on Christmas Eve where there were grandchildren to enjoy. My mother was kind enough to accentuate her reason for going in front of Amanda as if the mere mention of grandchildren would make her ovulate. Amanda's mother was on a cruise around the world so neither of us had people we needed to be with. I was invited to also join my sister and her husband at their house; it would be a big family feast, but a quick discussion regarding Amanda's plans led to our decision to spend it together. Honestly, it was a lot more enticing than being uncle Tempest the ride-on horse for the day.

She and I had only been dating for a few weeks, but I was smitten; I could admit that to myself, but it took me back to the question of what would make an appropriate gift at this time of year? I passed jewellers and a lingerie shop, a florist, and a confectioner selling imported pralines from Belgium. Items from any or all of these might be appropriate, but what would be considered over the top and what might make me look cheap?

It made my head hurt.

My musings took me all the way back to the office, where I shouldered my way through the front door with thoughts of hot, dark coffee on my mind.

I walked into a stand-off.

There were two men in their late thirties ten feet in front of me. Each was broad shouldered with scruffy, short hair; however the standout feature was their matching leather jackets with matching motifs. They were part of a biker gang, which didn't make them bad people. Their actions, however, did.

They had their backs to me and were faced by both Amanda and Jane, who looked nervous enough to put me on immediate high alert. I needed less than a second to assess the situation and only the rest of the same second to reach a decision.

I dropped the dogs' lead, threw the box of donuts onto the reception counter, and as my actions drew their attention, I stepped into their personal space.

I didn't want a fight inside my office, but it wouldn't be the first time I didn't get what I wanted. I was going to have one shot at defusing whatever situation I'd walked into. After that, these men were leaving by force.

'Good morning, gentlemen. What seems to be the problem?' The words came out through teeth that were very nearly clenched as I did my best to make my posture seem relaxed.

Amanda answered, 'They wish to hire you, Tempest.'

I narrowed my eyes, never taking them from the two men's faces. 'Is that a problem?'

'Apparently so,' growled the man to my left. He had a three-day stubble and a thin line of scar tissue running along the left side of his face from his chin to his ear. 'According to miss Sugar Tits here,' I didn't need to see Amanda's face to know that she just cracked her knuckles at his comment, 'we are known criminals.'

'Yeah,' said his partner. 'Neither Bear, nor I have ever been convicted of a crime. She besmirches our good character.' He managed to sound forthright and wounded though I barely noticed it because I was still wondering about his name.

'Indeed,' complained Bear. 'We find ourselves eternally stereotyped because of our clothing choices and preferred mode of transport.'

Amanda snapped, 'I arrested you twice myself, Bear Knox. Once for possession of a firearm. You only got off because you had a good lawyer and the weapon had been wiped clean of your fingerprints.'

'That's slander!' he protested. 'You have no proof my fingerprints were ever on it.'

'A fine example of the discrimination we suffer daily at the hand of bigots,' added Bear's colleague.

Amanda's eyes flared but he had her; there could be no proof his fingerprints were ever on the weapon. They were not being overtly threatening, so I pushed forward, hoping we could soon wrap this up and get them out of our office.

'Then tell me, gentlemen, what is it I can do for you today?'

They glanced inward toward each other in confusion as if I ought to already know the answer to my own question. 'We wish to hire you?' said Bear.

Oh, yes. Amanda already told me that.

I invited them to join me in my private office at the rear of the building. There were two of them, one each for Amanda and me, though we were now working out how to share two between three detectives. If Jane was going to take on cases of her own, then she deserved equal treatment.

Closing the door defused the situation between the men and my ex-police girlfriend, Amanda. I would get a full blow-by-blow account from her later, but for now, it felt right to indulge their request, listen to their story, and then kick them to the kerb.

The two men were called Bear Knox and Ellis Jarrett, though their club names; the ones they wished to be known by, were Bear and Elk. I got the impression all the club members would have animal names like it was the boy scouts or something. They matched each other in height, haircut, facial hair, and clothing. Beneath their faded brown leather jackets, each wore a grubby white t-shirt, dark denim jeans and black leather boots of a style I thought of as biker boots. They were both full members of the Whitstable Riders' Motorcycle Club.

When I asked what they did for a living, Elk said, 'Various entrepreneurial enterprises.' It was deliberately vague and supported Amanda's claim that they were criminals.

I repeated my question from earlier, 'What can I do for you, gentlemen?'

'We need to hire you,' said Bear for the third time.

'More specifically,' I begged. 'I assume you have a case for me to investigate.'

Elk shifted in his chair, the leather of his jacket squeaking against the leather of the chair in the quiet of my office. It was Bear who replied. 'Two of our club members were murdered,' he announced.

Murder in Kent is rare enough that it tends to make the news, yet I'd heard nothing about two men being killed.

Seeing my frown, Elk added. 'Their deaths were listed as animal attacks. That's why you haven't heard about it.'

His comment connected the dots in my head. There had been a small article in the local newspaper last week. Two men were found partially eaten in woodland close to the coastal town of Whitstable. I couldn't recall anything else about it.

'So, you want me to find out what happened to them?' I enquired. 'You believe they were murdered?'

Both men stared at me, their eyes hard. 'We know they were murdered,' said Elk.

'And we know who did it,' supplied Bear.

'But we have no evidence,' cut in Elk again.

'And we want you to find it,' finished Bear.

I met their eyes as I considered their claim. It caused several questions. I led with, 'Tell me who did it.'

'The Herne Bay Howlers.'

The answer came from Elk, the men taking it in turns to speak as if it had been agreed in advance. I didn't know who the Herne Bay Howlers were but guessed correctly that it was a rival biker gang.

'Motorcycle club,' Bear corrected me. 'We are not a gang. The term gang is synonymous with illegal activity and carries unwarranted negative connotations.'

I had to admit the two men spoke more eloquently than I expected: their range of vocabulary far beyond the average person. It meant they were educated, but that, if they were engaged in criminal activity, just made them more dangerous.'

'This sounds like a case for the police,' I stated to see how they would react. Had they avoided the police because they didn't want the authorities looking at their activities?

Elk nodded. 'As we already expressed, Mr Michaels, the coroner recorded the deaths as animal attacks. The police have nothing to investigate.'

It was a fair point. 'What makes you think they were murdered?'

Bear leaned forward to get his face closer to mine. 'We know they were murdered. The Herne Bay Howlers have been taunting us. They are using terror tactics to scare our members into leaving and our president believes they are trying to move into our turf to take over our operations.

'What operations?' I pressed them again.

'Various entrepreneurial enterprises,' Elk repeated, his voice emotionless. I would have to find out for myself if I chose to take their case. I still couldn't see where I came in.

Finally, Bear stopped beating around the bush and explained why they chose to single me out for their case. 'The Howlers are werewolves, Mr Michaels, and the animal attacks are exactly that. We have seen them in their transformed state.'

As was their habit, Elk took over. 'Our ability to defend ourselves against werewolves is limited. We are currently seeking a supply of silver bullets, but we cannot predict where and when they might attack.'

'At night seems obvious,' added Bear. 'However, we do not know how much of our supposed knowledge about werewolves comes from fiction and how much is accurate. That is why we approach you today. Will you help us, Mr Michaels?'

'We may be a little rough around the edges, but the men who were killed were our friends. We want justice for them, and security for ourselves.' His final point delivered, Elk sat back into his chair. Both men watched me to see what I might say.

On the face of it, this case was right up my alley. A gang of bikers posing as werewolves to augment the fear factor as they attempt a hostile takeover? Just my cup of tea. Maybe they did murder the two men, it felt plausible, but why then would the coroner state it was an animal attack? I would have to look into it. Bear and Elk were asking me to investigate a double homicide and offering to pay me for it. Why would I want to say no? In my head, the answer floated back instantly: because they are most likely criminals and their various entrepreneurial enterprises could be anything from drug smuggling to prostitution and everything in between.

Should I take the case or not? That was the question.

As the silence stretched on, I rapped my knuckles on the desk and made a snap decision. 'Ok, chaps. I'm willing to perform a preliminary investigation.' I met their eyes, first Elk and then Bear. 'I want you to know that I will not associate myself with criminal activity. If I get the sense that your ... enterprises,' I used their word, 'might cause my business embarrassment, I will walk away. Is that understood? If I see anything I don't like, I'll bail.'

'Understood,' said Elk.

That appeared to be all they had to say on the subject. I let go of a breath I didn't know I was holding and pushed back my chair. 'We need to discuss fees.' I was going to walk them through my usual explanation of charges and expenses but with an additional tariff added on because I still wasn't entirely convinced taking the case was a good idea.

Before I could get into it, Bear took a fat white envelope from the inside pocket of his leather jacket. 'This should get you started,' he said, placing the envelope on the desk. 'That's ten grand.'

I looked at the envelope. That much cash suggested they operated a cash business, doing deals under the table and claiming none of it to the tax man. There was nothing illegal about me taking their money, provided I filed my tax assessment correctly. That did not, however, make it all above board. I was making assumptions about them that were yet to be proven true. They complained that the world possessed and employed a bigoted view of them; refusing to take their money would be the same thing. I picked it up. 'I'll get you a receipt.'

Bear said, 'There's no need. We are more interested in stopping the Howlers than we are in the money. The cash is yours if you can solve the case.'

His statement made my right eyebrow raise. It was a large amount of money for one case. What if I solved it in a day? I started the business because I had bills to pay like everyone else, but the days of trying to make ends meet were far behind me. I could refuse this case and never think twice about the wad of cash in the envelope. However, the case was intriguing me, and I wanted to see what would motivate them to just hand over such a large sum.

Bear asked, 'How soon can you start?'

I stood up to shake their hands as gentlemen should. 'Straight away. I need an address from you, and I need some details about the Herne Bay Howlers.' Actually, I needed a lot of detail since they claimed to be certain the accused were werewolves; something had to have caused their certainty. 'I will come to you later today.'

They gave me their address, complete with postcode. It was the name of a business, a car repair place by the sound of it. There being nothing left to do at this juncture, I opened my office door and led them to the front of the building.

I'd left Bull and Dozer roaming free in the main part of the office, which was never a good thing to do as they tended to attack people when they came in. Not actually attack, you understand, but bark at them menacingly the way a small dog does. They were not visible, and neither was Amanda. Her office door was closed, so I drew a simple conclusion and, when Elk and Bear were gone, I knocked on her door.

A Difference of Opinion. Friday, December 16th 1212hrs

DOZER AND BULL BOTH barked the second my knuckles touched the wood of her door. I knew they would and had listened for a second to make sure she wasn't on a call. I opened it and went in as the two sausage shaped idiots climbed over each other to get out.

'How did they take the rejection?' she asked, not looking up from her computer screen.

I felt my forehead crease. 'I took the case.'

Amanda's head and eyes whipped around so fast I thought her eyeballs might rattle in their sockets. 'You have to be joking.'

'Um, no,' I replied, feeling that the ground beneath my feet might not be as stable as I believed. 'I considered it, but they have a legitimate case ...'

'They are criminals, Tempest!' Amanda snapped. It was the first time she had spoken to me harshly or raised her voice since we started dating. 'You cannot represent them or be associated with them. It will damage the business.'

She looked genuinely upset. Trying to placate her, I said. 'I believe you over-state the case. They want me to investigate a double murder which they are convinced was perpetrated by a rival gang. I committed only to a preliminary investigation.'

'Oh, cut the crap, Tempest. We both know you'll see it through to the end. Once you get a sniff of a mystery, you're like a dog going after a rabbit: nothing will sway your course.' Amanda was still sitting in her chair, but it felt like she was in my face all the same.

Folding my arms as I scrutinised her features and posture, I asked, 'What is it, Amanda? Why do these guys bother you so much?'

'They don't,' she argued irritably. 'Your decision to take their filthy criminal money does. This is a bad call, Tempest. I think you should call them and say you have reconsidered.'

I couldn't stop my frown from forming. This wasn't what we did. There were three of us at the business and we each took our own cases from the pile that came in. Sometimes we discussed who might be best suited to take a particular case, but I never enforced my will. As owner/establisher of the firm, I had every right to run it as I saw fit, but it wasn't in my nature to impose hard rules. This was out of character for Amanda and it was beginning to feel like we were having our first fight.

When I said nothing, she glared at me. 'Are you going to?'

'Ditch the case? No,' I replied, doing my best to keep my tone even. 'I'm going to look into it and I'm going to start as soon as I have had some lunch. Can I get you anything?'

I got a stern, 'No, thank you,' from her, which was followed by a, 'Please close the door on your way out.' When I took a step back.

Flustered by her response, but refusing to let it show, I gathered my things, clipped the dogs back onto their lead, and went out the back door to get to my car. Just like that, all my Christmas cheer and visions of Christmas Day spent intertwined watching old movies in our pyjamas went up in smoke.

I would talk to her later when she calmed down, but I couldn't deny my anger at being snapped at. Pushing it to one side, I made a plan for the afternoon and got started.

How was I to know she couldn't have been more right? I should have ditched the case and stayed at home.

Coroner's Office. Friday, December 16th 1407hrs

I TOOK THE DOGS home and grabbed lunch while I was there. I have a four-bedroom detached house in the nearby village of Finchampstead. It is bigger than I need, but smaller than I can afford, and I like not only the quiet location, but also the easy access to nearby towns and cities via the motorways which run nearby. I bought the house when I was still in the army. I had a plan to leave the service and that lifestyle and needed a place to be mine – I wasn't moving back in with my parents, that was for certain.

I had friends here too. An old school friend call Jagjit lived ... actually, I had been about to say he lived in the village with his parents, but he'd just moved out and into a new place with his wife. They'd met and married in a whirlwind romance just a few weeks ago. Despite the swiftness of their nuptials, they were well-suited to each other.

Then there was Big Ben. Benjamin Winters stands six feet seven inches tall and due to a terrible accident, which killed both his parents a few years ago, he lives the lifestyle of a rich person. He works for me as hired muscle semi-regularly because he gets to thump people. Big Ben is what many would call a force of nature. His main goal in life is to get women naked. As many of them as possible, as often as possible and getting several of them naked at the same time, while a feat most of us only fantasise about, is a weekly occurrence for him. How he achieves this remains something of a mystery to me, but he is gifted with a Hollywood smile and body most men would kill for.

Given that it is Friday today, I would see both men at the pub tonight. It was a regular Friday night fixed point in the diary and one I looked forward to. Joining us would be Hilary, whose real name was Brian Clinton. Until Jagjit's wedding, he'd been the sole married in the group and the one who stood as a template for why men shouldn't marry according to Big Ben. I had to admit, Hilary tended to look and act morose. However, a near-death experience a short while ago, when he saved both me and Big Ben from a murderous witch, gave him a new attitude. Until then, his wife had been the one wearing the trousers, but things were more even now, and his new disposition came with a more positive outlook.

Finally, the last member of our regular Friday night drinking quartet was Basic. James Barnham was dumber than gravy. Or so we thought. I couldn't ask the question – such things are vulgar – but I suspected he was making a small fortune for himself. Being dumb enough to give it a go, he tried to sell an air guitar on a popular global sales platform. It worked, and he'd sold thousands of them since. So many, in fact, that he'd started selling different versions of the guitar. Each owner received the box the air guitar came in and a certificate of authenticity. It was bonkers, but I honestly wanted to get to the pub tonight so I could ask him how it was going.

I daydreamed about cold, refreshing amber liquid while I quietly ate my turkey sandwich and drank my pint of water. I try to stay healthy and exercise regularly. This is partly due to habit after a number of years in the army, partly due to vanity because I have a girlfriend and want her to want to see me naked, and partly because it's hard to chase down bad guys if you are out of shape and overweight.

Bull and Dozer looked up at me expectantly. Perhaps that should be hopefully because I rarely gave them treats during the day; I wanted to look after their waistlines as well. My plate went in the dishwasher, but I got them some ready-sliced pieces of carrot from the fridge and tossed them into the living room. The carrot pieces bounced in every direction, creating a game for the dogs to play as well as giving them a healthy snack. Then I left them to it and went back to work; I was heading to the coroner's office and the dogs would not be welcome there.

I was known at the coroner's, an institute where everyday people didn't get in without a reason and an appointment. I was able to circumvent that by making a phone call. It was picked up by the receptionist. 'Maidstone morgue,' she announced. 'How may I direct your call?'

'Good afternoon. This is Tempest Michaels. I wish to speak with Elizabeth Clement, please.'

There was a brief pause before she said, 'One moment, please.'

A second later, Elizabeth's voice came on the phone. 'Tempest is that you?' I knew Elizabeth because one of her former colleagues got killed in my house. Victoria Mallory was the insane serial killer pretending to be a witch who gave Hilary his near-death experience. Elizabeth turned up to deal with the body, Big Ben seduced her, and she's been bugging me ever since because he won't answer her calls.

'Hello, Elizabeth. I need a favour.' I got straight to the point. The case was geographically way outside of her area, but I was confident she could access the files.

'It's going to cost you,' she replied instantly. 'I want a date with Big Ben.'

'I'm not sure I can swing that,' I sighed.

The coroner wasn't taking no for an answer. 'You'll just have to, Tempest. I work too hard and I get too little play time. That's my price. Call your friend and have him call me. Do that and you can have your favour.' Then, sensing that she had jumped forward and missed a vital element of our deal, she asked, 'What is it?'

'I need the details on two bodies recently killed in an animal attack in Copthorne Wood outside of Whitstable. Their names are David Blake and Hugh Brydon. The whole file on each one would be nice, please, Elizabeth.' I knew their names because I'd looked them up with a simple Google search while I ate my lunch. 'I'll call Big Ben now.'

Which was what I did, the call connecting from my car's handsfree kit.

'Alright butt maggot, what's going down in spooky town?' his voice echoed in my car. Like me, he was ex-army. Unlike me, he is a dickhead.

'I have a case to investigate down in Whitstable, but I need some information from the coroner and Elizabeth won't give it to me unless you agree to go on a date.' You might think this would be an instant and easy thing to arrange with a single man, but it wasn't. An attractive woman wants a date and by date she means going to his place to get naked, but Big Ben operates a once only rule – he sleeps with each woman once only, with only one exception that I knew of.

When he agreed without hesitation, I almost lost control of my car. 'I said, okay,' he repeated when I prompted him.

'What about the once only rule?' I countered, feeling like there was a punchline coming.

He sighed. 'I keep breaking that with Patience.' Patience Woods is Amanda's best friend. They were both police officers and Patience still is. Big Ben hit on her when they first met just because she has a heartbeat, but to his surprise and that of his friends, he had entertained her several times since. Amanda sneakily set him up on a blind date with her last weekend at an eightieth birthday dinner party. It went a bit south, the party that is, but their blind date sounded like it hadn't ended yet. He tutted. 'Give me her number. Maybe this will help to shake off the funk I've fallen into.'

Doing so required that I use my hands, so I ended the call by thumbing a button on my steering wheel, then found a side street to pull into. Once Elizabeth's number was forwarded, I continued onward, arriving at my destination a few minutes later.

By the time I got into reception, I was expected; Elizabeth had seen my car swing into the morgue's carpark. 'Thank you, Tempest,' she said as I shook her hand. She didn't say anything else on the subject of her date and I had no wish to discuss what she might have arranged with my friend. 'You wish to see the files and ask me questions?'

This was an unexpected bonus. I might get to quiz her about why the medical examiner in this case had drawn his or her conclusions. She invited me through to her office where a small table and four chairs were set to one side for meetings. On the table, she'd set out a laptop.

'All the files are in a central, national database,' she explained. 'I have to leave a digital fingerprint which records my accessing them, but there they are. There's not much to read.'

I plopped into the chair in front of the computer and touched the mousepad. The screen flicked into life to a page showing me two files. I opened the first of them, a password request popping up to check my access rights.

Elizabeth leaned around me to get to the keyboard, her perfume, exotic and heady, hitting my nostrils when she got close. 'There you go.' As she stood up again, I leaned forward to scrutinise the screen. David Blake came up as the first victim alphabetically, so it was his mutilated body I saw first. Dressed in his biker outfit still, the white cotton of his t-shirt was almost entirely red. His jeans, too, were stained with his blood. His jacket was missing. I filed that away as I read the report on his injuries.

He died from loss of blood, the medical examiner concluded. His jugular had been penetrated but that was just one injury on a long list which went on to describe the parts of his body that were not found at the scene. In the coroner's opinion, the missing parts had most likely been eaten.

I moved on to read about Hugh Brydon. The photographs and descriptions were very similar. Both men died gruesome deaths, eaten alive by wolves. The coroner was clear about exactly what kind of animal had attacked them, referencing the bite marks by shape, penetration depth, size of tooth etcetera. I scan-read the next few lines, looking for anything that stood out. The coroner determined the bites came from at least six different animals, which he could tell, once again, by measuring the bites.

There was a line at the bottom of the report which I had to go back and check appeared on the first one too. Both men had stab wounds to their left deltoids. The coroner stated the wound was made by a double-edged blade to a depth of approximately two inches. It was fresh, but was not the cause of death.

Absorbing all there was for me to know, I wanted the answers I hadn't found. 'Where can I find if their jackets were found at the scene?'

'Their jackets?' she repeated, crossing the room again; she'd left me to my own devices so she could work at her desk. Leaning over me once more, she clicked the mouse and moved a finger around to shift the document between pages. Squinted at the screen she said, 'It makes no mention of clothing or other items found remote to the bodies.'

I pushed back my chair and thought for a while. Did the missing jackets have any significance? Had their club jackets been taken? If so, had they been taken before they were killed or afterward? Two men killed by wolves in a country where there were no native wolves and hadn't been for centuries. The police would have been involved when the bodies were found ...

'Do you know, or can you find out, if the police are following up to find out where the wolves came from?' I asked. Tilting back in the chair, my eyes were on the ceiling tiles when I asked the question. Levelling out again, I swivelled around to look at the her.

'I'll ask a question,' she offered. Elizabeth was focused on her work; whatever it was she was doing on her desktop computer.

I thanked her and stood up to leave, shooting my cuff to see the time: 1448hrs. It would take most of an hour to get to Whitstable and the same again if not longer to get back through rush-hour traffic. I was due at the pub at 1900hrs and needed to eat before then. It was definitely time to get going.

Coastal Delights.
Friday December 16th
1532hrs

I DISCOVERED THE DISTANCE to Whitstable was less than expected, arriving some twenty minutes earlier than predicted. My car ate up the miles efficiently, of course, the sleek, red German sports car making the journey a pleasure not a chore.

I couldn't remember the last time I visited the quaint Kentish coastal town, but what I did remember was how pretty and enticing it was. On a sunny day, which this wasn't, people from local inland towns would flood to the coast, making parking and even traversing the narrow pavements, a nightmare. The small town boasted an abundance of shops, eateries, and public houses and had for centuries been a mecca for seafood due to the abundant oyster beds sitting just off the coast.

I had no time for any of that today, plus the December temperature killed any desire to explore I might have otherwise felt.

The supplied postcode and my satnav led me directly to the Whitstable Riders. However, nowhere outside did it say I was looking at a motorcycle club. The property now filling my windscreen was indeed a mechanics repair shop but didn't look like it operated as a business to attract customers. The gates were padlocked and there were no signs to suggest customers should come in. It was a clubhouse then, where the members would take their own machines.

I rang the bell for attention as a sign outside the gate instructed and waited to see what might happen. It was already getting dark, which meant I could easily see inside the building through several long windows. Heads popped to see who was there and I saw, but could not hear, a conversation take place between several men.

Then, one of them, a young man of about twenty, jogged out of sight to emerge a few seconds later through a door at the front of the building. He came to the gates, unlocked the padlock, and threw them open. Before I could pull my car forward, he put out a hand to stop me and jogged to my window.

'Boss says you have to hand over your weapons before you come in.'

I blinked at him. 'I'm not carrying any weapons.' It seemed an obvious statement to make but the question had to have been born of experience which suggested most visitors were armed.

The young man assessed me, decided I was either telling the truth or crazy enough to lie about it, and waved for me to go. 'You can park down by the doors. Don't go in until I get these gates shut though, okay?'

On the back of the young man's jacket were the words, 'Probationary Member' a status which probably dictated he was the one who ran out to open and close the gate every time someone showed up.

I waited for him to finish and escort me inside, but the door opened to reveal Elk. 'Come in,' he beckoned. 'No need to wait outside.'

'Your probationary member asked me to.'

'Don't mind him. He doesn't understand your status. You're a guest of the club.' I raised an eyebrow. 'You have to be to come inside our headquarters,' Elk explained.

I chose not to challenge it or even ask what that meant in practical terms.

Inside, the bikers' headquarters looked and smelled like a mechanic's garage. The scent of old oil, burnt brake linings, and grease filled the air. There was something else mixed in with it, something floral.

A man with a beer belly stretching the front of his white t-shirt and an almost white beard approached me. I stuck out in most crowds because I choose to dress in smart clothes when most around me wear sportswear. Buying good quality office wear, because that is my preferred uniform, is one of my few indulgences, but among the biker club, who all wore derivations of the same outfit, I was a rhinoceros at a unicorns only event.

The white-haired man wore a material badge stitched onto his leather jacket that said 'President'. He stopped a few feet short, and as his men fanned out to surround me, he said, 'The fellas said you'd be stopping by to ask some questions. I'm Moose. I'm the president of this club. You're going to help us get justice for our boys?'

Selecting my words carefully, I said, 'I'm prepared to investigate the circumstances of their deaths. If that is still what you want.'

He nodded slowly as I talked. 'I want justice for them. They were good boys and they didn't deserve to be eaten.'

'Your ...' I struggled to find the right word. 'Members,' I guessed, 'Elk and Bear suggested the attackers are werewolves. Do you also believe that to be the case?'

'Damned straight I do. I saw them with my own eyes, young man. As sure as we are standing here right now, those Herne Bay Howlers are straight from hell itself. You wouldn't be here if they weren't, we'd take care of this ourselves.'

'I still say we can, Moose,' argued a man wearing a badge that said 'Deputy'. 'I don't buy this whole werewolf nonsense. I'm going home tonight to see my old lady.'

'You're staying here with us during dark hours, Brother Salmon. That's what we agreed on,' barked Moose. 'This club sticks together. I'll not be burying any more members.' When Salmon didn't argue any further, Moose turned his attention back to me. 'What do you say, Mr Michaels. Can we shake on it? I want justice for them killing Hugo and David. You track them down and tell us who they are and where we can find them, and we'll rid this area of their menace.'

He meant every word. It wasn't the first time I'd come across a group of people all sharing the same delusion. Amanda had witnessed it too and Jane used to be part of a vampire wannabe cult. His intention to kill the offenders didn't surprise me all that much, but if Bear and Elk knew about it before now, they'd been wise enough to hide it.

It was something I needed to straighten out right now. The only problem with that was that if I tried to tell them they were wrong, and the werewolves were nothing of the sort, they would reject it. It happened every time. So reliably, in fact, that in cases of mass delusion, it was better to just play along.

'Moose, I will find out who they are, but I will not be complicit in a revenge killing.'

His face creased in startled confusion. 'Revenge killing? You think we plan to kill them?'

Now it was my turn to look confused. 'Um. You want to rid this area of their menace,' I repeated his words.

'Well, yes, Mr Michaels. I mean, obviously we want the ones guilty of killing Hugo and David to be arrested and tried, but the rest of them we're going to sue for damages. It's the twenty-first century, man. No one opts for violence anymore.'

I glanced around. Surrounded by members of the motorcycle club, they were all looking at me like I had just suggested something otherworldly and ridiculous – like they try quiche for lunch. Giving my head a quick shake to clear it, I had to ask, 'I thought you were convinced they are all werewolves?'

'Yeah, so? That doesn't mean we can't get a lawyer to litigate against them. We don't know who they are, though,' Moose complained.

'Yeah, it's a real drag,' added Bear. 'We don't have an address for their clubhouse, and we don't know who any of them are, so we don't know where any of them live.'

Elk joined the discussion. 'They just showed up two weeks ago. We heard rumblings that there was a new club in the area, but no one could tell us anything about them. Only the name. We planned to greet them like brothers.'

'Yeah,' said Bear. 'There's no need for rivalry. But they showed up here one night and they threatened us. One of them got off his bike and walked up to the gates with a set of bolt cutters. Before any of us could react, they were inside our compound. He was the only one who spoke, acting as their spokesperson while the rest looked on. He said we were all under threat of death. If we disbanded our club and left, they would let us live. Otherwise, they were going to hunt us down and kill us all.'

'I laughed at him,' said Moose, sounding rueful. 'I told Rattlesnake and Vole to send him away. He was standing ten yards ahead of the rest of them. I told them to escort him from our premises. If he resisted, I was filming so would have footage of his trespass and refusal to leave. That's irrefutable when it comes time to sue.'

Noting that there was video footage I could see, I pressed him for more information. 'What happened?'

Moose hung his head. 'He beat the crap out of them, right in front of us.'

Bear said, 'That's when they showed their supernatural nature. All the others were just watching. None of them saw the need to get off their bikes.'

Elk took over. 'As that one guy threw Hugh and David across our yard, the rest of them took off their sunglasses to show us their inhuman eyes and pulled down the masks covering their faces. We were all just about to run to help Rattlesnake and Vole but when they started growling and showing their teeth, it stopped us dead in our tracks.'

'Then they repeated their ultimatum,' Moose finished the tale. 'They gave us a week to abandon our business and leave the area. I figured we could wage a legal battle against them, but in two weeks, we haven't been able to find out anything about them and they seem to know our movements. We are still operating our business but there is this constant threat that they will attack us. We all travel together when we go out to make our deliveries, I think that's why they haven't challenged us. But as soon as the week they gave us ended, Rattlesnake and Vole vanished.'

I raised a hand to make him pause. 'Is that David Blake and Hugh Brydon?'

Moose replied. 'Yes, but we use our club names at all times. They vanished last Thursday. Up until then, we'd been going about our lives as usual; the Howlers hadn't shown themselves since that first time. But then the half-eaten bodies were found, and we knew it was the Howlers making good on their threats.'

'Did the police come here to question you?' I wanted to know.

'They did, but we didn't let them in,' replied Moose. 'I came out to speak to them through the gate.'

'Why didn't you let them in?'

Moose looked surprised by my questions as if the answer should be obvious. 'We have a reputation to uphold. We can't just be talking to the police.'

I held up a hand to stop him. 'It's cards on the table time. I know you want to be mysterious about your business interests, but I won't be able to help if you don't give me the truth. I need to know what criminal activities you are engaged in.'

Moose met my eyes with a hard stare. 'Before we tell you anything, you need to be sworn in as an honorary member of the club. This status isn't granted lightly, Mr Michaels.'

Beginning to feel like Alice down a rabbit hole, I almost chuckled at my situation. The serious expressions of the club members stopped the amusement I felt from making it to my face. Seeing this as the simplest way forward, I asked, 'What does that involve?'

In Da' Club. Friday, December 16th 1612hrs

THE CEREMONY WASN'T WHAT I expected. Not that I was sure what to expect at all, though I admit a moment of fear that they might demand to tattoo me. To be an honorary member, all I had to do was put on one of their jackets. They sent the probationary member, who they referred to as Gopher, to fetch it from a back room. The jacket had the word 'Honor' spelt the American way, stitched into the leather above the right breast and the emblem on the back was in white stitching only, not the full colour the members got.

I wore it, recited some words from a card they gave me, which basically had me pledge to uphold the secrets of the club and defend its honour at all times and against all foes. I felt ridiculous, but I did it anyway.

Once complete, Moose lifted his hands into the air. 'Gentlemen, please welcome our newest member, Brother Weasel.'

'Weasel?' I couldn't help but complain. 'Come on Moose, you've got to have a better creature in reserve than Weasel. How about Brother Eagle or Brother Wolverine?' I asked picturing Hugh Jackman looking fierce. Yeah, I could get behind a name like that.

'Ooh!' said Gopher. 'How about Brother Sasquatch? Because, it's like this mythical beast and he's a paranormal investigator.'

I thought about that. Big, scary ... 'Yeah, I could go for sasquatch.' I volunteered and got a grin from Gopher.

'No. It's Brother Weasel,' argued Moose. 'Weasels are a proud and ancient animal. They're natural hunters known to take on far larger creatures as their prey.'

I blew out an exasperated breath that flapped my lips. I didn't want to join the stupid club in the first place. Now I had to be called Weasel every time one of them addressed me. 'Fine. Fine. Let's move on. I kept the jacket on and pressed Moose to reveal the nature of their operation. 'It's clear you didn't pay for those bikes with buttons, guys. If you want me to continue with this investigation, I need to know what the Howlers are trying to force you out of.'

Moose exhaled slowly through his nose while holding my gaze. I could tell he was still concerned about revealing the truth. Finally, he said, 'Flowers.'

My head tilted to one side of its own accord. 'Flowers?'

'Flowers. We import flowers to supply the market traders in London and the south east of England.'

I rolled my eyes. 'Okay. What do you really do?'

'We really import flowers,' Moose replied, his tone so deadpan I was beginning to believe him. 'It's surprisingly lucrative, Brother Weasel. Of course, we are bringing them in at night under cover of darkness and paying no import tax. That's how we undercut our competition.'

'You've got to be kidding me.' I couldn't get my head around the idea. They presented themselves as rougher than a badger's arse, but they were florists.

'Not at all,' replied Moose as if surprised at my disbelief. 'We are doing a surprisingly good trade with freesias at the moment.'

'Got to love freesias,' said Elk.

I turned my head to check if he was serious but before I got there, Bear said, 'And gerberas. They have such a wonderful array of colours. So many different shades.'

A man I hadn't heard from yet, who was most likely called Porcupine or Skunk or something chipped in his two penn'orth, 'The problem with gerberas is the need to wire the stems. It increases the effort for the florist with no accompanying increase in profit. The same with tulips quite often.'

Bear shook his head. 'You're missing the visual impact one gets from using a bold statement flower such as a gerbera. Freesias will never be more than a background bloom.'

Moose raised his voice to call for quiet. It was about time someone called a stop to the floral discussion. I was shocked they weren't all wearing pink jackets and carrying secateurs on their belts. 'I think,' Moose started, 'we can all agree, that if one wants a statement flower, the lily is the only safe way to go.'

I slapped my face into my palm. 'Okay, okay, I get it. You're illegally importing flowers and making a pile of money from it. Is that it? Is that the extent of your operation?'

Moose looked hurt that smuggling tulips into the country under the nose of customs wasn't enough. 'We sometimes dabble in Christmas trees,' he added defensively.

Still struggling to believe that anyone would kill for it, I summed up. 'The Howlers are demanding you cease all trading and disband the club. You think they killed two of your members, and want to take over your operations, and this is all over some flowers? Are you still importing?'

'Yes,' Moose nodded. 'We have to make the deliveries at night because the market traders need them fresh first thing every day. I think it's only a matter of time before the Howlers target our convoy and that's why we do the importing part during the day. It runs the risk of customs catching us, but I don't see any choice.'

'But it's safe during the day because ...' I wanted him to make the picture clear.

He looked at me like I was being particularly dense. 'Because they can only transform under the moon.' He said it like he was questioning how I didn't know that. 'We have to keep them here overnight and risk a run to the markets early in the morning. It's not ideal but we recognise the need to make it work until we can rid ourselves of this scourge.'

Absorbing it all, I needed time to think and it was already nearing the time when I ought to be home feeding the dogs. However, I had another question to ask, 'Hugh and David ...'

'Rattlesnake and Vole,' Moose corrected me.

I rolled my eyes. 'Yes, Rattlesnake and Vole. They were found without their jackets. All their other clothing was with their bodies. Would the Howlers have taken it?'

Moose nodded, a dread look on his face. 'They'll have claimed them as trophies. Wherever their hideout or clubhouse is, they will have them hung there now. It's like capturing the flag of the opponent's army; something to be displayed.'

Now I got it. A few centuries ago, capturing a French Eagle from Bonaparte's troops was the biggest achievement possible. Greater even than victory in some senses. I shot my cuff to check the time: 1639hrs. It was time to get going.

The last hour had been bizarre, but it was nothing compared to what I had coming.

Chief Inspector Quinn. Friday, December 16th 1640hrs

BACK OUTSIDE THEIR COMPOUND, I eased my car along the dark streets of Whitstable. The Riders were tucked out of the way at the eastern end of the town which also placed them close to the neighbouring town of Herne Bay. Once their property no longer filled my rear-view mirror, I pulled over to think.

My situation was perplexing. To start with, I was fairly sure Amanda was right and that the Riders were criminals. I saw no sign of that when I visited, but they knew I was coming and if they were under police scrutiny, they would know to keep their activities hidden. That they claimed to be florists fooled me for not one moment. I would sooner believe they were ballet dancers. So they were lying about what they were into. Was it drugs? Guns? Something else? I could legitimately walk away from the case and never think about it again, but I worried the Riders might take it upon themselves to retaliate. If I read about an innocent being killed as a result of my not preventing such a course of action, I would never forgive myself.

I parked that part of the quandary to focus on the case. First, I needed to track down the Howlers. If the Riders couldn't locate the Howlers' base, they couldn't retaliate which was a good thing. I had to find it, and then find a way to determine who among them was a killer. Maybe it was all of them, maybe it was none. I would need evidence to secure a conviction; that was the task and what I always strove for. I wanted to give my clients a solution that was ironclad

40

and could be used by either the police or a legal team depending on the nature of the case.

With little to go on, I would focus on what I did have. The coroner's report stated the saliva in the wounds was from wolves and that gave me a start point. It also demanded I find out what the police were doing about it.

Blowing out another exasperated breath, I dialled a number I never choose to ring without good reason.

When it was answered, the voice at the other end was equally displeased to hear from me. 'Mr Michaels, to what do I owe the pleasure of this call?' asked Chief Inspector Quinn. His tone made it quite clear he used the word pleasure in a sarcastic sense.

'Chief Inspector,' I started formally by using his rank, anything else might have given him cause to hang up. 'What do you know about two men being eaten by wolves a week ago?'

I heard him make a tutting noise. 'Is this another of your wonderful investigations, Mr Michaels? Let me guess, they were actually killed by a werewolf, yes?'

'Doubtful,' I replied. 'There's no such thing. They were members of a biker gang in Whitstable, the surviving members of which have hired me to find the killers. They believe a rival biker gang, the Herne Bay Howlers, are, in fact, all werewolves.' Quinn made a scoffing noise. 'They are wrong about that, but they may be correct in their belief that the men were murdered.'

'A person cannot be murdered by an animal, Mr Michaels. The owner of the animal can be held accountable for a death, but I am not aware that a successful conviction for murder has ever been achieved in such circumstances. My time is precious, so I'll ask that you get to the point.' This was typical behaviour for the chief inspector. He liked to have people acknowledge that he was in charge and once he felt he held the cards, which he did this time because I called him, he would leverage his power. I felt it made him look small.

Refusing to react, I said, 'Is there a police investigation into the two deaths? They were recorded as animal attack by the coroner, but I assume still that there must be a hunt for the dangerous creatures involved.'

He drew in a breath through his nose and let it out again, a habit I'd seen him perform dozens of times when trying to reach a decision. Arriving at one, he said, 'There has been an investigation. To my knowledge, its results were inconclusive. The wolves are most likely part of a private collection. This was not my investigation, of course, it is out of my area. However, I know the man who led it and have no doubt he was thorough. I know that his team checked zoos and animal parks, and found no animals were recorded as missing.'

I cut in, 'The bodies were found in public woodland. From the coroner's report, they were killed where they were found. Surely, that rules out a private collection as well?'

'As I said, Mr Michaels, this was not my investigation.'

He was looking to wrap up our conversation, but I wasn't letting him go yet. 'Known associates of the victims believe this was murder and have hired me to prove it, Chief Inspector. Are you really telling me the police are not looking into the biker gangs operating along the south east coast? How many times will I have to be the one to do your job for you?'

Pushing him was the wrong thing to do apparently. 'Mr Michaels, I do so enjoy our little chats. This is a police matter and will be handled and contained entirely by the police. If I require your interference at any point, I will be sure to let you know. Good evening.'

The line went dead. I swore quietly in the darkness of the car. One day I was going to work out how to manage the chief inspector. He was a good cop, I could acknowledge that, but his determination to climb the promotion ladder made him too much of a politician. Maybe I would get lucky and he would be promoted. Perhaps his replacement would be easier to deal with.

He didn't answer the question about whether there was an ongoing police investigation, but I felt certain there had to be. I had criminal biker gangs and at least one of them was prepared to murder the others. If I could answer why that was the case, it would form a nice start point for my investigation.

Slipping the gear lever into first, I checked my mirror and eased out onto the road again. I needed to go home and do some research, but about a mile later, just as I was threading my way along the coast road to re-join the motorway, I spotted bikes going the other way.

They whipped past on the other side of the road. I already knew it wasn't the Whitstable Riders because they were behind me and weren't going out at night. I didn't know how many biker gangs there were in Kent, but I'm a big believer in coincidence, so I checked my mirrors, plipped the accelerator and swung my wheel hard. The nifty red Porsche spun through a hundred and eighty degrees as it crossed lanes. Truly, I didn't really have enough room for the manoeuvre and had to gun the car to get away as an oncoming truck bore down on my tail end.

The bikers, doing forty in the other direction, were mere pin pricks of light in the distance already, and I would have to break the speed limit to find out if they were my quarry.

So that's what I did.

Howling Mad. Friday, December 16th 1646hrs

MERCIFULLY, I SPOTTED NO cops as I got above seventy on the coast road. As soon as I could distinguish the shape of the bikes ahead instead of just their lights, I began to slow, cruising up behind them as I squinted my eyes to read the motif on the back of their jackets.

I had to get closer, and then closer still, but as the rear bike passed beneath a streetlamp on the way into Herne Bay, I got a clear view of the rider's jacket. His back was dominated by an embroidered patch, the design that of a howling werewolf standing on two legs. Around it in a half circle were words which I could not read, but the werewolf design was sufficient to convince me I'd already found the elusive gang.

Having identified the design, I could see it repeated on the other bikers, each of them wearing a thick denim jacket against the cold winter air.

My phone rang: it was Amanda calling, but I knew I wouldn't be able to hear her over the rumbling thrum of the large-engined bikes I tailed. I let it ring off knowing she would understand.

Sweeping into Herne Bay along the coast road, two of the bikes detached from the main group, turning right into a side street. The rest carried on. I counted sixteen bikes in total, every one of them a powerful, chopper-style motorcycle with an abundance of highly shined chrome. It was down to fourteen now with the departure of two. Then two more peeled off, taking a side street and vanishing.

My goal in following them was to locate their base. It was nearing dinner time and it was both dark and cold outside thus my hastily drawn conclusion that they must be on their way back to their club house or whatever they called it, seemed a solid hunch. Or they were all going to their homes and the chaps peeling off were heading to houses in that direction.

Two more peeled off, but we were most of the way through the town now. The coast road running along the edge of the beach had the sea to one side and the town to the other. Herne Bay isn't a big place; at forty miles an hour, it takes just over a minute from the first house to the last. Curious, I kept going, foolishly watching ahead of me, and paying little attention to what was behind until I heard them.

Suddenly, I had six of the bikes behind me and ten in front and they were deliberately sandwiching me between them. The bikes that peeled off weren't going home, they were circling around to get behind me. You might think a car against a bike ought to be a sure thing, and it is, but do I really want to knock any of them over?

We continued like that for half a mile as I tried to work out if they had malicious intentions. When the first one bumped my car from behind, I decided that they probably did. The jolt was nothing more than a nuisance, but the intention was to make me pull over and that was precisely what I wasn't going to do.

The bike that hit me flashed his headlight and flashed his indicator for me to pull in. I didn't know what had given me away, or if they just didn't like sports cars, but if I wasn't going to stop, my only alternative was to go.

There was a gap in traffic coming up on the other side of the road. I could floor my accelerator and power around them in heartbeat. It felt a little like running away from an unknown threat, but it was the right thing to do at this juncture. I could regroup and find them again tomorrow.

The gap approached. I gripped my gear stick, ready to downshift, but they were way ahead of me. Just as I dipped my clutch, two of the bikes in font of me swerved into the gap to block it and one of those behind swung around to come alongside my door. His face was no more than a few feet from mine, so when he turned his head my way, I got to see his glowing red eyes. Then he reached up with his left hand to tug his face scarf down. It revealed his distorted upper and lower mandibles and the rows of razor-sharp teeth contained within.

He grimaced in a way which was probably supposed to be a smile, but just looked horrific from where I was sitting. I was looking at a werewolf and he was looking at me. Were it not for my unshakeable belief that such a creature did not exist, I would have believed it, and I understood why Moose and his gang were so convinced.

Before I had time to react, he swung his left hand at my car. What I took to be a glove, was a hairy paw which ended in several terrible talons. His first swipe tore my door mirror clean off from its mount.

It shocked me, but forcing myself to be calm, I lifted my right hand to my mouth and made a show of yawning at him.

His face registered surprise at my lack of fear, but a second swipe clanged against my door, raising sparks. Then another bump from behind, this one more aggressive than the last, let me know I was in more trouble than I thought. They meant to run me off the road and I could only guess what they might chose to do then.

I didn't fancy fighting sixteen men all at once, which was what would happen if they cornered me, so I stilled my centre, waited for the headlight behind to surge forward again, and slammed on my brakes.

The rider aiming to rub the bumper of my car, got the whole car instead. To my right, the man doing a great impression of a werewolf, shot ahead of me, unable to react swiftly enough to stop. My back bumper was probably trashed, but it would be nothing compared to the damage the large man did as his head hit the canvas of my convertible car's roof. I heard the material rip and shot my head around to see if the rider was about to fall into my passenger seat. Squealing brakes from behind let me know the other bikers were all trying to stop, and flaring brake lights ahead told me the message had reached them already.

My car was slowing fast, and I could not allow it to stop, so just as the biker came to rest on my roof, I snapped the gear stick into second and floored it again. The car took off once more, but now I had little room for manoeuvre. Their bikes were big and heavy. It I hit one, it would smash out of the way, but packed so close together as they rode in formation, I would need to hit more than one to fight my way clear and doing so would probably prove too much. Worse yet, if I hit them, I had no idea what damage it might do to the rider. Yes, they were overtly aggressive and pretending to be werewolves, but it would be their word against mine if I chose to use my car as a weapon.

Amazingly, it was time for me to get lucky. Our slower pace meant the gaps between cars going the other way lasted longer. Just as I mashed my accelerator, a space opened. With no time to question whether I had enough room, I yanked on my handbrake. Cranking the steering wheel and firing the engine, I spun the back end around once more, and this time, when I burned rubber from my rear tyres, the car found itself with room to escape.

Which was when my luck ran out.

Tense Situation. Friday, December 16th 1652hrs

I WAS GOING TOO fast and paying too much attention to the bikers as I fled the scene. I whipped by them, trying to get a good look, however, failing to pay enough attention to the road meant I didn't see the van pull out of the junction I sped towards.

There was nowhere to go and no way to avoid hitting it unless I ditched my car. So that was what I did, mounting the kerb with a jolt that grounded out my suspension and slammed my body. I missed the tail end of the van, but now mostly on the pavement and barely in control, I ploughed through a litter bin and had to fight the wheel as I stomped the brake pedal.

When the car slewed to a stop, now half on and half off the pavement, its nose was less than two inches from the steel pole of a street sign. On the coast road between towns, there were no houses and no lights, but the beams from oncoming headlights illuminated me well enough and the bikers were coming back for me.

It wasn't like I could run away. Even if I wanted to, there was nowhere to go except the sea. Beyond the pavement on the shore side were tufty lumps of sand dunes. Gritting my teeth and setting myself to be ready for a fight, I pushed my door open and got out.

I didn't even make it to my feet before I got hit.

Standing up, someone came over the top of my car in a leap that ended with a kick to my right shoulder. It caught me by surprise; I thought they were all still to arrive, but I managed to go with the blow as I fell. My plan was to roll and spring to my feet, but my attacker had followed me down, and as I attempted to get my feet facing the right way, he punched me in the mouth.

Whoever he was, he was strong and there was plenty of him. He had the upper hand, striking me again, this time connecting with my right eye socket as I tried to get my hands up. I needed to find something to grip hold of. If I could just work out which bits of him were where, I could strike back.

I was on my back, a strong position if a person knows how to fight, and when the next blow missed my constantly weaving face, I wrapped my arm around it and kicked out with my left leg. My assailant got the full force of my rage in his gut and sailed backward as I let his arm go. My head swam and I could taste blood, but the rest of his gang had to be upon me. In the second of respite, I flipped onto my feet to face them.

'It's the cops!' I heard the shout just as the bikers were all getting off their parked machines. A heartbeat of indecision followed as they stared at me and I stared back. Hopelessly outnumbered, if they rushed me now, there would be little I could do to defend myself and the lone set of flashing lights tearing along the coast road behind them wouldn't be enough to save me if they decided to stand and fight.

I think that might have been their decision had a helicopter not appeared overhead. One moment, the bikers were black shapes silhouetted by their own headlights as they advanced toward me, the next they were bathed in light from a giant spotlight high above.

It was a freakish sight. Each of them had glowing red eyes and more than one had their hands exposed to show the same hairy paws I'd seen on the one who ripped my door mirror off. I glanced at my car where his raking claws had carved deep cuts into the steel of the door just below the window. If they hit flesh, they would go straight through it.

I saw a silent gesture from one of the bikers, presumably the leader, though perhaps they referred to him as the alpha, and they all went back to their bikes.

From high above, the helicopter pilot ordered the bikers to stay where they were, but with the squad car bearing down on them, they gunned their bikes and ignored his instruction. I got a malignant stare from more than half of them as they rode away, my pulse pounding a staccato beat even though I knew the danger had passed.

Twenty seconds after the Herne Bay Howlers roared into the darkness, the squad car blew past. I caught a face looking out of the driver's window as it sped after the bikers. The helicopter had already departed, following the bikes back to Herne Bay and I was all alone on the coast road for a moment. Cars were coming from both directions, though none were currently within a hundred yards of me, and I could see two more police cars in the distance, heading toward me from Reculver, the next inhabited spot along the coast.

Is my car still driveable? I asked myself as I walked around it. It looked like crap. The back bumper had a crack where the bike had hit it; the whole thing would need to be replaced. The folding roof was caved in on one side and where the mechanism appeared to have been bent by the weight of the human landing on it, the canvas had ripped. That would be the expensive part to fix, I estimated. The driver's door mirror was completely missing, and the driver's door had claw marks in it. Otherwise, the car appeared to be in working condition; the tyres were inflated, the lights and engine worked.

Berating myself for being annoyed at damage to something as unimportant as a car, I climbed back in to use my visor mirror to assess the damage to my face. I could tell I had a cut, the skin by my eye was sticky, and sure enough, the blow I took there had opened up the skin. A thin trickle of blood had run down to my cheek. My lips were cut too, both top and bottom fattened when his first punch landed.

It could have been a whole lot worse and I would heal in a week. I needed time to assess what I'd seen, but it would have to wait for the drive home because the cops were about to arrive. Before they got to me, I sent a quick message to Jane. I'd memorised two of the bike's number plates; something I could use to identify their owners and obtain addresses. It was my first step toward solving the case. It cost me a big chunk of the ten thousand I took, although, to be fair, my insurance would cover the damage. It also cost me a fat lip, a price I would gladly recoup from the person who gave it to me if the chance arose.

Jane's response came back moments later to tell me the number plates I'd given her didn't exist; had I got them mixed up? I popped my phone away as the cops approached. My memory worked well enough; the Howlers were using fake plates.

There was no time to deal with it now, and my plan for a cold pint was going to have to wait.

Girl Trouble. Friday, December 16th 1802hrs

THE LEAD OF TWO cop cars did as the earlier one had and flew past me without slowing down. The rear one slowed and stopped behind me. I was getting out by the time their car came to a stop. They wanted me to get back in, but I had no interest in following their instructions.

I got a second, 'Get back in your car, sir,' before the man giving the order accepted that I wasn't going to obey: I was the victim, not the criminal and would do as I pleased.

'I'm fine,' I told him before he could ask. Both cops were out of the car now, advancing toward me but not looking nervous. I could see the beam of the helicopter's searchlight way off in the distance. It was hovering over Herne Bay, but something told me they would have no luck catching the Howlers tonight. I watched the beam of light moving around for a few more seconds, then accepted that I would have to deal with the cops if I wanted to get home tonight.

It took an hour.

More cops arrived. My car was causing a partial roadblock, so they controlled the traffic and supervised my getting it back onto the road. Then they wanted to look at it to be content it was safe to drive. I thought for a moment they might impound it, but the damage was all minor and nothing was hanging off.

After numerous rounds of questions to determine why the bike gang might have targeted me, they took a statement and let me go. Back in the car and heading for the motorway, I called Big Ben.

'Hey, knob jockey, your pint is getting cold. Where are you?'

'Good evening, Ben,' I replied. 'I am going to be late.'

'You're already late. You're telling me you're going to be later.'

Thinking he was being unnecessarily pedantic, I accepted his point and moved on. 'Can you get my dogs?'

'Um, sure. Where are you?' I could hear Jagjit and Hilary in the background asking the same question. Not being at the pub at seven o'clock on a Friday evening was a rare occurrence for any of us.

I explained about the case and my run in with the werewolves. He wasn't impressed.

'They sound like a bunch of dicks to me.' It was a typical Big Ben response but not one I could disagree with.

'I should be there in thirty. The boys will want some kibble, mate.'

'No problem. I'm drinking your pint though.'

Big Ben and I had keys to each other's places, an exchange of convenience that had proved useful many times. My dogs knew him well enough to not attack him when he went in, not that they were likely to attack anyone when it was two hours after their dinner time. Anyone choosing to break in would be greeted as a potential meal provider and lavished with love even if they were burgling the place.

I checked my face in the mirror again: my lips hurt from being punched. Flicking the visor shut with an angry swipe, I remembered Amanda's call and hit the button to bring up my voice activated phone book.

She was uncharacteristically slow to answer. 'Tempest.' That was all she said, which was also uncharacteristically monosyllabic.

Telling myself, her coolness existed only in my imagination, I smiled mentally and gave her my happy voice. 'Hi, Amanda, how was your day? I didn't see much of you.'

'That's because you accepted a case working for criminals, Tempest,' she replied with ice dripping off her words. Okay, so the coolness might not be just in my imagination.

'What is it about this case that bothers you, Amanda?'

She sighed; a huff of disgruntled breath that displayed how disappointed she was with me. 'They are dangerous, Tempest.'

I frowned in the darkness of my car. 'How does that make this case different from half of the other ones I tackle? Or those which you take on? Or Jane for that matter? We find ourselves in rough spots most weeks.'

'And this is worse,' she insisted. 'Seriously, Tempest, I am worried you will get hurt.' I thought about the cut by my eye and my swollen lips. Telling her about them now would only strengthen her argument.

'How is this worse?' I asked.

I got a beat of silence as she switched tactics. 'If I asked you to, would you drop the case?' When I didn't answer straight away, she said, 'What if I told you I'd been shopping in Ann Summers and had something adventurous to show you? Why don't you come to my place right now so we can discuss it?'

Her purring voice went straight to my groin where Mr Wriggly was instantly awake and limbering up for a battle. 'I can't,' I protested. 'It's Friday night. The guys are already at the pub with my beer getting warm and Big Ben has gone to get my dogs.' My night at the pub was a single man's tradition that I would lose at some point. I accepted it stoically, but I was also determined to hold on and protect it for as long as I could. If the two married guys could get there, and Big Ben could take a night off from his quest to shag every woman in England for a few hours, then I could be there too.

You might think it odd that I have run towards enemy fire, and gone hand to hand with multiple opponents too many times to mention, yet found myself cringing as I waited for my girlfriend to respond after I spurned her advances.

She was going to say something cutting I knew it, so when she sobbed, it caught me completely by surprise. 'Okay, Tempest. I'll see you tomorrow at the office. Goodnight.' The line went dead before I could respond and sitting in the car at a steady seventy miles per hour, a mile short of my exit, I found myself utterly bewildered.

'What the hell just happened?' I asked myself.

No answer came back.

I couldn't remember if I had ever heard Amanda cry before, not that I could be sure she was crying now, but it sure sounded like it. Was she lonely? Was she genuinely that worried about me? My foot twitched as I approached the off ramp. Did I go to her place instead? It felt like the right thing to do. Yet it also felt like I was giving in to her trying to dictate how I operate and to breaking up my routine. Big Ben would tell me I was three steps away from picking wallpaper and arguing over toothpaste brands.

With a flick of my indicator, I took the off ramp and made my decision. This did not seem like the time to start allowing my relationship to start dictating other parts of my life. Besides, there was a principle in play: my long-standing commitment on a Friday night was to my friends. They were friends who had all saved my life at one time or another. If I was going to bail on them ever, it wouldn't be at the last moment and would be for a better reason than hot sex with my girlfriend who might very well have turned on the waterworks to see if she could influence me.

That was what I told myself.

I am such an idiot.

Pub O'clock. Friday, December 16th 2022hrs

THE FLASH OF MY headlights, as I swung my busted car into the carpark of the Dirty Habit, caught the attention of my four friends. They were sat two yards beyond the window that overlooked the pub's carpark at a table for four. We always sat in the same place and managed to squeeze an extra chair in despite Big Ben's broad shoulders and Basic's general girth.

I guess they saw the damage to my car because they all left their drinks to come outside for a look.

'Hey, guys,' I chuckled at myself as I slid from the car and stood up. 'I had some car trouble.'

Big Ben had the dogs held in check as they strained to get to me, but let their extendable lead run out when he got close enough, I bent down to fuss them both, glad to see they were fine and being looked after.

'Did you roll it?' asked Hilary, his eyes agog.

I shook my head. 'Nope. The damage to the roof is from a werewolf landing on it.' My comment was intended to startle and might have done with a different group. For my friends it was nothing shocking at all.

Big Ben handed the dogs' lead over, then bent down to squint at my face. 'Is that from the accident or from meeting the werewolf?'

'The latter,' I admitted.

He stood up again. 'You should learn to duck. Come on, punch bag, there's a fresh cold one waiting in the tap.'

I locked the car, and trudged inside, where Natasha, the usual Friday night barmaid was already pulling me a pint. Big Ben collected it, making a comment to Natasha that I didn't hear, but which earned him a flick of spilled beer and a scowl. Natasha and I had almost been a thing a short while ago. I messed it up through my inability to manage my own love life, but I wasn't unhappy about it as I had Amanda now.

Big Ben, however, had been trying to get into her knickers for as long as I could remember, and she continued to show no interest. It placed her into a very small subset of women who could resist his charms.

He placed the cold beverage in front of me. 'Here you go, shiner.'

'Shiner?' I repeated. 'Do I have a black eye?' I blurted the question, horrified that might be the case. A cut to my face and a split lip I could deal with. A black eye was a whole different thing.

Jagjit inclined his head. 'Sort of. There's a bit of colour at the edge of your right eye.'

I swore and stalked to the men's room to check in the mirror. Only then, with proper lighting, did I see that I looked to have been in a bar brawl. My jacket was scuffed and essentially ruined. It was dirty too, and my shirt was skewwhiff. I used a paper hand towel to clean the blood from my face and then examined the bruising to my right eye. It wasn't too bad, but it was visible.

I was as tidy as I was going to get without going home to change, something which wasn't going to happen, so I went back to my pint.

The chaps were bound to have questions for me about the car and werewolves and all that was happening to me, but I didn't come out to spend the night talking about myself. 'What've I missed?' I asked, before anyone could get a chance to quiz me first. 'Basic, how's the air guitar thing going?'

Basic said, 'S'right.' He wasn't known for giving stimulating conversation.

Hillary, to Basic's right, piped up, 'I've gone into business with him.'

I paused with my glass halfway to my mouth. 'Really?'

Hilary nodded. 'He needed some help with banking and other admin stuff. But we got to talking, and I couldn't help but suggest that he might want to branch out. The next thing I knew, I was helping him to make a website.'

I finally got the glass to my mouth and took a long draught from it, quenching my thirst in the way only a cold beer can. 'So what new ideas have you got?' I asked, setting the beer aside.

'Wicked air and radical skids,' grunted Basic.

I looked at him, hoping he might expand on his statement, but that was all he had to say on the matter.

Hilary helped me out. 'The air guitar thing has become so popular that it seemed obvious to try to replicate it. I suggested he sell in the same format only with different air-related products. It was a sort of cramming session where I attempted to reignite the spark that led to the air guitar's sales. Basic came up with ...'

'Wicked air,' Basic filled in the blank.

Hilary nodded. 'That's right.'

I narrowed my eyes. 'I'm lost. What exactly is wicked air. Fervently I hoped my friends were not somehow selling farts on the internet.

'Like when you do a jump on your bike and don't land for several seconds,' Jagjit explained. 'You and I used to see who could jump over the most Hot Wheels cars when we were kids.'

'I still have a scar on my left elbow from you moving the last car,' I reminded him. We were six at the time.

Hilary pushed on. 'Anyway, we went down to the local skate park and took a load of footage of Basic doing jumps on his BMX and his skateboard, then threw in a pogo stick for good measure. Once we had enough shots of wicked air, he started selling them.'

The concept was making my head hurt. 'What about the skids?'

'Radical skids,' Basic corrected me.

'Sorry, yes, radical skids.' Since the wicked air wasn't farts in a jar, I felt safe to assume this wasn't a product one might associate with it.

Hilary did his best to explain, 'Basic goes really fast on his bike and then jams on the brakes. His tyres leave a skid mark.'

It beggared belief. 'What exactly do people get when they buy the skid?' asked Big Ben, beating me to the question, his face the same mask of disbelief mine had formed.

'A photograph,' replied Hilary, looking embarrassed as he took a quick swig of his pint.

'You send them a photograph?' I tried to confirm.

'Nah,' said Basic, 'Sselectonic, innit.'

Hilary translated. 'We send them a jpeg. Basic has performed hundreds of skids. We've gone through three sets of tyres already.'

'How much do they go for?' asked Big Ben.

Now Hilary looked really embarrassed. 'Well, um ... we started selling them for ten pounds each.'

'A tenner for a jpeg?' I blurted incredulously.

Big Ben couldn't believe it either. 'I wouldn't pay that for a naked picture of Scarlet Johansson.'

Jagjit pulled a face. 'I might,' he admitted.

Ignoring them both, Hilary hadn't finished yet. 'They were more popular than we expected. We were getting emails from people who wanted to buy one, and we couldn't make them fast enough - demand outstripped supply. That was when we tried putting some into an online auction. Then it really took off.' Seeing our faces, he slipped into salesman mode. 'It's the uniqueness, you see. We only sell each skid once. The jpeg is signed electronically by Basic and the rarest ones fetch a fortune.'

'Did a double tyre crossover yesterday,' grunted Basic. 'That's not easy.'

Hilary knew I was going to ask, so explained before I could. 'That's where he has enough speed to get both tyres to make an individual line and then, by shifting his weight, he makes the back one cross the line the front one is making to one side and then the other.'

'S'right,' said Basic. 'Double tyre crossover.'

'Basic came up with the name.' Hilary was looking thoroughly pleased with himself. 'That one went to a collector in Utah for almost two thousand pounds.'

'What!' Big Ben and I both cried out in shock at the same time, drawing the attention of everyone else in the pub.

'This is literally unbelievable.' I felt genuinely in awe. 'I'm sitting opposite an internet millionaire.'

'Not yet,' said Hilary proudly.

I finished my pint and bought a round, ordering myself some food at the same time because dinner never happened. A bowl of chips at the pub was hardly going to improve my waistline but I was already drinking beer. I could worry about it in the morning and get to the gym early.

Inevitably, the guys wanted to know about the werewolf case and my car. I told them what I knew and what happened on the coast road earlier.

'I don't like werewolves,' said Basic, who most likely thought they were real. 'They're all hairy and nasty.'

Big Ben laughed. 'You're hairy and nasty.'

It made us all laugh, even Basic, who then proceeded to peel his polo shirt up. Wondering what he was doing, we soon saw when he began to expose his middle. 'Maisy wanted me to wax.'

'Didn't that hurt?' asked Jagjit, whose eyes were as wide as mine. Basic's belly and back, which used to be a rug of hair a Wookie might be proud of, were now as smooth as a baby's.

Basic slurped his pint, spilling some on his shirt as he rolled it down again. 'Nah.'

That Basic had a girlfriend at all surprised us when he first showed up with her. That she was attractive surprised us more, but it was almost a month since they met, and she was still seeing him. I liked the guy, but he looked like, acted like, and had the intelligence of a caveman. His girlfriend is an engineer in the aerospace industry.

Seeing my thoughtful face, Big Ben leaned his head down to mine. 'I know what you are thinking: Gold-digger, right?'

I didn't want to admit it out loud, but the thought had occurred to me. 'To be discussed later,' I whispered back. I hoped it wasn't true, but Basic had money. Lots of it, it would seem, and that could be a very attractive quality for some people.

Letting the subject drop, Big Ben nudged my arm. 'Tomorrow, you're going after the werewolf case again, right?'

'That's my plan.'

'Cool. I'm coming with you. You clearly need wheels anyway. I'll be your wingman.'

I felt like I ought to argue, but truthfully, I was glad of the support. If there was one thing Big Ben excelled at, it was fighting people. Where I baulked at the chance to fight sixteen men earlier, he would have waded in.

Decision made, we agreed a time he would pick me up and got back to the serious matter of drinking.

Unexpected Guest. Saturday, December 17th 0700hrs

I AWOKE WITH A dachshund's ear tickling my nose. It's only right that I clarify this to be a semi-regular occurrence. The dogs can get on the bed so even if I tuck them into their own bed, which sits underneath mine, they just snuggle in with me as soon as I am asleep.

The ear belonged to Dozer, the dopier of my two dogs, who is also the more affectionate. His brother, Bull, could normally be found at the far end of the bed, tucked under the duvet with just his nose showing – what I like to refer to as coming to periscope depth. I pushed Dozer off me and sat up. Having imbibed my usual limit of four pints last night, I felt no ill effects from the alcohol. That was good because I now planned to beat myself into a sweaty pulp at the gym.

Leaving the dogs to snooze, I left the house five minutes later, ran to the pub where I collected the car, and returned a little more than an hour later in need of a shower. Unlike a lot of people whose working lives are governed by office hours and kids attending schools, I had no such limitations. I could just not work if I fancied a day off, but in general, I worked every day. That's not to say I was slavishly committed to the job, but even on a Sunday, when I would typically be giving myself a later start and visiting my parents for a roast dinner, I could be found putting effort into research on one or more cases. Sometimes, the natural run of a case demanded I work on a Sunday or it might be that I am

63

out all night on a stakeout and only get to bed in time to sleep through the day. It's just that kind of job.

This morning, I was heading to the office where I expected to find both of my colleagues. From there I would be heading back to Whitstable and Herne Bay to do some more digging.

That was my plan.

My plan didn't make it past breakfast.

When my phone rang, I was just finishing the last piece of boiled egg with my final toasted soldier. I didn't recognise the number, so I gave them my professional answer. 'Good morning. This is Tempest Michaels at the Blue Moon Investigation Agency. How may I help you today?'

'This is Bear. Salmon is missing.'

That was all the information he gave me, but it was all I needed to join the dots. Salmon was the one whose sewn on badge said 'Deputy' yesterday. I remembered he was the one who wanted to go home to see his old lady. Those were his words.

'Am I to gather he left the club house last night?' I asked.

'Moose thinks he must have snuck out at some point in the night. We got up this morning and his bunk was empty. His wife never saw him, so unless he is shacked up somewhere with another woman, then he is missing.'

'Thank you for letting me know.'

'Moose wants to see you.' Bear made it sound like an order to be obeyed.

'And I wish to see him too. I will be along later today.'

Bear tutted. I imagined him shaking his head at the other end of the phone. 'Right away, Mr Michaels. One of our members is missing. You can't take our money and then just mosey on along when it feels convenient.'

Keeping my voice calm, I replied, 'I work my own hours, Bear. You can have the entire amount back right now if you wish to challenge me. I will not be at the club's beck and call. The Howlers' targeted me last night. When I get to you later today, I would like to discuss how it is that they knew to do so.'

I heard muttering in the background and muffled noises as if someone had put their hand over the phone. The next time someone spoke, it was the voice of Moose. 'The Howlers came after you last night?'

'Yes. My car is trashed. I need to get it in for repairs. Also, I have research to do, solving these cases often requires a lot of time sitting in front of a computer.'

'I expect to see you later today, Mr Michaels.'

'And you shall. Please let me know when you locate your missing member. What is his full name, please? His real name?' I added quickly before he could give me phylum and classification for a salmon in Latin.

I got the information I needed, and the call ended. My need to get on with the case became more pressing with a missing man to locate. Yesterday, he used the words 'old lady' but I took that to mean his wife. Even if he wasn't married, he might very well have kids at home, and I worried that he might already be dead.

Sucking air between my teeth as I thought, I played a hunch and called Chief Inspector Quinn again. He was just as pleased to speak with me now as he'd been yesterday.

'Yet again, Mr Michaels, I have to question what I have done to warrant such constant attention from you?'

'A person linked to the two deaths we spoke about yesterday has gone missing overnight. Have you heard the name Matthew Kaddish in the last few hours?' If a mutilated body had arrived in any of the morgues across the county, Quinn would know about it.

'No, Mr Michaels. You say he is connected to the two animal attack deaths? How so?'

'By association. They are all members of the Whitstable Riders Motorcycle Club. If you are not already hearing his name, I would put no further thought to it.'

'Yes. I'll take that under advisement, thank you. Is there anything else? Or can I get back to my job?'

Several rude responses formed a hasty queue in my head. If Matthew Kaddish was dead, then his body was yet to be found. Hopefully, though, he was still alive and would appear of his own accord at some point. I said, 'Thank you for your time, Chief Inspector.' And thumbed the button to end the call.

The clock ticked through 0830hrs and it was time to go. Unless I have reason not to, I get to the office just before 0900hrs each day. I like the routine of it. Jane usually beats me and has the coffee machine running before I park my car, but when someone knocked on my door, the sound loud in my quiet house, I wondered if I might end up being late today.

The dogs exploded in a fit of barking, each trying to be louder than the other I swear. Having just finished my breakfast, they were still hanging around next to the breakfast bar in the eternal hope I might have left them something. It meant they got to the door ahead of me where they continued to bark insanely at the shadow outside.

The shadow looked worryingly familiar.

'Hey, kid,' said my dad when I opened the door. Bull bounced over the top of Dozer to be the first to greet him, Dozer somehow losing his balance and falling to land on his side. The sausage shape of his body caused him to roll so all four paws were pointing to the sky for a second.

I scooped the stupid dog before his flailing paws could get him back up the right way. 'What'cha doing here, dad?' I asked, taking in the small bag by his feet.

He frowned at me as he petted Bull. 'I'm staying for the weekend, remember?'

A small ball of worry formed in my core as I wracked my brain. I didn't remember. I said, 'Um,' but dad could already tell by my expression that I'd forgotten whatever plan we might have made.

'Your mother says this is why you've stayed single so long, you know: You cannot remember appointments. You arrange a date with a girl and then forget all about it because your brain is filled with everything else. A busy brain: that's your problem. Well, whatever you thought you were doing this weekend, you're doing it with me now. Your mum is at a Cliff Richard concert with her friends.'

The penny dropped. I could remember a conversation about this, but it hadn't been mentioned in weeks so, like my father said, it slipped my mind. A little flustered by the sudden change to my plans, I stepped back inside my house, saying, 'Right. Okay, dad. Have you had breakfast already?'

'Indeed, I have. Your mother made me get up early so she could drop me off on route to collect her friends. I'm all set for a day of whatever you have planned.' He placed his overnight bag on my breakfast counter and began to rummage inside it. Producing a bottle of rum triumphantly, he said, 'Tots of rum to get our bodies ready for the day?' Before I could stop him, he'd snagged two glasses from my cupboard and there were two tots waiting to be drunk.

My eyes widened at the sight of the dark liquid. 'Wowza.' Dad is a retired Royal Navy officer and served back when they still handed out a daily tot of rum. A tot, you might think, doesn't sound too terrible. Don't be fooled though, a tot is an eighth of a pint and the rum used is highly alcoholic. I chuckled. 'I've no desire to be a party pooper, but I need to drive so it would be best if I abstain. You crack on though.'

'Don't mind if I do.' Dad downed his glass and gave a full body shudder as the alcohol hit. I love my dad. I think he is great. Growing up with him around was a lot of fun and our relationship hasn't changed much since then. He does, however, have something of a gregarious personality which is kept in check day to day by the presence and stern tone of my mother. He'd been without her for five minutes and was already misbehaving.

'I have to get to the office, dad, and I'll probably be heading to Whitstable later this morning.'

'Ooh, fish n chips by the beach. Sounds great, kid.'

I couldn't argue but felt it necessary to caveat his luncheon plans. 'I'll be there to work, dad. I need to investigate a case.' I clicked my tongue to get the dogs moving, the pair both trotting back toward the door, ready to be let out. With a final pat of my pockets to make sure my keys, phone, and wallet were in place, I slung my bag loosely over my right shoulder. I had everything I needed, and I was already ten minutes late leaving.

At the door, I plipped the car open so dad could get in it, then glanced back inside to the breakfast bar where, sure as dammit, the second glass of rum was now empty. I sighed and hoped he might just fall asleep.

I wasn't that lucky.

Busy Office. Saturday, December 17th O900hrs

WITH CLEAR ROADS, WE got to my office on the stroke of nine but both Amanda and Jane were already there. Inevitably, upon seeing the crumpled roof, missing door mirror, and other damage, dad asked about my car. I explained the incident with the Howlers much the same as I had the previous evening when the chaps asked.

Last night, it was too late to arrange for it to be repaired and today I felt too busy, yet it wasn't a task I could delegate, so while dad sat in the client area reading a tatty paperback he'd pulled from his coat pocket, I called the Porsche dealership in Tonbridge. I didn't have to take it to the Porsche dealership, others could do the job and certainly Porsche would charge me more per hour for the repairs than anyone else, but I felt confident the work would be done correctly there. I also knew they would come to collect it.

Task complete and the collection arranged, I went to the coffee machine. My typical routine would be to make coffee and then catch up with both Amanda and Jane. Amanda's door was closed; it felt like a cold shoulder though I told myself I was being silly. Proceeding as if nothing untoward had occurred, I found Jane.

As usual, she was hunched over her keyboard. 'What are you working on?' I asked, conversationally.

'The Sandman case still. He's vanished, but I don't think that is a positive thing.' The Sandman was a case she stumbled across when I was tackling a Yeti in the French Alps. At the time, neither Amanda nor I knew Jane was taking on cases of her own. We gave him the nickname because he sang the song Mr Sandman to his victims.

A woman called Karen Gilbert wandered into the office one day and hired Jane to find out why she was having vivid dreams about a man singing to her at night. Jane then snuck into her house that night for a stakeout, but the place got burned down – not by the Sandman, but because Jane was involved in another case. Do you see how complicated this can get?

Anyway, Jane found several other instances of the Sandman targeting victims who then ended up dead. Karen Gilbert ran away to live with her sister in Dudley and hadn't been visited at night since, but the Sandman, whoever it was, sent Jane a copy of the record *Mr Sandman* by the Chordettes and promised to sing her to sleep. It was no surprise that Jane was taking the case personally now. She wanted to solve it, but almost two weeks after starting her investigation, she'd got no closer to working out who the mysterious Sandman is.

'You have surveillance equipment set up at your place, right?' I confirmed.

'Yes, plus silent alarms on the doors and windows so we'll know in advance if anyone tries to get in. I'm still working on the theory that he's some kind of counter-intelligence operative or something. Whoever he is, he's able to get into the victim's houses without leaving any trace of his method of entry. This time I really do feel like I'm chasing a ghost.'

'What other cases are you working?' I knew she had several because the Sandman case was without a client. Karen hired the firm initially, but when her house burned down, we were lucky to get away without being sued. Jane needed paying cases.

She swivelled the screen to show me several tabs at the bottom. When I first hired her, Jane devised and created a file naming system to organise incoming cases. It was hard to imagine what I might do without her if she were ever to leave. 'I have a haunting over in Twydall that will turn out to be a rodent in the attic. I have a woman who claims her grandmother-in-law has a pet cemetery in her garden and is bringing dead animals back to life and I have a rather worrying enquiry about a pyromancer.'

'A pyromancer?' Echoed Big Ben, barging his way through the front office door with a tray of coffee in his hand. 'I don't even know what that is.'

'Good morning, Ben,' said Jane. I gave him a high five, downed my tiny porcelain cup of espresso and took a tall Americano when he offered it. Jane explained, 'A pyromancer is someone who can conjure fire.'

'Actually, that's not quite right,' said Amanda from behind me.

I hadn't heard her leave her office but there she was, looking as lovely as ever. Normally, I would get a smile or a gentle touch on my arm, but it was noticeably absent today. I tried to catch her eye, but she was taking a coffee from Big Ben as he offered them around and, it seemed, trying to avoid looking at me.

'A pyromancer,' she continued. 'Is a person who uses fire for divination purposes – they attempt to tell the future by conjuring fire. The point, of course, is that they can conjure fire. If they then choose to use that skill for destructive purposes ...'

'Is that like in the Stephen King film *Carrie*?' asked Big Ben.

This time it was Jane who supplied the answer, 'No, she just had telekinetic powers; the ability to move things with her mind. She didn't conjure the fire, she simply manipulated fire that was already there.'

Big Ben's face was screwed up like he had a bad taste in his mouth. 'You lot have been hanging out with Frank too much.'

'Did someone say my name?' asked Frank. He'd come through the door and was in the office, but Big Ben's height and girth had hidden him until he spoke. The office this morning was a regular meeting place. Usually it would be Amanda, Jane, and me, plus a client maybe. Today, we had three extras already. The dogs were climbing Frank's legs to get attention. When none came, they gave up and returned to the seats where my father would continually scratch their ears as an idle habit.

Everyone said hello to Frank as he joined our conversation. 'We were just talking about pyromancy,' I told him. 'Jane believes she has a case.'

'I'm not sure I have time to pursue it,' she butted in quickly. 'That's the point I was trying to make. I think it's worth investigating, but so far we don't have a client.'

'What do we have?' asked Amanda.

'Twelve fires in a small area which appear to be linked. I got an email with no name yesterday. Or rather, the firm did. It came to the firm's central business email account. I was going to trace the IP back to the sender to see who it might be but hadn't got that far yet this morning.'

'It's only 0933hrs, Jane,' I pointed out.

She bit her lip, deep in thought. 'Whoever it is, wanted us to see it, but didn't want to tell us who they are. The fires ... I say they are linked, but the thing linking them is this email more than anything. Geographically, they are not spread over a large area, and they are house fires, car fires, two cases of spontaneous combustion.'

'There's no such thing,' scoffed my dad from his chair in the client waiting area. It proved he wasn't asleep at least.

Frank opened his mouth to speak. Undoubtedly about to tell us all about spontaneous combustion and why it happened - I cut him off quickly. 'Jane, can you send me the file, please? I'll have a look at it. Please find the sender though if you can make time later today.' Turning my attention to Frank, I said, 'Frank, old buddy, I have some questions for you since you are here. What was it you came in for?'

Frank waggled his eyebrows. 'I heard about your little run in with the were-wolves last night. I came to see that you are in one piece.'

'He's not in one piece,' remarked Amanda, looking at the cuts and bruises on my face. 'Are you, Tempest? You told me you were okay. I didn't expect you to lie about it.'

Her comment caught me off guard. As Big Ben's right eyebrow raised in question, Jane and Frank found other things to do, suddenly discovering that her printer was out of paper and needed them to collect some from the back store.

I couldn't help but narrow my eyes. My girlfriend was calling me out in public and I had no idea why. 'I didn't mention it because it wasn't worth mentioning, Amanda. Since when have we ever talked about on-the-job minor injuries?'

'These are not minor injuries, Tempest. This is the start of a trend. I've seen your car. The broken roof won't buff out.'

Feeling an argument brewing, I chose to diffuse the situation. 'I think we should talk about this later, Amanda. I have my father staying this weekend,' I let her know. 'It was something I arranged a few weeks ago and then forgot about.'

'Slipped his mind,' my father raised his voice but didn't take his eyes off the book in his hands.

'Indeed,' I agreed. 'Do you still want to get out for dinner tonight with a plus one?' I already knew the answer; I wasn't deliberately playing games, but I had no desire to be the one to tell her our usual Saturday night date was off.

She pursed her lips and skewed them to one side as she scrutinised me. 'I think we should leave it for the weekend. It will let you concentrate on this case.' Without a further word, she turned and went back to her office.

Unhelpfully, Big Ben leaned down to whisper. 'I think she's got the painters in, mate.'

I doubted that was the case, not that we'd been dating long enough for me to have recorded her menstrual cycle, but this was something else. Something about the bikers and her time as a cop perhaps. I would find out when she felt like sharing. For now, I seemed to have little choice but to pursue my case and wait for her to come around.

Frank and Jane passed Amanda as she went back to her office, both carrying boxes of printer paper.

Pushing thoughts of Amanda's unexpected mood from my head, I focussed on Frank. 'How did you know I met the Howlers last night and how do you even know about them?'

Frank laughed at me. 'Come on, Tempest. There isn't much supernatural stuff going on around here that I don't know about. Kent has been clear of were-wolves for more than a decade, so this new lot were soon clocked when they arrived last month.'

'Last month? They're that new?' Then I remembered Moose saying they first saw the Howlers two weeks ago.

Frank nodded at my question. 'They are. Or at least, that is when the activity started. To answer your first question, I know because I have contacts in the Kent League of Demonologists, and some of them are prominent politicians, policemen, and other public figures. I can't give you names obviously, but your name was taken at the scene and immediately flagged when the right person read it.'

I'd met a few of the KLoD, as I liked to call them. Frank discouraged the abbreviation which made me use it all the more. They were an odd bunch, as one might expect, but I'd never guessed they might also have serious jobs. The KLoD held no interest for me, the Howlers did. 'Frank, what can you tell me about the Howlers?'

He sucked in a deep breath through his nose and exhaled it hard in a sigh. 'Not much, I'm afraid. They're dangerous, but you already know that. We have classified them as Loup Garou because the sightings thus far have all been of upright bipedal weres. Does that match what you saw?'

I stifled a laugh and nodded. 'They were riding motorbikes.'

'That is not typical dog behaviour,' snorted Big Ben, not bothering to hide his mirth.

Frank tutted. 'These are not dogs, Ben. They're no closer to a dog than you are.'

'Dude, I'm the alpha dog!' argued Big Ben.

I rolled my eyes and tried to move the conversation along. 'They are upright werewolves, got it. What else? How about, how do I find them? I need to understand what they are doing and why. That is my first focus. They appear to have targeted a rival biker gang, one which I believe is involved in criminal activity, most likely smuggling and such. My question is why?'

'Why are they here?' Frank echoed. 'Why are they bikers? Those things I cannot tell you. I know why they are targeting the other biker gang though; it's purely territorial. Two packs will not share the same hunting ground. The Whitstable Riders might not be werewolves, but the Howlers' natural instinct to clear their turf had caused them to target the Riders anyway. They won't stop until they are all dead or dispersed.' Frank had a habit of making himself sound ominous.

My phone rang, the trill sound muffled inside my pocket. Fishing it out, I found the name displayed was someone I hoped I wouldn't hear from because his call would only mean one thing.

I put the phone to my ear. 'Hello, Chief Inspector.'

Murder Spree. Saturday, December 17th 1115hrs

WE ARRIVED AT THE address Chief Inspector Quinn gave me to find a police car blocking our path. A uniformed cop posted there to stop people getting closer to the scene raised an arm to bar our way.

'You'll have to go back,' he said when Big Ben powered down his window. 'There's been an accident.'

'There's been a murder,' I corrected him, leaning across the car to speak through the driver's window. We were in Big Ben's car; even if mine wasn't to be collected later today, it wouldn't fit more than two of us anyway. With dad already along for the day, and Frank insisting he had to come with us, Big Ben's beast of an off-road vehicle was the only choice.

The police officer, a man in his thirties with a trim beard looked unsurprised that we knew the truth, but I followed up with another statement before he could respond, 'We're here to meet Chief Inspector Brite,' I told him. 'I'm Tempest Michaels. He's expecting me if you wish to check.'

He nodded and stepped away, tilting his head down to speak into his lapel microphone. My father chose that moment to snore loudly. He was slumped in the back seat, the rum having caught up with him to act as a sedative. He shifted in his sleep, one leg lifting slightly to the sound of escaping gas.

'Time to go,' I announced, shoving my door open with a shoulder. Frank, his eyes wide on the seat next to my father, wasted no time in exiting either. The dogs, both asleep on my lap, got a rude awakening as I thrust them from the warm car and into the chilly onshore breeze.

'Please, stay in the car, gentlemen,' demanded the officer.

Big Ben held on for a second longer than the rest of us so he could power down the remaining windows before he too bailed out. 'Not a chance, mate. The environment inside my car is not survivable.'

The officer was going to argue, but his radio crackled with a response to his question and he waved us through. Big Ben needed to park the car which he did with his head hanging out of the window so he could suck on fresh air.

My father came around as the car bumped over the grass. 'Cor, did someone let one go?' He announced with his face screwed up in disgust.

We were at Tankerton Slopes, a piece of rough, open grassland with nary a tree in sight. On the eastern end, where it met Swalecliffe, a patch of scrubland set apart from the nearby houses and shops was dominated this morning by a white tent. Inside the tent was the decapitated body of Mathew Kaddish. It sat beneath a grey sky, a bank of clouds travelling along the coast threatened rain, and moisture, carried on the air, was doing its best to dampen our clothes and hair. The sea beneath the sky churned and chopped, a lone windsurfer ripping over the surface at incredible speed as he braved the cold.

The call from Chief Inspector Quinn confirmed what I hoped would not be true: Mathew Kaddish had met with a sticky end. In a surprising display of cooperation, he then gave me the location and told me the chief inspector here wanted to speak with me. It wasn't cooperation though; that I had known about the murder in advance was deemed highly suspicious.

I didn't have to go to them; I could have forced them to come to me, but I wanted more detail before I spoke with my client and this was where I would get it.

With the two sausages pulling me along, we traipsed through grass worn flat by feet that morning, eyes watching us from the tent area around which was a hastily erected barrier.

The barrier was being controlled by another junior officer, this one a woman in her twenties. She had ginger hair and freckles, and a button nose that could only ever be described as cute.

Big Ben pushed in front of me, 'Hi, I'm Big Ben.' She raised an eyebrow. 'Yes, babe, that's right. I know you've heard of me. It's important to let you know that all the rumours are true, but don't be alarmed,' he hit her with a smile intended to melt her will. 'I'll be gentle with you.'

She ought to have taken out her baton and whacked him with it, but instead, like all the other women he tried to charm, she blushed and giggled. If you could bottle what he had and turn it into a spray-on deodorant, womenkind would be helpless the world over. It was probably a good thing there was only one of him.

I elbowed him out of the way. 'Chief Inspector Brite?' I asked.

Hearing his name, a man looked up. He was busy talking to the crime scene guys working inside the tent, but I guessed correctly that it was him. He smiled as he approached, which already made him a vastly different beast from Quinn.

'Tempest Michaels,' he boomed as he extended his hand. 'And I see you have your colleague, Benjamin Winters, with you.'

Big Ben and I exchanged a glance. We'd been in the papers a few times but getting recognised wasn't exactly commonplace. The chief inspector was a swarthy man, his dark complexion matching his almost black hair. His racial heritage had to be mostly Caucasian but the rest of it might be African or possibly even Caribbean. I wasn't going to ask him but whatever his ancestry, it made him barrel-chested and thick-limbed. When he shook my hand, he crushed it like he was trying to crack a walnut.

I like a firm handshake but I almost winced when he let go and my bones could move back to their original positions. 'Chief Inspector Quinn suggested you found my foreknowledge questionable.' I said it as a statement, challenging him to question me.

'Not at all,' he assured me, which made my brow furrow. He leaned forward to speak at a volume no one else would hear, but as he was about speak, Frank shoved his head between Ben's arm and mine.

'Wot'cha, Angus. All quiet on the eastern front?' CI Brite engaged Frank in a handshake that saw their two middle fingers folded in so the knuckles met, and their thumbs held high as if about to perform a thumb-war.

'You're one of the KLoDs,' I remarked, putting two and two together.

The policeman's eyes flicked to mine.

Frank tutted. 'Tempest, I've asked you not to call them that. You cannot abbreviate the name of an ancient secret order.'

I shrugged, my eyes locked on the chief inspector's. 'Whatever. How is it that you are even allowed to be a police officer and mess around with all that demon nonsense?'

'It's not nonsense, I can assure you, Mr Michaels.' CI Brite's smile was still firmly in place. 'The work of the league has kept this country safe for generations. The Kent league is one of the oldest in the nation, with traditions going back to Anglo-Saxon times.'

I waved for him to stop. 'Heard it all before. If you know who I am, then you know I don't believe a word of it. Is there anything here to indicate who killed the victim?'

Brite huffed. 'I cannot put it in the official police report, but this is clearly a werewolf killing. The victim has been decapitated; his head was bitten off.' I'd heard that already from Quinn.

'Ewww,' said Big Ben. 'That's nasty.'

It sure was. CI Brite looked cheerful though. 'The League have driven the wolves from this land once before. We can do it again.'

I stared at him in disbelief. 'What about catching the criminals? What if they are not werewolves at all but are pretending to be as a terror tactic? Mathew Kaddish deserves justice, does he not?'

'And justice he shall get!' trumpeted the chief inspector as if he were rallying troops to storm a beach. I began to wonder if the man might be a little unhinged.

I switched tack. 'Chief Inspector, since you are local, you must know what the Whitstable Riders get up to. They hired me, but it's obvious they are engaged in illegal activities.'

His face took on a more serious expression. 'The Riders have always been very careful to never get caught. During my time in uniform, we have only ever been able to make misdemeanour charges stick. I believe they are smuggling something in from the mainland, but we have never been able to catch them in the act. It's likely they have their fingers in other pies, but other than a few parking tickets, and an occasional bar fight, they are clean. Their leader likes to employ good lawyers whenever one of them gets into trouble.'

'Really?' I couldn't stop my face from frowning as I struggled to understand. 'You've been investigating them for years and haven't been able to make anything stick. In this rural seaside community where they wear a uniform and badges to make them easily identifiable, you cannot catch them in the act of committing a crime?'

Brite began to bristle from my barrage of doubt. 'If you wish to take over the investigation, Mr Michaels, you can do so at any time. They are your clients after all. Why don't you solve their case, prove we do not have a werewolf problem, and then serve the Riders on a platter for me to arrest.'

I rubbed my chin. 'All right, I will.'

'Excuse me?'

'Thank you, Chief Inspector. I feel quite motivated now. Three deaths here in a week, the victims linked by being members of the same club and you want to pretend it's werewolves. There's a murder spree happening, and it will continue unchecked if someone doesn't stop them.' I felt filled with purpose suddenly. Amanda didn't want me to take the case, but she would understand when this was finished, and the dust settled. I thumped Big Ben's arm. 'Come on, buddy. We have work to do.' Just as I spun around to head back to the car, I paused to ask another question. 'What happened with the Howlers last night? Your officers were chasing them, and you had a helicopter overhead. Did you manage to catch any of them?'

CI Brite did not look inclined to answer my questions. Yet despite my deliberate challenge, he provided an answer. 'We did not catch them. They vanished near the pier.'

'Vanished? Like in a puff of smoke?' I attempted to clarify.

CI Brite made daggers with his eyes. 'No, Mr Michaels. They simply disappeared. It's how men like Frank and I know they are supernatural. You will undoubtedly look for a rational explanation. I wish you luck in finding it.'

I smiled at him. 'Thank you.' His mention of Frank made me check what he intended to do now. 'What's your plan?' I asked him. 'Are you coming with us or hanging out with the KLoD?'

He looked torn for a moment but made his decision. 'I'm coming with you. It's where I will be of most use. I just need a moment with the chief inspector first, if I may.'

'We'll be at the car.' I left him behind, wondering, not for the first time, how the world got filled with so many crazy people. Frank's decision to come with me would be due to his belief that I was running towards a supernatural enemy that would kill me unless he was there to give me advice. That and because he wanted to be there when I came up against something I couldn't explain. I entertained him because he spoke the same language as the crazy idiots I was both helping and trying to catch. He regularly proved invaluable.

'What's our next move?' Big Ben wanted to know.

I leaned against his car as I compiled a mental list. 'We need to find out what my clients are doing because I think that might show us why the Howlers are prepared to kill them. The flower trade is a cover for what they are really doing. If we get to the bottom of that, maybe we can figure this thing out. Then I need to find the Howlers since no one knows where they hide out. Finally, we need to find evidence to prove they are behind the murders. The victims are killed by wolves, but someone is controlling the animals.' Bull and Dozer snuffled around near my feet, happy as always to be out and doing something.

Big Ben had a doubtful look. 'If your client isn't telling you the truth about what they are doing, surely you have grounds to ditch the case. Wouldn't that ease tensions back at the office?' He was talking about Amanda.

He was probably right. 'My clients usually lie to me. Possibly not to such a degree, but they rarely tell me the whole truth and I have to figure it out for myself. As for Amanda, I am not of a mind to obey when she will not explain why she wants me to drop the case. Too late now, anyway: I told the chief inspector I would solve it.'

Frank was coming, his face split by a wide smile as it was often was. 'We need to make a pitstop on the way home if that's all right with you.' He rubbed his hands together in excitement.

I deferred to Big Ben; he was driving, and it is his car. 'Sure,' he said. 'Where are we going?'

Frank's eyes sparkled. 'To see a silversmith.'

Pet Names. Saturday, December 17th 1237hrs

'WHERE ARE WE OFF to?' asked my father, awake again after his little nap, and full of life. 'I could do with a coffee and the gents.'

I turned to Big Ben. 'Coffee?'

'Sure. There'll be a place we can stop on the sea front in Whitstable.'

It took less than a minute to find a place to park just off the High Street, Big Ben electing to stay in the car with the dogs while the rest of us went for coffee.

The grey sky was just the same here, but the wind, which had buffeted us on the exposed slopes, was less challenging now among the shops. The coffee shop, a franchise place unfortunately, served good coffee despite my reservations. More importantly, it had a toilet for my father to use.

Waiting for him, I considered my next move and what I might be able to cram into the rest of the day. The silversmith was in the village of Charing, a charming little place located just off the M20 motorway. I knew why Frank wanted to go there but it held no interest for me; I wasn't going to shoot anyone with a silver bullet. It wasn't on the way home either, not without driving back roads across the county to get there, but we could squeeze it into our trip for Frank's sake.

A full day into this investigation, I hadn't got very far and had more questions than answers. I had a few ideas to explore, not least because I wanted to know how the Howlers knew to target me; I wasn't buying that their attack was random. Either way, we were going to the Riders' clubhouse next.

Back in his car with bladders empty and large cups of coffee to refill them once more, Big Ben found it easily with my directions. Back at their gates again, I had him honk his horn to be let in. I doubted word of Brother Salmon's death had reached their ears yet because the police would inform the next of kin, not the victim's friends or co-workers.

Leaning forward to look between the front seats, my dad asked, 'This is the clubhouse of a motorcycle club?'

I nodded, watching the building ahead for signs of life. 'Yes.' Yesterday, when I arrived, it was already dark, so the lights inside made it easy to see the bikers working on their bikes. In the daylight, I could see no movement at all, but a door soon opened, Gopher appearing just like yesterday, jogging over to the gate to let me in.

Big Ben powered down his window. 'Just park anywhere?'

Gopher pointed to a spot in front of the roller door. Then shot me a wave. 'Hi, Brother Weasel.'

I sighed. This wasn't going to go away any time soon.

'Brother weasel?' asked my father.

Big Ben turned his head with deliberate slowness, a giant grin spreading across his face.

I narrowed my eyes at him. 'Just park the car, you big doofus.'

The car moved forward but he carried on staring at me, his wide grin stuck in place. 'Did they pick the name, or ...'

'Yes, dickhead. They picked the name. They all have American animal names. Their leader is called Moose.' He sniggered. 'The three guys killed so far are Salmon, Rattlesnake, and Vole.'

Big Ben cackled. 'Is there one called Turkey? Please tell me there is one called Turkey.'

'How come you got a name at all?' asked dad as he opened his door to get out.

I figured I might just as well get on with it and admit the truth. 'I had to become an honorary member just to get them to tell me about what they do and why the Howlers might be targeting them.' I slid from the car and put the dogs on the ground. They both stretched and shook themselves.

Dad nodded in understanding. 'What did they say?'

I wagged a finger at him. Ha! 'You're not an honorary member. You're not allowed to know.'

'That's right,' said Moose coming around the car to shake my hand. He caught the dogs by surprise, Bull barking a warning, which made Dozer bark in re-action. I tugged their lead to shush them both. Moose had Elk, Bear, and others with him. 'I'm glad to hear you are protecting the business of the club, Brother Weasel. We take transgressions seriously.' I could only imagine what the punishment might be - probably a light spanking with some daisies.

Big Ben failed to stifle his snigger, which elicited looks of discouragement from all the club members.

'Something funny, friend?' asked Bear.

Big Ben did his best to straighten his face. 'I think it's cute that you all have pet names for each other,' he replied. It was one of Big Ben's most reliable traits; he rarely masked the truth, he just let people have it. On many occasions, like this one, it was not the best decision.

Bear squared up to him. Elk was on his shoulder and backed by half a dozen more as the bikers moved in to circle my large friend. Frank, the only one of our group on his side of the car, took a step back as the circle of danger closed.

Bear lifted a finger to prod Big Ben in the chest and I cringed for what was to follow. 'I think you should apologise,' said Bear.

Elk leaned his head forward. 'Yeah. I think you are being disrespectful.'

'Moose,' I tried, leaning in to speak quietly so no one else would hear. 'My colleague will go through your men like they are ballerinas at a rugby match. He's just amusing himself. If you invite him inside, he'll apologise.'

Moose looked at me with disbelieving eyes. 'There's just one of him against my entire club. Or are you proposing to stand with him?'

Big Ben raised his hands. 'Look, guys, I had no intention of insulting anyone, okay? Your naming culture caught me by surprise, that's all.' He was being sensible and defusing the situation. I breathed a sigh of relief. That is until he winked at me. 'Now, which one of you is Brother Turkey?'

Bear threw the first punch, a swinging right fist coming around in a big circle. He wasn't alone though, the second his body tensed, two men whose names I didn't know came at Big Ben from the side and rear, and Elk sidestepped his partner, Bear, to throw his own punch. In total, I counted six men all surging toward my large friend.

I leaned on the car to watch.

Big Ben's left arm shot up to parry Bear's swing, a large right leg powering upward at the same time. With his back against the car, Big Ben's right foot caught Elk in the chest before his punch could make it halfway through the distance to its target. One moment Elk was surging forward, the next he sailed backward to be caught by the club members behind him. Big Ben's left arm whirled around in a wide circle to trap Bear's arm, whereupon he grabbed, yanked, twisted and pivoted off his back leg to throw Bear at the two men closing in on his blind spot.

Bear had to weigh over two hundred pounds, but Big Ben got him off the ground and moving through the air like he was a throw cushion. All three men went down and suddenly there was a wide semi-circle around that side of Big Ben's car with him standing at the centre.

No one moved.

'Where did you find him?' asked Moose, his voice filled with awe. Big Ben had put four men down without actually hitting any of them, and the other two of the six who chose to attack him were now pretending they hadn't moved.

'Everyone okay?' he asked, now sounding genuinely concerned that he might have hurt someone.

Just in case any of his club members felt like wading in for round two, Moose shouted, 'That's enough!' When all eyes turned his way, he said, 'Let's take it inside. Brother Weasel must have some news for us, or he wouldn't be here.' More quietly to me, as his men filed inside, he said, 'The marks on your face are from the Howlers?'

I nodded. 'I think it would have been much worse if they'd got the chance. I had a lucky escape. It's why I have him with me now.' I jabbed a finger at Big Ben.

Moose pursed his lips. 'I can see how that might help.'

As we moved toward the clubhouse, Gopher blocked our path. 'I'm supposed to collect your weapons,' he announced.

'I am the weapon,' Big Ben replied. Nevertheless, just like yesterday, we all got patted down before we went inside.

'We can't discuss club business in front of non-members so your friends will have to wait here,' Moose insisted once we were inside. I was going to be taken to a back room to speak in private, but the garage part of their property had a rest area with tables and chairs, and it was warm enough with the doors closed. I left my father with Frank and Big Ben but swear I heard my dad ask if they had anything to drink as I was being taken through the back.

'Is he dead?' asked Moose the moment we were in private. They had a room in the back set up for meetings. A long table ran down the centre of the room with a dozen wooden chairs around it. At the head was a larger chair with the word 'President' carved into it. At the other end, the word was 'Deputy' which meant Brother Salmon had been Moose's second in command. I'd let the dogs off their lead once the door was closed; they were small and well-behaved. They both vanished under the table, audibly snuffling air in and out of their noses as they searched for interesting smells.

To answer Moose's question, I said, 'Yes.' There seemed no point in beating around the bush. 'He was found on Tankerton Slopes this morning by a man out walking his dog. It is the same as before. The same as Rattlesnake and Vole.'

Moose took the news well, perhaps expecting it and thus prepared. Elk and Bear were with us and less reserved in their reactions. There was some swearing. Okay there was a lot of swearing, but Bear punched a wall, leaving a four-knuckle dent and Elk looked ready to kill.

Elk spoke through gritted teeth. 'When the guys find out, we are going to lose some of them, Moose. They've got wives and kids. Most of them anyway, and they'll want reassurances that they'll be safe to make the run tomorrow morning.'

Moose wasn't going to take any crap from his subordinate. 'Look, if we lose a couple of the guys because they chicken out and run, then so be it. I'll get us through this, but listen, Brother Salmon would have been fine if he'd stayed here. He snuck out against club orders and that's what got him killed. If he'd stuck with us, he'd be here now. We need to make the deliveries tomorrow just the same as every other day. We go together; strength in numbers.'

I stayed quiet and listened, hoping they would give something away. I was beginning to believe their claim to be smuggling in flowers, but I struggled to believe that was all they were doing. They talked about delivering flowers as if it were life or death. It made me want to believe there was a lot at stake for them if they failed and that didn't sound like the flower industry to me. I would find out the truth eventually.

'How are you going to get us through this?' Bear demanded more detail.

'You need to name a new deputy,' said Elk.

Moose curled back his top lip. 'Don't you two boys think you can challenge me. Neither one of you has what it takes to run this club. The senior council will discuss Salmon's replacement at the next meeting. You'll both be involved.'

I butted in with a question, my investigator's mind wanting answers. 'How did the Howlers know he left the clubhouse?' I let the question hang while I made eye contact with each of the three men. 'He snuck out in the middle of the night. How far away does he live?'

'About a mile, back toward the motorway on the way out of Whitstable,' said Elk.

'Completely the opposite direction to Tankerton Slopes then. He had only a mile to go, maybe a couple of minutes. Not long enough for anyone to react unless they already knew he was coming. How would they know that?' I got no answer from the three men facing me. 'Here's a better question: how did they know about me at all?'

Now I had their attention.

'Do you think they are watching us?' asked Moose.

I wriggled my nose; it was one option. 'Maybe. Have you swept this place for listening devices or cameras? Have you looked outside? They could place a camera across the street and watch the place remotely. They could even have drones above you.'

My questions were dishonest because I thought the truth was something else entirely.

A noise drew my attention across the room where Dozer was sitting on his backside and trying to scratch his ear. Dachshunds are not very well designed, and Dozer isn't very well balanced, so he managed a few swipes of his back foot and then fell over. Casting my eyes in that direction brought something to my attention I might otherwise have not seen: a large, wooden plaque bearing all the names of the previous presidents. It went back to the late sixties, each name having a pair of dates beside it to show the period of tenure. In stark contrast to their practice, the plaque showed real names, not animal club names. The most recent, showing just one date because he is still the president, was Davis Milnthorpe.

One name had been crossed out. Or rather, it had been burned out. I could just about make out what the letters were and squinted to form a name.

'Brother Weasel, did you not hear me?' asked Moose, breaking my concentration.

I turned to look at him. 'I'm sorry, what were you saying?'

'I asked what your next step is?' he repeated.

Wondering the same thing myself, I said, 'I need to visit a silversmith.'

There was nothing more I needed from the Riders right now; I wouldn't solve the mystery of the Howlers by talking to my clients. I found dad with a rum and coke in his hand, chatting with one of the Riders. Approaching their conversation, I could already hear the connection: they were both former Royal Navy.

'You know my son, of course,' my father turned his conversation to me. He was talking to one of the club members I hadn't yet met. 'Tempest, this is Brother Muskrat.'

We shook hands quickly. 'Dad, we need to go. This is a working day for me, even if you are taking it easy.'

Behind him, Big Ben held up three fingers and made his eyes go wobbly with his tongue lolling out: It was my father's third rum and coke. I'd only been gone ten minutes.

'But I'm just discussing membership,' dad protested.

'No.'

'No what?'

'Just no, dad. You are not allowed to join a motorcycle club. Ignoring the small matter that you don't own a motorcycle and haven't been on one since the seventies, mum would shoot you if she ever found out you'd so much as considered it and then she would sell my testicles to medical science via the internet. It's a hard no.'

He downed his rum and coke. 'I don't think I need your permission,' he grumbled snippily. 'Nor your mother's. I bet none of the brothers had to ask permission to join. Did you, fellas?' he raised his voice to get their opinion. He got a resounding chorus of nos from anyone within earshot. 'Thought not.' Feeling he'd proved his point. He handed his glass back to Brother Muskrat and started back toward the door we came in through.

Walking in front of me, he tottered just enough for me to put my hands out in case he fell. He stopped, got his centre of balance back and stared accusingly at the floor behind him. 'Fellas, you have an uneven patch of floor there.' It was as smooth and level as an ice rink. 'Might want to get that checked out,' he suggested.

I nudged him to the door. 'Let's just get back to the car.'

It took some effort but mercifully I got him back to the car and strapped into his seat.

'Where to next?' asked Big Ben with the car in idle.

The clock on his dash displayed the time and it was already getting late for lunch. My stomach rumbled its emptiness.

From the back seat, a slurry version of my father said, 'Fish 'n' chips on the beach?'

Fish 'n' Chips. Saturday, December 17th 1412hrs

IT TOOK NO TIME at all to get back into the town centre and to the chip shop there. With a sign outside boasting that it opened for business in 1708, I hoped they'd changed the oil since. We opted to eat inside in deference to the winter temperature and stiff breeze we would face on the beach.

Large pieces of cod, deep fried in batter, alongside heaping mounds of deep-fried soggy chips smothered in salt and vinegar, landed in front of us just a few minutes after walking inside. The air was thick with the smell of hot oil and I had to wonder if the workers ever managed to get it out of their hair. It was a rare treat; not the sort of food I would allow myself except on an occasion such as today. Despite the amount of rum in him and the slurry speech, my father acted as if completely sober. He fell upon his plate of food ravenously, but then the rest of us did too.

The dogs were allowed in and went under the table where they pawed my legs and attempted to jump up to my lap in turns. They wanted fish and chips for lunch too.

In between bites of food, I chose to indulge Frank and ask him about the silversmith. 'I take it this chap is making bullets and that is why you want to see him.'

Frank shifted the food around in his mouth so he could reply. 'It's not a man,' he told us around a gobful of chips. It came out a little distorted, but we all understood what he said.

Big Ben raised an eyebrow. 'Let me guess: its an elf. No, hold on. It's an elf warrior prince stuck on Earth after disgracing himself before the elf king and now he makes mystic weapons for the KLoD as a means to pay his rent.'

Frank frowned at him. 'No. It's a woman.' Big Ben's expression changed to one of interest. 'Actually, it's three women. They're sisters. Beverly, Chloe, and Zoe.'

Big Ben's face took on a hopeful look. 'Are they old?' he asked with bated breath.

Frank had to think about that. 'Depends on one's perspective, I suppose, but I think they all turned thirty last month.'

Big Ben's jaw fell open and a piece of fish fell out. He didn't even notice. 'They're triplets?' he gasped as if he'd just been offered something magical.

'Yes,' Frank replied, wondering what all the fuss was about.

Big Ben reached out to grab my arm. 'We have to go. We have to go now.'

'I haven't finished my lunch.'

'Get eating, Tempest,' he insisted. 'Do you not understand how rare this is? Triplets of an eligible age. It's been on my list since I wrote it and I've never even had a sniff of a chance so far. Of course, quads and quins are on there too but the chances of that are up there with a big lottery win.'

I couldn't help but chuckle at his desperately needy face. 'What makes you think you can bed any of them, let alone all three? What if they are married?'

'They're not,' mumbled Frank around another piece of fish.

'What if they are ugly?' I asked.

'They're stunning,' said Frank. 'Golden blonde hair and blue eyes. They look like shampoo advert models.'

I thought Big Ben was going to start dribbling. He got to his feet. 'I need to check how I look. Eat up you lot. The Big Ben-mobile leaves in five with or without you.'

As he ran to the men's room, Frank picked up another piece of fish. Inspecting it critically on the end of his fork, he asked. 'Do you think I should tell him they are all lesbians?'

I damned near choked on my chips.

We Silversmiths Three. Saturday, December 17th 1538hrs

BY THE TIME WE arrived in Charing, the light was already fading fast. Darkness would descend in the next twenty minutes and though the village wasn't far from civilisation, or the motorway even, it was remote enough that it picked up no ambient light from anywhere else.

The address Frank had for the silversmiths wasn't even in the village though. We passed right through it and out the other side, reaching our destination just a yard or two before the sign announcing drivers were leaving Charing.

Big Ben rolled the car up a gravel driveway to a cottage set between trees. Frank hadn't been here before, he explained. He first met the sisters when they came into his shop several years ago, though he'd heard about them before that because their reputation proceeded them. They were metal crafters by trade, all three following a family tradition that went back centuries to a time when their ancestors were blacksmiths forging armour.

According to Frank they still did that today, but were better known for providing weapons, trinkets, and artefacts to the occult trade.

Big Ben checked his teeth and hair in his visor mirror before shutting off the engine, then turned around to snag Dozer from the backseat.

'What're you doing?' I asked him with a curious frown.

'All guns blazing,' he replied. Then, seeing that none of us got it, he explained. 'Great hair: check. Devastatingly handsome: check. Athletic physique to prove I am clearly good mating stock: check. Throw in a cute, sausage-shaped, floppy-eared dog, and the irresistible level goes right off the chart. Plus, he's sausage shaped, and I want them to make the association between him and my own ...'

'Give me the damned dog,' I took Dozer out of Big Ben's hands.

'Dude!' he protested.

An evil thought crept into my head. 'I think this challenge is beyond you,' I was throwing down the gauntlet. 'I don't think you can seduce any of them, let alone all three.'

His eyebrows rose to his hairline as a smile creased his stupid face. 'Oh, Padawan, where do I begin?'

'I'll go so far as to bet money on it.'

He pushed out his bottom lip in thought. 'A wager. I like that. It really ups the ante. Name your price and terms.'

Feeling like a cheat and loving it. This would teach the womanising git a lesson and take him down a well-deserved peg. 'A grand. I wager a thousand pounds that you cannot get even one of the sisters into your bed. Or any bed for that matter. And proof is required.'

He stuck out his hand to seal the deal. I feel it necessary to make it clear I would never engage in such a bet where I thought the woman or, in this case, women, were going to be exposed to anything they might disapprove of. Big Ben is a rogue, but he would never do anything to compromise their free will. However, since Frank was certain they had all grown up gay, I was quite content this would be an entertaining interlude for all parties. Except Big Ben, of course. He was going to suffer. I'd let him know the truth later and make him buy me a pint, not hand over a grand.

He bounced from the car with vigorous steps, Bull and Dozer chasing after him excitedly as if sensing the purpose in his strides.

My father ambled up next to me. 'Your friend has some issues.'

'And a skewed sense of what is important in life, but he seems happy. I figure he'll meet someone eventually, but maybe he won't.'

Frank speed-walked around us all to get to the door first. This was his show after all, the rest of us were just here because he asked us to make a detour.

The house was more accurately to be called a cottage. It was double-fronted, with windows either side of the front door and all set on one floor. The low roof was in need of repair and the windows were wooden with glass, not a modern double-glazed material.

'Do they live here?' I questioned.

Frank knocked on the door with his knuckles but looked over his shoulder to say. 'I don't know. My guess would be that one of them does, maybe. There's a forge at the back, I know that much.'

Any further discussion of the subject was cut off when a light came on behind the front door. It shone through a small glass panel above Frank's head height. With no light outside, my eyes were already beginning to adjust to the dimness and the bright square was hard to look at. More so when the door opened.

Big Ben made a small squeaking noise of excitement which got a look from the woman now illuminated in her doorway. She was most of six feet tall and would tower over me if she wore heels. Glancing down, I saw that she wore calf-length leather boots with a low chunky heel. They had buckled straps up the sides. Covering her body was a summer dress of an aquamarine colour though I noticed, when she moved, that other subtle hues ran through it. Her arms were exposed, the flesh there goosepimpling in the December air. She was delicate and petite despite her height, her neck an almost cartoonish pin on which her head balanced. Above all, she was seriously attractive – and there were two more of her somewhere.

I began to see Big Ben's interest.

Frank waved his hand in an arc. 'Hi. I'm Frank. We met a couple of years ago,' he began to introduce himself.

'Yes, I know who you are, Frank. You are the collector.'

To Frank, I whispered, 'The collector?'

'It's what the League call me,' Frank hissed back.

Standing in the doorway, the woman said, 'I received a call from the League; they told me to expect you. I was not advised that you would have company.' She nodded her head at me. 'This one looks familiar.'

I stepped forward to extend my hand. 'Tempest Michaels. You've probably seen me on the television.'

Frank reached across to push my hand back down. 'She doesn't shake hands. None of them do,' he hissed from the side of his mouth.

'I do not like to be touched by men,' she announced.

Big Ben's smile fell. 'Say what now?'

'Please do not be offended,' she implored me. 'You should all come inside. It is cool this evening.' Without a further word, she turned around and walked away, back into her house along a narrow corridor. It branched off to the left and right, but what lay beyond the closed doors remained a mystery.

Falling into step beside me, Big Ben whispered. 'She doesn't like to be touched by men? What does that mean.'

Cruelly, I just shrugged. 'Looks like you've got your work cut out, old boy. I hope you brought your A game.'

'Ha! Watch and learn.' His cockiness was a joy to behold.

The hallway ended in a wider room that appeared to be the hub of the house. The woman, who was yet to give us her name, crossed it at an angle to go through a door with light spilling from it. Inside, despite a complete lack of chatter, I could tell there were more people: her sisters we discovered, when we too entered the room.

Again, Big Ben made his small noise of excitement as all three women were identical. Identically beautiful. One wore jeans and a t-shirt with a pair of plastic sandals, the third a tight-fitting pair of leggings and a sports vest with running shoes on her feet. None of them were dressed for winter because the room was a workshop and they were working with heat.

'The collector is here,' announced the woman who met us at the door.

Frank said, 'Hello,' to all three women and waved his hand through the air again.

The three women were all looking our way. They were gathered on one side of a large oak table looking back at the four men gathered on the other side. On the table were all manner of trinkets and weapons. Set along one side were axe heads. They were without the shaft to heft the weapon but looked to have been recently forged; their blades were still dull. I saw daggers, some of them silver, one which appeared to be solid gold, and a sword which looked very familiar.

Frowning at it I asked, 'Is that Vermont Wensdale's?

My question attracted three sets of surprised faces from the ladies. 'You have a good eye,' said the sister in the sports gear. 'That is his weapon. It was damaged in a fight with a hydra and required to be reworked.'

'What's a hydra?' asked my father. Then, dismissing the question as insignificant, he said, 'Good afternoon. No one seems likely to do introductions, so I'll kick them off. I'm Michael Stormcloud Michaels. This is my son, Tempest Danger Michaels, and I guess you know Frank.'

'I'm Big Ben,' said Ben proudly.

The women all but ignored him, but they did introduce themselves. The one in the dress said, 'We are the Paxton sisters. I am Beverly.'

Jeans and t-shirt said, 'I am Chloe.'

Sports gear said, 'And I am Zoe.'

'You came for the munitions,' said Beverly to Frank. 'They are ready as request-ed. You will distribute them?'

'Many are already waiting for them,' he replied. 'This new threat has the League and other defenders highly agitated. It has been so long since a lycanthropic threat endangered our lands that the weapons required to defend ourselves have been all but retired.'

I listened with rapt fascination but couldn't help asking. 'What munitions are you here to collect, Frank?'

'Why, silver bullets of course,' replied Chloe.

'And the guns to use them with,' added Zoe.

Big Ben tried to get in on the conversation. 'A normal gun will not suffice?'

This time the women looked at him. Then Beverly levelled a finger at me to draw her sisters' attention. 'This is the disbeliever.'

'We know of him,' the sisters chimed in perfect unison. 'What is the large one? Is he a were bear?'

Big Ben grinned at them. 'I have some bear like qualities, ladies. Anatomically, I have often been compared to a bear once I get my ...'

I cut him off. 'We ought to be getting back, Frank.'

'Yes, yes,' he nodded. 'We won't take up any more of your time. If you have what I came for, we'll be on our way.'

However, Beverly wasn't done with me yet. Her piercing blue eyes met mine. 'Why is it that you refuse to believe when there is so much evidence around you?'

Aware that I was in her house, I did my best to be polite. 'I see no evidence. I have investigated vampires, ghosts, boogeymen and pixies, yet none of it was real. Every case I tackle shows me the supernatural has no foundation. I know

Vermont Wensdale because he has shown up to chase the very monsters I reveal to be men. The werewolves are no different as I will prove when I get to the bottom of what is going on.'

'You see what I have to put up with,' commented Frank. 'A were would bite him under a full moon and he would still deny it was real.'

Behind me my dad mumbled, 'They're all as nuts as each other, kid.'

I wasn't going to let myself be drawn into a conversation. 'It really is time to go, Frank. Ben and I need to get organised for a stakeout. Do you need a hand carrying things to the car?'

Chloe's jaw dropped. 'A stakeout? You propose to hunt the wolf pack? Based on the premise they are nothing but men in what ... costumes? You will breathe your last breath this night.'

'I think we'll be okay, toots,' chimed Big Ben, doing his best to look big and imposing. 'If they come near us, they will get a good twatting.'

Her hands scrambled over the table. 'Here, take these. I insist.' She thrust silver necklaces at us. 'These pentagrams will help to counter the weres. If they are newly changed, it may even force them to revert to human form.'

I looked at the five-sided symbol. The workmanship was excellent; delicate like filigree almost. Each pendant was two inches across and bright silver as if brand new, which they probably were. I cast a glance at Frank. 'A pentagram?'

Chloe handed one to my father as well and kissed his cheek. 'Bless you, sir, for your bravery. May this keep you safe from your son when he falters and they turn him.'

I rolled my eyes.

Frank sighed. 'Yes, Tempest, a pentagram.' He looked at the sisters with a hopeless expression. 'I have to explain everything to them.' Settling into lecture mode while the sisters left the room to fetch his weapons and munitions, Frank said, 'The inverted pentagram has been long associated with the werewolf. Inverted, it forms the symbol of the goat with its chin in the bottom point and its horns filling the top two points. Pagans performing dark rituals will invert the pentagram and perform their spells within it, orientating the bottom point to the west.'

'Why the west?' I interrupted.

'Because that is where the sun sets. The wolf resides within the evil of the inverted pentagram. Ignoring daft comedies like *Teen Wolf,* which completely misrepresents the truth, most movies get some of the legend right. Werewolves are a primal force. They cannot be convinced to behave, they are very hard to kill, and you should not go up against them unless you are prepared for the fight of your life. The pentagram in your hand is of limited value,' he whispered the last sentence so the women wouldn't hear him. 'Yes, displayed the right way up, it can counteract the magic that permits the werewolf to transform. However, a sufficiently powerful were; one who has been born that way or first transformed many years ago, will most likely be unaffected.'

Chloe came back into the room carrying a heavy box. Big Ben darted forward to help her but was shooed away as the strong-willed woman demonstrated she could manage. 'Those are imbued with wolfsbane. It strengthens their effectiveness.'

Frank nodded as if it was an obvious step for her to take. I wanted to ask what wolfsbane was, but that would just stretch things out even further.

Zoe and Beverly followed their sister into the room, each carrying a similar box to Chloe's. Frank opened the first of them and I couldn't help step forward to peer inside when he flicked the clips holding it shut. Big Ben and my father were equally curious.

Inside were rows and rows of silver bullets, each pressed into a tight hole in the foam which filled the base. To the side were automatic pistols; two to the left and two to the right. I said nothing but my brain was screaming that these were illegal weapons and getting caught with them would mean jail time. There are no guns in Great Britain.

Frank lifted one of the weapons, a small calibre beretta with a customised handle. Expertly, he worked the mechanism and inspected it. 'Fine work, as always,' he nodded his approval. 'The other cases?'

'Shotgun shells and another set like these,' said Chloe.

Zoe produced a shot gun from her back where it had hung unseen from a sling.

Dozer barked his impatience because no one was paying him any attention. I looked down to see my two dogs staring back up. 'All done, Frank?'

He placed the weapon away and closed the case once more. 'All done. Thank you, ladies. I shall make sure they go to the right people.'

Ten minutes later, we were back in Big Ben's car with a boot full of illegal firearms and a bewildered Big Ben.

'They barely even looked at me.' The concept of a woman being able to resist him wasn't a new one, but it didn't happen very often.

'I'll let you off with paying out the grand, buddy. I knew they were gay when I made the bet.' I had to admit the truth; Big Ben was questioning the foundation of the universe as the Earth shifted beneath his feet.

He squinted down at me, his eyes attempting to bore a hole in my head. 'Tempest, such mistreatment demands reprisals. It shall be necessary to exact vengeance.' He said it as if he were the Godfather and I had just admitted to killing his brother or something. He was already in debt to me for about fifty practical jokes and he knew it. Nevertheless, I could expect him to be extra dickish for the next few days.

Batman Cometh. Saturday, December 17th 1707hrs

WE DROPPED FRANK OFF at his book shop, my dad and I helping him to carry the cases inside and up the stairs where he had us place them on the counter. It was just after closing time, so we arrived to find the shop still occupied by his assistant Poison. She wasn't alone, answering a question I had never asked about who was running his shop today.

'This is my cousin, Athena,' she told me as I placed the heavy case down.

Athena looked much like Poison, though a couple of years older by my reckoning. That would make her twenty-two and I felt glad Big Ben was waiting in the car in case a traffic warden came because she was every bit as delightfully attractive as her younger cousin.

I waved a quick hello, backing toward the door the moment the box was out of my hands.

'That's the one?' Athena asked of Poison.

Poison bit her lip and smouldered her eyes at me. We'd had a long-running tension brought about by her proposal to give me everything I could possibly want and my continued resistance. Now both girls were looking at me as if

I were a dainty morsel to be devoured. Continuing to back away, I reached behind to grip the doorframe. It led to stairs and down to the street outside.

'Come on, dad,' I begged.

'Hold your horses, kid. I'm not as fast as I used to be.' A display of DVDs had caught his eye. Frank's bookshop specialised in all things supernatural or science fiction; two genres my father enjoyed watching.

'Ben is double parked, dad,' I reminded him.

'And we're all going on a stakeout tonight so I wouldn't get to watch it anyway,' he moaned.

I wasn't sure I'd heard him correctly. 'Stakeout, dad? Surely you will stay at home with the dogs and a bottle of rum. Get a movie if you want one. I'll settle up with Frank later. My treat.'

'And miss all the fun? Not a chance. I'm coming with you boys tonight.' I groaned inside and let him slip by me to head down the stairs. His voice echoed back up as I waved goodbye to Frank and the girls. 'Say, have you got a spare one of those Batman suits you wear?'

Night Ops. Saturday, December 17th 1817hrs

I HAD ANOTHER COUPLE of goes at convincing my father to stay at home, but he was having none of it. My argument that the dogs needed a sitter met with a considered argument because what did I normally do? Normally they went next door to Mrs Comerforth when I wasn't sure what time I would get back. She liked the company as much as they did.

That's where they would go before we left again, but we were home for more than an hour, getting dinner – I had some chicken breasts in the fridge and rice is easy to steam – and changing our clothes. Big Ben and I have long favoured hard-wearing clothes of a similar design to those we wore in the army. Choosing black over olive drab or any other military environment colour, we wore rip-stop trousers, hybrid boots, that were as much a mountain hiking boot as they were designed for military use, then, depending on temperature, a t-shirt or jacket. Tonight, we needed the jackets; it was too cold for anything else. Then we added our usual Kevlar vests and Kevlar-knuckled gloves.

I had spares of every item because I used them so often, so my father became the third musketeer decked out in head-to-toe black. He didn't really look the part, truth be told. His silver hair stood in stark contrast to the outfit, like a woman in her seventies dressing like her granddaughter. However, nothing was going to put him off, and he even abstained from drinking more rum as we got ready.

At 1817hrs, we were ready to go and had no reason to delay any longer. The Howlers were in Herne Bay somewhere and I planned to find them. According to Chief Inspector Brite, they vanished somewhere close to the pier, so that was my start point. Taking two backpacks from my office, one each for Big Ben and me, we loaded the car and were about to set off when my phone rang. I pulled it from my pocket and glanced at it.

My blood froze.

Seeing the look of dread on my face, dad said, 'It's your mother, isn't it?'

Reluctantly, I thumbed the green button to answer it. 'Hello, mother. How is the concert?'

'It hasn't started yet,' she replied quickly to deal with my question so she could ask one of her own. 'Where are you? You do not sound like you are in the house.'

How on Earth could she tell? We were in Big Ben's car, but the engine wasn't running yet. 'Um, no. We are in the car?' I tried tentatively to see if she would buy it.

'Well, where are you going?' she demanded to know.

Now I was caught. I didn't want to tell her the truth. The best thing for dad and me was for her to believe we had a quiet weekend watching action movies and walking the dog to the pub while a chicken roasted in my oven. It sounded idyllic but I wasn't the type who just lied to people. Most especially not my mother. I couldn't tell her the truth and I wasn't going to lie.

On the backseat, my dad just shrugged unhelpfully.

Because I hadn't answered straight away, mum asked, 'What are up to?' Then she raised her voice. 'Michael, are you there?'

'I am here, kitten. Are you ready for Cliff Richard? Are the Shadows with him this time?'

'Don't you be all sweet with me, Michael Michaels. You two boys are up to something.' She gasped. 'Tempest, I had better not find out that you got him involved in any of your daft capers. Why couldn't you have been a dentist? I never get any of these problems from your sister, you know. She doesn't give me heart palpitations.'

I motioned for Big Ben to start the engine. 'Yes, mother. I believe the subject of my career and your disapproval of it has been covered before. Must we go over it again?'

'Must you continue associating yourself with weirdos and hoodlums?'

This was an old argument that was impossible for either side to win. I would never willingly have the discussion again, but my mother liked to pick at scabs when she could.

Dad leaned through to get his face closer to the phone. 'Darling, we're just off to the coast to spy on a gang of motorcycle werewolves. Enjoy the concert, dear. I hope it is worth the trip.'

'You expect me to believe that, do you? Motorcycle werewolves indeed. I'll find out what you two have been up to when I get back. You're too old to be out galivanting, Michael, you daft old codger. Go home, put your slippers on and try to avoid drinking rum.' There were some words in the background, a short conversation with someone else before she returned to the phone. 'I have to go. Just you be warned.' The line went dead, and I took a breath for the first time in several minutes.

Dad relaxed back into his seat and looked out the window. 'I love your mum,' he told me. 'But she can be a real pain in my bum sometimes. If I have so much as a scratch on me when she gets back, I'll never hear the end of it.'

I faced the road and hoped he could manage to get through the night un-scathed. To be fair, the most likely cause of injury would be head collision with a blunt object due to imbibing too much rum, so I figured we were safe enough unless he had a bottle stashed about his person.

It took forty minutes to get there, a casual drive past the pier gave us a refreshed view of the area; we needed to select a place to position ourselves and a direction to approach from. Ideally, this would have been conducted in daylight with people around so we could walk and poke about in our normal clothes and not look like we stood out. Now we were just going to have to wing it.

Big Ben parked his car at the far end of the sea front. Ahead of us was the beach and the sea. Behind us was the seaside resort, or what was left of it now its heyday was a century in the past. Brite's claim that the Howlers had vanished near the pier was incongruous because there was nothing there. The long stretch of exposed steel and wood ended where the shore met the coast road.

Curious enough to check it out anyway, we skirted along the coast with the black sea behind us. From land we would be all but invisible as we crept along toward the old skeletal feature. Four hundred yards took us five minutes across the sloping uneven and shifting surface, but we reached the underside of the pier without seeing another soul.

'It's a bit nippy,' observed my father.

He wasn't wrong. The frigid winter air this close to the water was laced with ice-cold water and an onshore breeze did its best to rob our bodies of heat. We would gain nothing by discussing the cold though, it would just attune our senses to it more starkly.

'There's nothing here,' said Big Ben, echoing my thoughts. 'That Brite character was having us on.'

We were underneath the pier, which the Howlers could get to only if they drove their bikes across the pavement and down the beach, but there was no secret entrance to a hideout down here. I'm not sure what I expected to find but I got crabs, limpets, litter, and a sort of rotten fish smell.

I pulled my backpack off and started back up the sloping beach toward the sea wall. Glancing at Big Ben, I asked, 'Do you think they'll fly in this breeze?'

He shrugged. 'Kind of an expensive way to find out if they don't.'

'Who fly what?' asked my dad.

With the backpack unzipped, I slid a large drone from inside along with a complex handset to control it. Big Ben did the same. They were a recent investment and yet to be used in anger. Thus far, we'd had a few test flights to get used to the controls, but I'd spent the money to get the infrared technology cameras installed. I wanted to be able to find things at night.

'The bikers are out here somewhere, dad. That much we know. They can't just vanish, and they are not werewolves, so task number one is to find out where they are. Once I know that, I can watch them to find out what they are doing.' Satisfied by my answer, dad fell silent as the drones' rotors came quickly to full speed and lifted them gently into the air.

The breeze buffeted them slightly, but they were stable enough to operate even as we took them higher. The control box came with a strap to go around our necks and an eight by six-inch screen to show live footage. For now, I had it in standard video mode, the picture dark until I got it over the town.

The instructions boasted a two-hour battery life, but I wasn't sure if I could trust it and didn't want to find out what happened when the drone died high above Herne Bay. Ninety minutes in, I was not only getting bored, an emotion I expected to face on a stakeout, but also nervous about the drone conking out. A display in the corner of my screen promised me a further forty-three minutes of run time, but we had been circling the town, Big Ben at one end and me at the other, with not one sight of a motorcycle gang. We hadn't even found a hopeful but ultimately disappointing target to explore.

'I'm calling it,' I announced, aiming to bring the drone directly back to me. It was disappointing to get nothing, but we could still cruise the town for a while and see if we spotted anyone: maybe they were all in a bar and that's why there was no sign of them. We could look for parked bikes more easily from the car.

Big Ben didn't respond when I spoke, and when I checked, I could see him scrutinising his screen with interest. 'I might have something,' he told us, not sounded very sure of himself.

Dad went over to check the screen too. 'What is it?'

'A guy on a bike. That's unremarkable, I know, but I can see the patch on his jacket; it's one of the Riders. I thought they were all hiding at their club house in Whitstable.'

'They are. Or, rather, they are supposed to be. Moose wanted no one to go anywhere until the threat could be neutralised.' My drone was on its way back to me, but I could take my eyes off the screen for a half second or so as I brought it closer. Edging closer to Big Ben, I flicked my eyes to his screen and caught sight of the biker. 'Wow! How close are you?'

He flicked his eyes down to his screen. 'Height above ground is fifteen feet. These things are silent though, and even if they weren't, he'd never hear it over his bike.'

I snorted an exasperated laugh. 'I'm more worried about you hitting a street sign.'

The moment I said it, the drone's camera suddenly spun end over end as the drone flipped helplessly out of control. The Whitstable Rider drove onward, oblivious to the drama behind him.

With no time to lose, I broke cover from our hiding position behind the sea wall. 'Get to the car! I want to see where he went. I'll land my drone, just pick me up on the way past.' We all recognised the street he was on; it was the inland road into the town from Whitstable. We would have to be fast if we were going to catch him, but it was worth a try. My favoured reason for the Howlers knowing about me was a mole in the Riders providing them with information – was this the mole?

Big Ben shed his control unit, chucking it to my dad so he could run unencumbered, dad stayed with me, accepting that he wouldn't be able to keep up with Big Ben running full speed.

Two minutes later, Big Ben's car was screeching to a stop on the tarmac two yards in front of me and my drone was just coming into land. Thirty seconds after that, he was burning rubber with dad and me inside the car.

The roads were quiet but not empty, forcing us to slow to match the speed of the cars around us. Big Ben took a left to get us off the coast road and wove around the old, narrow streets until he fetched up facing against the direction the Rider had been coming. Now on the same stretch of road, if he hadn't turned off, we would meet him coming the other way.

Eyes peeled, we searched the street ahead for a single headlight, but all we got was car after car. A moment of excitement came and went when a single headlight came toward us, but it was a racing motorcycle in bright colours; a completely different beast. In such a small town, it took less than a minute for us to accept he'd slipped away while we were racing to find him.

Big Ben carried on until we came to the area where his drone went down. Expecting to have to search for it or find a trail of parts strewn across the tarmac, I was pleasantly surprised to find it sitting at the side of the road looking intact.

Leaving Big Ben to swing the car around – we were not done in Herne Bay yet – I jumped out as he briefly paused in traffic. The drone had several busted blades from impacting the ground, but otherwise looked unscathed. I toggled the on switch to be rewarded with a blinking light on the power panel.

'Is it dead?' asked my dad as I clambered back into the passenger's seat. I shook my head and passed it to him.

'We need to have another go at trying to find that lone Whitstable Rider,' I told him. 'We might get lucky.'

Big Ben added, 'We can hang out for another couple of hours to see if the Howlers show up too. Maybe they will know the Rider is here and come looking for him.'

We'd lost sight of the Rider, the pier was a red herring, and we had no leads plus one of our drones was down and the other was almost out of battery. It looked bleak from an effort versus achievement perspective.

Little did we know, it was going to get a lot worse yet.

Unlucky Break.
Saturday, December 17th 2137hrs

AFTER SOME DISCUSSION, WE parked the car where we had a view of the main intersection in the town. Ninety percent of traffic moving into or out of the town would funnel through this spot which made it the obvious place for us to watch.

We hoped to catch the Howlers on their way to somewhere, but it not only sounded like a long shot, an hour later, with my dad quietly snoring on the back seat, it had begun to feel like one too.

'You feel like calling it a night?' asked Big Ben, breaking a silence which had stretched on for over thirty minutes by that point. We were both accustomed to long periods of inactivity from our army days, not that we thought of them as happy times, but one gets used to being silent and still.

I nodded slowly, disappointed that we hadn't had more luck. It was then that my brain caught up to me and I tutted at myself for being so dumb.

The gap between Big Ben's front seats is such that I could turn around and clamber through, not that I needed to; I got halfway and grabbed the drone remote. Before Big Ben could ask me what I was doing, I explained. 'We have footage of the Rider on your drone. It automatically backs up to the cloud.' I got an eyebrow in response. 'We can watch it, dummy. Maybe one of us will recognise the Rider. Or maybe we can identify who it is from the bike's number plate.'

'Worth a go,' he conceded.

A yawn from behind told us my dad was awake again. 'Did I fall asleep?' he asked.

I didn't turn around, my focus on the device in my hands. 'You sure did.'

'I need the gents,' he announced, stretching his arms out and making his neck click.

Big Ben jabbed a finger across the street. 'There's a bar just around the corner. The toilet is in the back.'

Dad slipped quietly from the car to vanish around the corner just as I got the machine working. We had to forward through the first ninety minutes of hovering above the ground and watch as Big Ben zoomed the drone's camera in and out whenever a motorbike appeared. Finally, he spotted the Rider and the drone dived toward the ground, whipping down to a low altitude where Big Ben followed the man and his bike along the road into Herne Bay.

The image was a little shaky which would have been fine, but the speed combined with the low light level made the picture too indistinct for us to see the number plate on the back. The man, too, had no defining characteristics to make him stand out. No long flowing blond hair flapping on the breeze as it hung from the bottom of the helmet. The lack of long hair ruled out some of the Riders, but like that *Guess Who?* Game, I needed more information to make an identification.

'Can you tell what kind of bike that is?' I asked.

Big Ben sucked in his teeth. 'Not my area of expertise, but I think we can ask. Maybe Moose will be able to tell you who it is.'

'Yeah, he's about the one person it can't be. He's too broad. That could be half of the other guys in the club though.' I blew out a breath, but then I saw it: the thing that gave it away. I knew who it was, without question. 'That's Gopher.'

'How can you tell?'

'His jacket.' I pointed at the screen. 'The stitching is an outline of the club's emblem. He won't get the fully embroidered patch until he is enrolled as a full member.'

'What do you get?' he asked, teasing me about my ridiculous honorary membership.

'Permission to speak and that's about it, I think. He's the mole,' I made it a statement. 'The Howlers attacked me minutes after I left the Riders' clubhouse. The only way they would know to do that is if someone told them about me or they were watching. I think it's the first of those and who would you suspect first: the newest member, right?'

Big Ben pushed out his bottom lip – he wasn't sure he agreed. 'Maybe. If there is a mole, it could be any of them. A member who didn't get his way or someone who has a beef with Moose.'

I understood his viewpoint but wasn't about to be discouraged. 'It's the Probie who is out on his bike and in enemy territory when all the Riders are supposed to be on lockdown in their bunker. If there's a mole, it's him. I'll talk to Moose in the morning.'

The back door to the car opened, giving Big Ben and me both a start. We spun around aggressively to repel the intruder, but it was my dad.

Our angry expressions and sudden reaction made him jump too, a hand going to his heart. 'It's just me, boys!' he gasped. 'I came around the back. There's a biker bar around the corner.'

'There is?' The news came as a shock to me. The real shocker was that it never once occurred to me to look for a biker bar and it should have.

'It's on the opposite corner to the bar you sent me to. I wouldn't have noticed it at all but two guys wearing leather doublets and denim came outside for a cigarette, so I went over to look through the window. It's half full and all the men look like they buy clothes in the same shop.'

Big Ben and I exchanged a glance, but we were out of the car in seconds. Muttering along behind us, my father got out again too. 'You boys are never in one spot for more than a few seconds, you know.'

'We haven't moved in over an hour,' I argued.

'Well, I was asleep for most of it so that doesn't count.'

Ignoring him, I started stripping my gear off. We couldn't go into a bar dressed as we were in combat gear. Going into a biker bar without looking like bikers wouldn't cause a problem – probably – but we would get some looks. If the Howlers were in there, it might be a lot of looks when they recognised me.

'What's the plan?' asked Big Ben, shucking his jacket to reveal a skin-tight t-shirt beneath.

'Go in. Have a drink. Look about, and if there is nothing to see, we leave and go home. If we get lucky, a couple of the Howlers will be in there.'

'Won't they spot you?' he asked.

'I sure hope so.' I was ready, Big Ben was ready, I glanced at my dad: he was still wearing his Kevlar body armour and gloves.

Seeing my expression, he narrowed his eyes at me. 'It's winter out and the cold gets into my bones. I've got a jacket over the top of it.'

He wasn't the problem though: we all were. Even without the Kevlar vests and gloves, Big Ben and I both looked like escapees from a dark ops military unit.

Seeing the problem too, Big Ben had an idea. 'Hold on a second.' He started rummaging around inside the compartments in his car. 'There's always some in here. Always.' A triumphant cheer heralded his exit from the car with makeup accessories in his hand. 'This will fix it,' he beamed.

I looked at his open palm in which a pink lipstick and a bottle of red nail polish now resided.

'We're going in as transvestite dark ops soldiers?' I questioned, hoping that wasn't his solution.

He threw the lipstick so it bounced off my head. 'No, dummy. Watch.' Using the red nail polish, he drew a carefree blob on his t-shirt. Then added another on his trousers by his groin, then another on his left shoulder.

A smile crept onto my face. 'You know what? That might be the cleverest idea you have ever had.'

I got a two-word answer in response, but walking into the bar minutes later, we all looked like we had just finished an evening session of paintball. Our clothes would have to be replaced, but no one gave us more than a second glance.

Except for one guy.

I clocked his surprised expression the moment we walked in. Using Big Ben to block what I was doing, I zoomed in on his face and took a picture on my phone. Then watched as he sent a hasty message on his.

'Ben, can you take a walk past him, go to the gents or something. I need to know if he is wearing a Howlers' jacket.' I wasn't sure what to hope for coming into an environment where I might meet one of them, but my best-case scenario was he would now lead us to the rest of them.

Before Big Ben could move, the man stood up. He'd been checking his phone and to me it looked like he'd received a message back to the one he sent: advise the club president that I'd been spotted, get an instruction back, then comply with the instruction.

This suited me better than sneaking around.

'He's heading for the back door,' whispered my father, seeing the man move.

I waited a few more seconds, just long enough for the man to swing his jacket up and on. As it settled on his back, the Howler motif was right there to prove his membership.

'Get the car?' asked Big Ben, poised to run for it.

I exhaled and made a decision. 'No. I'm going to corner him in the carpark out back.' There were no bikes out front, nor was there room for them. The building was most likely erected in the 18th century so there was a narrow pavement out front and then the road. Thus, it stood to reason, the bikes were behind the bar. 'It's just him. I think I'll ask him a few questions.'

Already moving toward the back door, my feet swift because I needed to get there before he started his bike, Big Ben said, 'Cool.' My dad was at my side too, the three of us intimidating enough to believe we could force the man to give us some answers.

Halfway through the bar, someone else got out of his seat. He was short in stature, kind of scrawny and thin with hair that was disobeying whatever style he'd attempted. He hadn't seen us, as he made to follow the Howler, but there was no mistaking who it was.

'Frank?'

He spun around to see who had spoken, an aggressive, determined, but ultimately worried look on his face. When he saw the three of us right behind him, his expression changed to one of hopeful joy. 'Oh, wow. Am I glad to see you guys! I've been in here waiting for one of them to appear. He's just gone out the back. Did you see him?'

I pushed around him. 'Yes, Frank, and I don't want him to get away.'

'That's the spirit!' Frank followed after me, his excitement bubbling over. 'Let's pick them off one at a time.'

When we got outside and the back door slammed shut behind us, I realised how blind I'd been.

Shotgun Hero. Saturday, December 17th 2159hrs

SKIDDING TO A STOP just beyond the back door, I turned to see who had closed it. Either side of the rear exit were two Howlers, making four to our rear and there were another four standing to our front. It made eight in total. With the back door closed, our only way out was through the four to our front. We were in a car park behind the businesses; the exit from it some fifty yards away to our left where it met the road.

All eight men were wearing dark sunglasses and bandanas which covered the lower half of their mouths. To my immediate front, the man's jacket had the word 'President' on a machine-stitched badge high on his left breast. With only some minor wardrobe changes, they could be the Whitstable Riders instead.

'Is this going to be a straight fight? Or did you chaps bring weapons?' I enquired through gritted teeth. I was angry at letting myself walk into an ambush; it was an obvious place to stage one. The Howlers might have been just arriving, or in the car park to do a deal. Or maybe they were just outside having a smoke. Whatever the case, the man inside warned his pals, then led me outside like the sucker I am.

'We don't need weapons, growled their president,' reaching up take off his sunglasses. Hidden behind them were bright orange eyes - the eyes of an animal. Then he tugged his bandana down to show his distended jaw. From it, a row of wicked teeth shone in the moonlight. To his left and right, and behind us, his men all did the same, then tugged off their leather gauntlets to reveal hairy, clawed paws beneath. Even the man I followed from inside the bar had them, the transformation swifter than I expected.

To Big Ben, Frank, and my dad, I whispered. 'Watch out for the claws; they are wicked sharp.'

'Use the Pentagrams!' hissed Frank insistently, producing his own and holding it aloft.

It created a brief pause as the Howlers all stared at it.

Just to my right, dad gasped. 'I can't believe that thing is working.' Then he started trying to hook his out from inside his top.

'What is that?' asked the Howlers' president.

My father's fingers paused from scrambling to locate the chain as Frank thrust the silver pendant at the president's face. 'It's a pentagram, beast. Back away and cower in fear!'

Frank got a curious look for a split second, then the Howler swiped the silver necklace with his right paw, sending it flying across the carpark where it hit another werewolf in the face and fell to the ground.

Frank darted back to stand close to Big Ben. 'Maybe the wolfsbane was picked under a gibbous moon. Its effects can be erratic at that time of the month.'

'What's this all about?' I demanded. We were about to fight, that much was obvious, but maybe they would answer some questions first. 'Why are you targeting the Whitstable Riders and why are you dressing as werewolves?'

The Howlers were waiting for their leader's signal. Big Ben was only waiting for the first of them to move, but the president held up his hand to pause proceedings. 'You think I might reveal my devious master plan to you? You hope that I will tell you why the Riders have to die?' I waited for him to continue. 'I'm afraid not. There's no need for you to give it any further thought though, my wolves are very hungry, and you will soon be very dead.'

Big Ben laughed. He laughed hard enough for the president to pause just as he was about to order the attack. 'You bozos think you can beat us? You need to get some reinforcements first.'

'There are eight of us and only four of you,' pointed out a man to the president's left. On his badge it read 'Master at Arms'. 'On second count, let's make that three and a half,' he was looking squarely at Frank.

Big Ben shook his head, still chuckling. 'No, no, no, no. no. Your maths is all off, little man. There are only eight of *you*. I can take eight of you out by myself. How do you expect that you can beat me?'

Just then the rumble of exhaust announced the arrival of their reinforcements as several more bikes rode into the confined parking area.

'You had to ask, didn't you?' I growled at him, my teeth still gritted.

Big Ben inclined his head toward the Master at Arms, whose distended face was pulled into a victorious grin. 'Good answer.'

Then he attacked.

Here's a thing about Big Ben: he's fast, he's strong, and his reflexes are off the chart. When you then take a person with that combination of skills and train them to fight, what you get is a hybrid cobra/grizzly bear/great white shark in the body of a man. I've personally seen him rip through a room of men and he's confident enough to only sort of hurt them. What I mean is, a terrified person fighting for their life, will do the most amount of damage they can in order to stop any immediate retaliation. Big Ben wasn't like that. He wanted them to get up again so he could have another go at hitting them.

I slapped my dad's arm as I too burst into action. I wasn't happy that he was here and would be going back to mum with bruises or worse, but there wasn't a damned thing I could do about it except fight my way out. 'Fight to the street, dad! I'm by your side!'

Except I wasn't. Not for more than about a second. I got hit from behind by two of the howlers and it took all I had to stop myself from pitching forward to land on the ground. If they got me face down and pinned it would all be over.

Mercifully, I fetched up against a bike and could right myself. Using it to drive back against my attackers, I spun off my right foot with my elbow high. It caught one of the Howlers high on his face and toppled him.

However, in tackling one, I exposed myself to attack from another. He swung at me with his claws leading. Nature tells us to duck away from danger. Training told me I needed to head toward it. I caught his arm before it could complete the swing, stepped backward, and pivoted to convert the energy into his swing and threw him at the bikes.

Then I got slammed from the side and lost my footing. The hit came with such power and strength it shocked me. I sailed over the top of a bike and caught a glimpse of my dad as I toppled to the ground. He was being held by one Howler and about to be punched in the gut by another. Pinned from behind, his arms held cruelly to stop his escape, I had to watch as he fought them.

The fight was about eight seconds old.

Surging to go to my father's rescue, I saw Frank throw his coat open. I hadn't paid him much attention in the bar; I was too keen to get outside, but now I saw he was wearing a full-length canvass duster and had a pair of shoulder holsters beneath it. He was going to start shooting the Howlers.

On the face of it, you might think that sounds like a good idea, but it would be life in prison if he killed one of them and he was easily crazy enough to do just that. Rising from the ground like a sprinter coming out of his blocks, I grunted in effort and threw myself at Frank.

His pistols, a pair of the Berettas from the Paxton sisters, were clearing his coat as his arms unfolded. I made a grab for them, pushing his arms upwards as the first shots went off. Two silver bullets hit the wall opposite, vanishing into the ancient brickwork, thankfully without passing through a person first.

'Tempest!' yelled Frank as I pushed him back and wrestled the guns from his hands. 'What are you doing?'

'They're not real werewolves!' I yelled back as I tore myself away from him to get to my dad. Stuffing the guns into my own pockets, I took the most direct route to where I needed to be.

I had to leap a car to get to dad but saw a punch strike home while I was in the air. It doubled my father over, but as the Howler's fist came backwards, I caught his crooked elbow and ripped it away. My whole body was going in the wrong direction for his joint; I was going to break his arm or dislocate his shoulder for sure.

Neither thing happened.

As my inertia yanked him off balance and spun him around, he caught me. To say I was shocked would be an understatement, but he then swung me into the air and dumped me hard on the bonnet of the car I'd just leapt. It drove all the air from my lungs and made dancing lights appear in front of my eyes. I gave the windscreen a shove and slid off the car to place it between me and him but there was no escape: the recently arrived reinforcement Howlers were closing in from the road having dismounted their bikes.

In the moment when no one was attacking me, I saw Big Ben. Expecting to find him standing on a pile of unconscious bodies I saw blood coming from a cut to his chin. He was winning, but they were using their claw hands to keep him back and there were enough of them to make his fighting skills ineffective.

Our situation looked hopeless and there were still bikes coming into the carpark. As they came for my father again, he landed a hopeful punch. It struck right on the jaw of the nearest Howler but, though he staggered slightly, it had almost no effect. It was the president, I saw. He reached forward with his left hand to grasp my father's head, getting a rough handful of hair as his raised the claws of his right hand to swing a death blow at his exposed neck.

My legs didn't need instruction. I was on the car and running over the roof to escape three Howlers converging on me, so I converted my motion and leapt again, sailing through the air to grab the president's hand just as it began to descend. Crashing to the ground, I looked up to see my father still fighting the president's grip, but the lead Howler's claws were missing, and in its place, held high in the air, was a human hand.

A deafening blast made everyone stop and I flicked my eyes to Frank, terrified that he brought more than just the pistols with him.

'The next Howler to move gets dropped!' someone shouted, and I heard a fresh round being cycled into a shotgun. From my position on the floor, I couldn't see who it was, but I recognised the voice.

A crash to my left was Big Ben taking advantage of the lull to break free of the men surrounding him. With a shove, I was back on my feet and could see the lone man holding an entire motorcycle gang at bay with his shotgun.

The president shouted, 'You can't take us all with one shotgun, son.'

'You be the first to try to take it then,' Gopher suggested fearlessly. That it was the probie coming to our rescue ruined my theory that he was the mole. Right now, I didn't care about being wrong, I was far too interested in not being dead. It hadn't been yet more Howlers arriving, it was just him and whether it was blind luck, or divine intervention, this was our one chance to get out of here alive.

My father smacked the president's hand away; it was still gripping his head, then took a step back and held a hand to his gut with a painful grimace.

Everyone faced the lone Whitstable Rider and his shotgun. He showed no trace of fear as he stared down more than a dozen men. Men who were most likely guilty of killing three of his club members. With a steady voice, he said, 'Come on now, Brother Weasel. It's time we were leaving.'

I wasted no time obeying his suggestion, pushing my father along ahead of me and checking to make sure Big Ben and Frank followed. As we neared the mouth of the carpark and the relative safety of the road beyond, one of the Howlers made a grab for me.

Gopher shot him. As the echo from the shotgun blast faded away, a siren wailed in the distance. The Howler caught the blast on his legs at a distance of maybe ten metres. At that range, the pellets had spread and would be non-lethal. It still hurt though as his screams denoted.

Gopher cycled another round.

One of their men getting shot startled the Howlers and no one else dared to stop us. I nodded my thanks to him as we reached the road.

'You got a car near here?' he asked.

'Just around the corner.'

His eyes stayed firmly on the Howlers, all of them staring back at him with hate-filled eyes. 'I'll hold them here a bit longer, you get going.'

'Ben, can you get the car?'

'Yeah,' he growled and started running. Frank went with him.

'Go, man,' insisted Gopher.

I wasn't about to leave him here by himself though. Not a chance. He'd rescued me already. I felt safe now and had my father with me. I was prepared to call it a night at this point; we needed to regroup, but Big Ben would only be a minute and I could wait that long if it meant the Howlers couldn't rush the young probie.

Sure enough, what felt like mere seconds later, the sound of Big Ben's car dopplered off the buildings as he roared it from its parked position to where we stood with Gopher. I slapped the young man's shoulder in thanks once more, then, just before the approaching siren was upon us, I dived into Big Ben's car and escaped.

Clues. Saturday, December 17th 2218hrs

I NEEDED TO ASK if my dad and Big Ben were okay, but my father beat me to it.

'How are you boys doing?' he asked from the back seat. 'Any bad cuts or broken bones?'

I leaned through the gap between the seats to check on him. 'I'm fine, dad.' I had a cut on my head where it hit the concrete but that was about it. 'How's your gut?'

'Sore,' he answered honestly. 'I'm not sure I've ever been hit that hard. I know I'm getting old, but they were incredibly strong.'

'They sure were,' I agreed. 'Ben, are you injured?' I asked, switching my focus to the driver.'

'My pride is,' he growled. 'They all had those claws. I just couldn't get close enough to do any damage.'

Then my adrenalin spiked. 'Where's Frank?' I demanded, terrified suddenly that we'd left a man behind.

Big Ben reached out with a steadying arm. 'His car was parked just a short way from mine. He got in it and left. He said he'd come to get the pistols later.'

Breathing a sigh of relief, I replayed the evening in my head. Within what we had seen were more mysteries and unanswered questions, but one good thing had come from the experience. Holding my hand aloft, I showed dad and Big Ben the president's claws.

'What'cha got there, son?' asked dad.

I smiled and waggled my eyebrows. 'Proof.'

Gopher didn't hang around once we were away from the bar's carpark. The Howlers would give chase, at least that's what I expected, so it came as no surprise when he accelerated away and chose a narrow alley to duck down. Big Ben's car couldn't fit. He clearly knew how to escape from the Howlers; maybe that was why he'd been allowed to go to Herne Bay in the first place. I expected to find Moose sent him on a mission to get something they needed and would ask him about it shortly.

Despite wanting to get home now, the evening had been taxing enough, the claw in my hand was the proof I needed to show the Riders what they were up against. None of us had been able to get to their facial prosthetics, for that was what I felt certain they were. Big Ben had levelled a punch right into one of their faces but hadn't been able to see the result of his blow and neither my father nor I had even got close. The glove, however, was all I felt I needed, and we were on our way to the Riders' clubhouse now.

I slipped it on and held it up to the light. It fit snugly over my fingers, but across the back of the hand and curving around the edges to the palm was a flexible, yet tough, plastic. It extended down the fingers where it formed four sharp claws. I could flex my fingers against the rigidity of the plastic, but it took effort to keep my hand formed into a fist. It was a stabbing or slashing weapon and that was how most of them tried to use them. That the one punching my father in the gut hadn't put his on was a Godsend.

Whoever made the gloves knew their stuff. An elastic cuff ended the glove two inches up my forearm where it would be hidden beneath clothing. The facial prosthetics were just as convincing to look at and would be why they all wore bandanas to cover their faces. I still didn't know why they wanted to dress up as werewolves, but their convincing act was coming to an end. That was only part one of my task, of course. I still needed to prove they had killed the three men and gather enough evidence to ensure a conviction.

It led me back to one of my first questions: what is this all about?

On the backseat, my father shifted around to get comfortable, then went a little cross eyed as he looked at his glasses while they were still on his face. Tutting, he reached up with his left hand to take them off while simultaneously delving into his right trouser pocket to find a handkerchief.

'That chap got his greasy fingerprints all over my lenses,' he complained.

I moved so fast it startled Big Ben and he swerved the car.

'What the hell, man?' he grumbled.

I snagged dad's glasses.

'What the hell, kid?'

Not bothering to reply to either, I flicked open the passenger's sun visor and held the glasses up to the mirror. A broad smile spread across my face. 'We have a thumb print.'

'Cool,' said dad. 'Can I have my glasses back now?'

'Sorry, dad. You're going to have to be blind for a while. I need this thumb print to identify who that man is. If we can identify the president, we can find an address for him. If we can do that ... well, let's just say we'll be getting somewhere.'

'But, I'm practically blind without them,' he complained.

Blind or not, I wasn't giving them back until I'd had a chance to lift the print. I could do that at home easily enough. Getting it checked against a police database was another thing entirely, but Jane had made a friend on the force so maybe she could leverage that to get a match.

Dad continued to grumble about his eyesight, but the glasses went into the glovebox where nothing would touch them.

Herne bay was far behind us, its lights fading into the distance when I next looked back. Dad had his eyes closed, probably because he didn't like everything being blurry, and I wasn't going to be shocked if he started snoring again.

Passing into Whitstable, my thoughts were of Chief Inspector Brite. I didn't know the man; our first encounter was this morning, yet I didn't understand how it was that he hadn't arrested any of the Howlers. Three murders in a week and we found them hanging out behind a bar. Maybe Brite didn't know to suspect them though. I accused them this morning when I talked to him, and he said they were werewolves. He acted as if he had a plan to deal with the werewolf problem as a separate issue to the murders. Additionally, he stated that the Riders managed to keep their noses clean, or at least, never get caught, which just sounded incompetent. Surely, he could gather enough evidence to justify a search warrant and storm their premises. Or he could get an undercover guy to infiltrate the club. It didn't sound all that hard though I admitted to myself that I had never tried to do such a thing.

Notwithstanding my lack of experience in deep cover police sting operations, I was beginning to wonder if Chief Inspector Brite might be on the take. It might also explain why Quinn was so tight-lipped about him.

I let it rest, we were nearly back at the Rider's clubhouse, but made a mental promise to be wary of the local senior officer.

At the gate, Big Ben hit his horn to get their attention when flashing his lights didn't work. My dad came awake with a jolt.

'What the hell!' He lurched from prone to upright, then groaned as his bruised abdominal wall complained bitterly about its mistreatment. 'Where are we now?' he groaned, leaning between the seats and squinting.

'Back at the clubhouse,' I told him.

The news brightened his mood instantly. 'Good. There's a rum and coke in there with my name on it.'

He wasn't wrong, but it wasn't Gopher who came out to get the gate this time, it was someone else. His face was familiar, but I didn't know his name; he was just another background face in the crowd of bikers.

He came up to the window. 'You know the drill, guys, right? Leave your weapons in the car, okay?' We nodded our acceptance, too tired to get into a discussion about not having weapons. It begged a question I had not yet asked: where did Gopher get his shotgun from? Not that shotguns were hard to come by. There are lots of places one can buy them. It's the tool of a farmer and ownership is managed by the police. All a person needs is a licence and a lockable cabinet to keep it in. That didn't mean it was okay to carry them around, of course. What Gopher did earlier would land him in jail without many questions being asked, but the same would be true had he been caught with it in his possession. Firing it made things worse from a legal standpoint, but not by much.

Dad was blind enough without his glasses that he needed to put a hand on my shoulder to navigate into the building. Once inside, though, he became miraculously able to see the bar area. This late in the day, no one was working on their bikes, but no one was drinking either, dispelling the image of hard-drinking hard men. It made me wonder why.

'Run out of Jack and Coke?' I asked as I steered dad into a chair. I made it sound like a joke, but I wanted to see how they reacted because a club full of men not drinking on a Saturday night was suspicious in the extreme.

A few of the men smiled and sort of mumbled replies. None of them committed to answer me but before I could press the subject Moose arrived. I still had the glove on my hand but changing my plan completely in the last ten seconds, I slipped it off without taking my hand from my pocket.

As Moose approached, I got my hand free, leaving the claws tucked safely away and thrust my hand out to shake. 'We just had quite the run in with the Howlers,' I reported. 'We were lucky to get away.' Several of his men were standing close by, so I had to lean in to say, 'We need to speak in private.'

He nodded his understanding. 'Get drinks or refreshments for these boys,' he ordered as he let go my hand. As my father willingly went back to where they were serving him rum earlier, Moose took me back through the door which led to the meeting room. That's not where we went though. He turned left and to a new room which was clearly his office.

While Moose pushed his office door closed, I looked around the room, my eyes seeing and cataloguing as much as I could take in. There were photographs of Moose through several decades; he'd joined the club as a young man. 'What is it you wish to say in private, Brother Weasel?' he asked now we were alone.

'Gopher rescued us tonight.' I made the statement and watched his eyes to see how he might react. Nothing happened. He gave no sign that the news surprised him which told me one thing for sure. 'You knew he was out there, didn't you? What was he doing out by himself and in their territory, if you believe it is so dangerous?'

Moose narrowed his eyes at my question as if he found it impertinent. 'He wasn't by himself. Not at first at least. Brother Beaver had an emergency at home and had to go. I sent five others with him as an escort. He lives just outside Herne Bay which was never an issue until the Howlers showed up. They lost Gopher on the way back. One minute he was with them, the next he wasn't.'

Holding his gaze, I said, 'I thought him to be the mole.' I got a questioning look. 'We haven't discussed this yet, but I suspect there to be a mole in your organisation.' Moose's eyebrows showed his surprise. 'He seemed a likely candidate, given his relatively new membership status. Then he came to our rescue tonight and shot one of the Howlers.'

'He shot one of them?' Moose queried.

'Yes. He produced a shotgun and faced down a dozen of them. When one made a move, he got a blast to his legs. It was brave, but now I think about it, I can't help wondering if he might still be the mole and the whole thing was concocted.'

Moose shook his head. 'It's not him. If we have a mole, it's not him.'

'How can you be so sure?'

Moose leaned his backside against his desk. 'He's my son.' I got why Moose refused to question the young man's loyalty. It wasn't unequivocal proof so far as I was concerned, but I saw no reason to challenge it. 'Is that what you came here for?' Moose asked. 'You thought you might have found a mole in my organisation and wanted to check my opinion.'

If there was a time to show him the glove, this was it. I chose not to, holding my hand until the next round because I needed to check something first. I shot Moose a tired smile. 'That's about it. It seemed important enough.'

Moose, who had been acting uptight since I arrived, now relaxed. Pushing off the desk, he raised an arm to guide me back to the door and out of his office. 'His mother, Cathy, died just a few days after giving birth.' It was a sad thing for him to have to remember, but he quickly pushed away his look of despondency and asked, 'Are you staying for a drink with your brothers?' He said the words without thinking I realised when a flash of panic rolled over his features.

I tilted my head inquisitively. 'None of the brothers are drinking, Moose. Why is that?'

'Oh, um, we're all on a health kick,' he lied, flustered and looking for something believable to say. 'Yes, that's it.' He patted his beer belly. 'It's time we all cut back a bit and thought about our waistlines.'

I didn't call him on the lie, even though that's what it most obviously was. They were going out tonight, that was my guess, and they didn't want anyone, not even honorary members, to know about it.

To reply, I said, 'Well, thank you for the offer, but either way, the case comes first. There is yet work to do.'

'Have you been working?' he asked. 'You look like you came here from a paintball event.'

We found my father and Big Ben back in the bar area of the garage/workshop. Dad had a freshly made rum and coke on its way to his lips. 'No time, dad.' I swiped the glass from his hand before he could get a taste and handed it to the nearest Rider.

'Dammit,' he swore. 'This is not the weekend I had planned.' His grumbling continued as I steered him toward the door and back outside. The same man who let us in, jogged to the gate to let us back out. 'That's Brother Bull Frog,' dad pointed out.

'We still haven't found Brother Turkey,' chuckled Big Ben.

'Not yet,' agreed my dad. 'Are we heading home now, or do we have something else to do?'

I wriggled my lips around as I argued inside my own head. 'You noticed they weren't drinking, right?' I asked the occupants of the car.

'Not even one of them,' commented Big Ben. 'I've seen more alcohol consumed at a Women's Institute meeting.'

'I think we need to watch them for a while.' Dad groaned but didn't say anything, his presence with us was his own doing. 'I think they are going somewhere, and I want to know where that is and what they are doing.'

'Still not buying the flower import story?' chuckled Big Ben.

'Not a word of it.'

'Stake out?' asked Big Ben.

Reluctantly, and doing so around a yawn which split my face, I said, 'Stakeout.'

It was going to be a long night.

Stakeout. Sunday, December 18th 0259hrs

BIG BEN OPTED TO take the first stint, waking me at 0100hrs to take over. Big Ben would replace me again at 0300hrs, and dad got off with a turn because he couldn't see without his glasses which I refused to give back.

To pass the time, I ran through some scenarios in my head. The Riders were smuggling guns into the country, that was the obvious conclusion, and they were using the legitimate flower imports to hide it. They import flowers because that gives them a reason to be moving goods around the county and into London or beyond. However, the real purpose is the shipment of guns which they would make far more money from. Was it a small operation? Or were they a major distributor? I couldn't guess the answer, and I couldn't take what I knew to the police because all I had was a smell.

We were staking the place out on the premise that they wouldn't want to hold onto the guns for very long: if the guns were there now, they must be planning to shift them soon.

At a minute to three in the morning, just as my eyes were beginning to close of their own accord, a light came on inside the clubhouse. Big Ben's car was tucked into a spot almost two hundred yards away from their front gate. We had line of sight to them, but they would never think to look for us. His black car with its matt black wheels would be invisible at this distance, but in the still night air, I could hear the bikes starting up.

I gave Big Ben a nudge. 'We have movement.'

He blinked a few times and wiped his mouth. 'Got anything to drink?' I passed him a cold coffee and we watched in silence for a minute.

Bikes pulled out through the gate to form up on the road outside. It looked like a military unit, paired off side by side and ready for inspection. A large panel van joined on behind and then a dozen more bikers formed up behind it. Someone gave the command and they all set off.

Needing no instruction, Big Ben eased his car out and began to follow. He kept his lights off, which away from the lights of the town, was the same thing as a cloaking device. That they didn't head for the motorway, choosing to navigate back lanes through the tiny villages and hamlets, was indication enough of their nefarious intentions. They were my clients, but like Amanda said, they were also criminals.

For more than an hour, Big Ben trailed them. Their route was predominantly west, heading along the coast. There was plenty in this direction, but I expected them to skirt most of the major towns and head directly into London itself. Their choice of route extended the journey to make it twice as long and it took time to conclude my first assumption was correct. Eventually, they had to join a main route, but just as I thought they were going to drive into the heart of the capital, they turned off.

At the eastern edge of London, where the Thames flows in, sits the docklands area. Beyond it is a lot of nothing.

Keeping his distance, Big Ben continued to follow. None of us said anything, apart from dad that is, who kept asking what was going on and what we could see since he couldn't see any of it.

Close to the river, in a spot facing the small City airport on the opposite bank, the procession of motorcycles came to a stop. Big Ben had already extinguished his lights as he followed the sound they made rather than keep them in sight, and as we heard them stop, he stopped too.

Above his head, he flicked the switch to stop the lights coming on when we opened the doors. Go on foot?' he asked.

With my hand on the door to get out, I said, 'We shouldn't be long, dad.' I planned only to get a look at what they were doing. If the flower trade was a front, and they were smuggling guns as I suspected, then I would feel it necessary to take what I knew to the police. How best to do that in a way that ensured their incarceration I could work out later.

For now, Big Ben and I were back in silent mode, advancing through the shadows around the side of a building he'd chosen to park behind. The Riders were on the other side somewhere, their engines off now and the quiet of night dominating. Next to the water, the air was cold and still, hints of ice forming at the edge of puddles as the temperature dropped.

At the corner of the building, a large factory by the look of it, I slowly peeked around to take in the scene beyond.

The riders were meeting with an equal number of rough-looking men, these ones dressed less uniformly in jeans and jackets. The Riders had formed a circle around a pair of Luton-style vans. Each had a roll up door which would ascend into the roof when opened. The entire scene looked tense and fraught with suspicion from both sides as they faced off.

Whatever was going down, it had to be illegal. My bet was guns or drugs.

We couldn't hear what was being said and there was no way to get any closer without exposing ourselves so we watched and I used my phone to video the exchange, zooming in when a man moved to the rear of the nearest van to raise the door.

It slid into the roof to reveal a darkened interior. I huffed out a breath through my nose, tension and excitement making my breathing rapid. Two of the men here to meet with the Riders jumped up into the van's loading area, vanished for a heartbeat and reappeared with the goods in their hands.

'I don't believe it,' Big Ben murmured.

Staring at the same scene, I found myself lost for words.

Then a shout drew my attention and Big Ben grabbed my shoulder. As he yanked me back behind the building, I knew we'd been spotted.

'There!' The shout followed after us, but we were already running. It was joined by other shouts and the sound of footsteps on the concrete as they gave chase.

The phone was gripped tightly in my hand as we pelted down the side of the building; they wouldn't catch us on foot, but Big Ben's car was easy to spot and even easier to remember. If any of the Riders saw it, they would instantly know it was us.

At the car, Big Ben hurdled the bonnet, ripped open his door, and had the engine running before I could get my backside into my seat. Then he slammed the accelerator to the floor and took off in reverse.

On the back seat, calm as anything against the backdrop of our panicked actions, dad said, 'Have you just remembered you left the iron on at home?'

Half a dozen men; a mix of Riders and their supplier, tore around the corner after us, but Big Ben hit the button to send power to a bar of lights on his roof. It blinded the men instantly, all of them raising their arms to shield their eyes or turning their faces away. They wouldn't have been able to see who it was and that gave us the clean getaway we needed.

After a hundred yards, and now doing forty in reverse, Big Ben threw the wheel around. His car performed a power-slide through a hundred and eighty degrees so it faced the way he wanted to go then took off like a sprinter at the gun as he mashed the pedal again.

Since neither Big Ben nor I had yet responded to his flippant remark, dad tried again. 'I take it you saw something of interest. Shall I guess what it is? Is it guns? Is it drugs?'

Lying my head wearily against the headrest, I sagged into my seat. 'No, dad. It's worse than that.'

'Worse?'

'Dad, it was carnations.'

Identity. Sunday, December 18th 0712hrs

I NEEDED MORE SLEEP than I got, my active brain forcing me from slumber at 0712hrs according to the clock by my bed. Traditionally, Sundays are a day when I would do very little and maybe go to visit my parents. There might be some rugby to watch over a cup of tea with my dad, or mum might have some jobs for me that required a younger set of limbs.

That wasn't going to be the case today. Sitting in my bed and idly scratching Dozer's ears, I thought about the flowers. The Riders really were dealing in flowers, buying and selling them, but they were doing it under the table. They had a legitimate import operation, bringing flowers in from the mainland, but from what I saw last night, they were also buying smuggled flowers and thus avoiding paying import tax on them. Hardly a heinous crime; almost victimless, one might say. That wasn't for me to decide. The point is that they were funding criminals bringing goods into the UK. It gave them an unfair advantage when selling because they could undercut the opposition and probably drove other traders out of business.

Knowing about it created a moral dilemma. I wasn't bound by client privilege or anything like that, I could take what I knew to the police or to customs and let them deal with it, but I needed to give myself time to consider that yet.

Pushing thoughts of illegal carnations from my mind, I picked up my phone and tried to send a message to Amanda. I still felt off kilter, her attitude toward me suddenly changed as if she were trying to distance herself before a split. I composed the text message no less than six times, deleting it on each occasion because it failed to convey what I wanted to put across.

In the end, I settled for, '*I missed you last night. I hope you have a relaxing Sunday.*'

Dad was still asleep, and I still had his glasses. I probably should have dealt with it when I got in, but at the time, fatigue demanded I go to bed. With an old-fashioned fingerprinting kit, I dusted down his glasses and lifted the print. Leveraging a friendship I'd made through Amanda and Big Ben, I sent a text message to Patience Woods. Patience is a beat-cop working out of Maidstone. It put her under CI Quinn's dubious method of leadership, but she seemed to give as good as she got most of the time.

I didn't expect a reply any time soon; she ought to be asleep like any normal person at this time on a Sunday, so I shuffled through to my kitchen where I pressed the kettle into service.

I needed tea.

To my surprise, a message popped up before the water could boil. I'd asked if she could check the fingerprint and it turned out she was working this morning. I'd have an answer in a few minutes. For once, Big Ben's libido worked in my favour, Patience dropping whatever she ought to be doing to get me an answer.

While my tea steeped, I went back upstairs to dig the dogs out of my bed. Other dogs might bounce into life the moment their owner's feet hit the carpet each morning, but mine were more likely to eye me suspiciously – they are inherently lazy by nature. I shooed them into the garden, rescued my tea bag, and watched them through the big kitchen window as they snuffled in the undergrowth.

My hope that the fingerprint would reveal something was rewarded not only with a name but an entire file. Evan Marlowe's headshot was tiny on my phone, but even so, I couldn't match his features to anyone I'd seen last night. The print came from the Howler's president, that much I was sure of, so I had a name and could work from there.

Taking my tea through to my home office, I found my route from the kitchen barred by two dachshunds who wanted their breakfast. I'd forced them to get up and so as far as they were concerned, that meant it was time to eat.

Two small bowls of kibble later, I sent the file from my text folder to my emails and opened it on my laptop. Then I settled down to read.

Evan Marlowe wasn't a career criminal. Or so it seemed. Once I had the photograph opened on a larger screen, I could see it was an old picture; the face it showed was still in its early twenties. The file gave me date of birth: Evan was fifty-one which correlated with what I saw last night. I wouldn't be able to pick him out of a line-up, his facial prosthesis making sure he was unrecognisable. Even his eyes, which I always found were an easy way to distinguish one person from another, were unfamiliar because of the glowing orange lenses they wore.

Wondering how they did that, I punched the question into a search engine. Wouldn't you know it? I could buy my own set for pennies right now. I was trying to get to a point where I could go to the police, but by then I needed to have already solved the crime. Not only that, I would have to be sure the person I went to was on the level and I remained unconvinced about CI Brite's motivations. However, until I could work out where the Howlers were or would be, and what they were up to, my concerns over the local police were moot.

My tea went cold as I began to piece together information about Evan Marlowe. His address was listed in Hoath, an inland village not far from the coastal town but the file was more than twenty-five years old and the address very possibly his parents' house. I made a note, both mental and physical, because his parents might still be there. If I couldn't find him by other means, I would knock on their door. I cross checked it and found the address listed in the phone book had the name Marlowe showing but with a different initial: It was his parent's place.

He didn't appear on social media; not that I could find, at least, but Jane might have better luck. I checked the time and noticed the skin forming on the surface of my tea. It was 0827hrs which I considered to be an acceptable hour to message my colleague. Pushing back my chair, I went to the kitchen to make a fresh cup and used my phone to text her while the water got excited.

I rarely thought of Jane as a man anymore. It was so rare for James to be the persona he/she chose. At this time of the day, while still in bed and without the hair, makeup and other things that transformed one to the other, I had to assume it would be James receiving the call.

My message asked her to look into Evan Marlowe and gave her the address. It would be all she needed to find the right person. She was a whizz at dredging for details, but rather than message back, she called me, her fake woman's voice sounding more convincing all the time and ruining my theory that it would be James I got for once.

'Hi, Tempest,' she said sleepily. 'You didn't wake me, I was already up.' I heard a man's voice in the background and wondered who it might be. I didn't ask though since it could be anyone and it was none of my business.

'Good morning, Jane. Are you free to do a search?'

'Sure,' she yawned. 'I have my laptop right here. I'm with Jan.' When I didn't say anything, she added, 'The cop?' she was checking to see if I knew who she was talking about. I knew she'd met him when Amanda and I were away on the Yeti case, but I'd only seen him in passing so far. 'Anyway, who is this guy? One of the werewolves?'

'I think he's their leader. I need to see what he does for a living, where he lives ... anything you can get really. Their werewolf thing is one of the most realistic I have seen, and he has a whole gang of them doing it. Whatever they are into, it must be big. The KLoD are going to move on them soon, so I'd better figure this out before more people get hurt. Anything you can give me will help.'

Around another yawn, she said, 'Okay, Tempest. I should be able to work something out in the next hour.'

She was about to hang up when I thought of something else. 'Can you find a patient? A man got shot in the legs with a shotgun last night. It wouldn't have been life-threatening, but it also isn't the kind of wound you deal with at home. He must have gone to A&E down near Herne Bay somewhere.'

'Sure. I'll get right on it.'

I let her go and actually took a sip of my tea. From the lack of sound upstairs, dad was either asleep still or possibly dead. I told myself it would be the first of those and thought about what I wanted to do to fill in time until he woke up.

I decided exercise was the right choice even if it felt like the least appealing. Arguably, the lack of appeal dictated that it was necessary. With a clock to time myself, I fell into a rigorous High Intensity Interval Training routine. It would work every part of my body and test my cardiovascular system without the need for equipment and space. I started with superman press-ups, performing reps for forty seconds before resting for twenty. Then, as the second hand swept by to the top of the clock, I started on burpees.

Forty minutes later, I was a sweat soaked mess, but the exercise required very little mental effort which gave me time to consider what I needed to do for the case and in what order. I had an itchy feeling inside my head that I couldn't identify. At some point, I'd been witness to a clue, but I wasn't able to work out what it was. There was something familiar about the name Evan Marlowe, however I didn't know why. Drying myself with a towel in the kitchen, I went through the contacts on my phone: he wasn't in there. I looked at old cases; ones which occurred near the coast, but his name didn't appear. I knew it, but I had no idea where from.

I called Big Ben. 'Bonjour,' said a woman.

I pulled the phone away from my ear to make sure I hadn't somehow misdialled and got a wrong number, but it was his name showing on the screen. 'Bonjour, Ben est là, s'il te plait?' I tried, unsure if I'd got the translation quite right.

She said, 'Oui. I'll get him.' Then I got to listen to her calling his name as she went looking through his penthouse suite.

I scratched my head in wonder. This was nothing new, of course. Big Ben picked up women by walking into a room and snapping his fingers. But he'd only dropped me off a few hours ago. Was she stashed in his suite waiting for his return? Or did he call her on his way back to his place after dropping me off? Like my questions about Jane's relationship with Jan, I wasn't going to ask, but it suggested he was moving on from whatever had been going on with Patience.

'Morning, Weasel,' Big Ben's voice arrived in my ear at twice the volume one should use on a Sunday. He sounded bright and lively and full of joy, most likely induced by whatever he and the French lady had been getting up to. 'Did you get any sleep? I barely got a wink. I'm about to get started on the energy drinks.'

I didn't need to hear about his lack of sleep. 'I got enough to keep me going for the rest of the day,' I told him. 'Does the name Evan Marlowe mean anything to you?' I asked.

'Didn't he play Rugby for Scotland?'

I shook my head. 'That was Max Evans, donkey. You'd be better at this game if you thought with your biggest muscle and not the one you like to think is your biggest.'

'Whatever. I can promise you women have no interest in getting hold of my brain, whereas ...'

I cut him off. 'I know the name from somewhere. I wondered if maybe it was someone back at the unit.'

Mentioning our time in the army took the jokiness out of my large friend and this time he gave it some proper thought. 'It's not ringing any bells,' he concluded after a while. 'I guess you've already gone through case files.'

'Not all of them,' I admitted. 'I don't think that's where I know him from though.'

'Who is he anyway?' asked Big Ben.

'The owner of the fingerprint I took from dad's glasses. He's the leader of the Howlers so I want to know who he is. I have Jane working on it now.'

'We're working again today?'

I sucked in a breath and considered the answer. 'I will be. I expect to be back in Herne Bay later trying to find the Howlers again.'

'You don't have a very good record for encounters with them,' Big Ben pointed out. 'Do we need to enlist more help?'

I didn't want to do that. It was bad enough that I'd put my father in danger last night. He would have sore abs for a week; I didn't want to place anyone else in harm's way. 'No. I think I might operate better alone. I'll be less visible that way.'

Big Ben didn't agree with my idea. 'You can get stuffed. Whatever happens, I'm going with you. I want a rematch against those guys.'

I thought about Frank. He was desperate to shoot someone last night. If I hadn't disarmed him, he surely would have done. It was in his nature to fight evil, even if it did turn out to be a prat in a costume. He would be back for a second round too.

'Alright, fine. Listen I ... hold on a second; I have an incoming call from an unknown number.' The French woman, whose name I didn't know and most likely never would, murmured something in French. She had to be standing right next to him when she said it and though I didn't understand the words, the timbre of her voice left little doubt about the subtext.

I didn't wait for Big Ben to reply to her or me, I flicked across to the other call. 'Good morning. This is Tempest Michaels of the Blue Moon Investigations Agency. How may I help you?'

A gruff man's voice answered. 'You're the fella working with the Riders, right?'

Wondering where this might be going, I said, 'They have engaged me to perform services for them.' My response gave the caller an answer but told him nothing.

'Yeah. Yeah, right. I need to talk to you.'

'We are talking.'

'Face to face,' he replied in his gruff voice. It sounded like he smoked a hundred cigarettes a day and I expected him to burst into a fit of coughing at any second.

Sensing a trap, I was cautious in my reply. 'Why can you not tell me the nature of your business over the phone?'

'Not safe,' he whispered. 'Listen, I'm on the wrong side of this. I can't go to the police.' His words were urgent and desperate. 'If they suspect me of talking to anyone, I'm a dead man. I need a safehouse to go to. Then I'll tell you all about the Howlers.'

'What is there to tell?' I pressed.

'Not until I'm safe,' he insisted.

'I don't even know your name. I don't know anything about you, and I have this aversion to walking into ambushes. I get the impression the Howlers want me dead. How am I to know this isn't a trap?' All I could hear was his breathing at the other end. I changed tack. 'You said you are on the wrong side of this. Which side are you on?'

He sighed. 'I'm a Howler,' he admitted with deep regret. This was both good and bad. If he was genuine, I might be able to find out everything I wanted to know. If he wasn't, then it surely was a trap.

'So you know Evan Marlowe?' I gave him the only bit of information I knew to see how he would react.

'Who?'

'Evan Marlowe,' I repeated. If I could see his eyes, I would be able to tell if he was bluffing. 'He's the Howler's president.'

'That's not the name I know him by.'

'Really? Then what name does he use?'

The line went dead abruptly. One moment I thought he was about to reply. The next second, he wasn't there, and my phone reconnected the call with Big Ben.

I could hear both him and the French woman in the background and from the sounds I could hear, neither was coming to the phone in the next few minutes.

I hung up the call and stared at my phone. Did I call back? Was he genuine and had to end the call quickly because someone was coming?

I went for a shower.

Jane's Skills. Sunday, December 18th 0940hrs

D<small>AD WAS MAKING COFFEE</small> by the time I got back downstairs. When he wasn't looking, I sniffed his cup.

'There's no rum in it, kid,' he frowned. 'It's a little early for rum.'

I shot him a doubtful look. 'It's later than you started yesterday.'

He pulled a face. 'Fair point. How long have you been up?'

'A while. How's your gut?'

He touched some fingers to it and grimaced. 'Bad enough. It'll be worse tomorrow.' Then a cheeky grin stole across his face. 'We took on a whole gang of biker werewolves, son. Doesn't it make you feel alive?'

I couldn't help but chuckle at him. 'They're not actually werewolves, but yes, I get what you are saying. I think we had a lucky escape and when we go back, we need to be better prepared.' Big Ben's suggestion of backup flashed into my head. It was something to consider, but how could I do that without being certain no harm could come to my friends. Giving my elderly father a level stare, I said. 'If I attempt to leave you here while I attend to this case, you'll just find a way to join in anyway, won't you?'

'Trying to protect your old man?' He made it clear he didn't feel that was my job.

I sighed. 'Trying to keep mother off my back.' It was mostly true. If dad got injured, I would never hear the end of it. As it was, she was likely to find out about his sore abs and nag me half to death.

Dad chuckled at me. 'Look at it my from perspective: if you're getting a portion of the grief, the amount I get will be less. Doesn't that sound like a good thing?'

I rolled my eyes. Before I could say anything else, my phone rang. This time it was Jane calling.

'Hi, Jane. Was there much to find?'

I got a cryptic answer, 'Yes and no.'

'That's not very helpful.'

'What I mean is ...' my father was gesticulating something; he wanted me to put it on speakerphone. I hit the button. 'Jane I just put you on speakerphone. My father is with me.'

She called, 'Hi, Mr Michaels.'

'No need for formalities. Michael will do. Or Stormy works too.'

'Um, okay,' replied Jane, probably wondering why he had given himself a nickname. I would explain it later. 'So, Evan Marlowe barely exists. It's his real name,' she added quickly. 'But since he left school, he has only had two jobs and the last of those he quit almost thirty years ago. Whatever he does to make money, isn't showing up anywhere. He pays no taxes and doesn't bother to claim any benefits.' It was a keen criminal indicator. 'He was arrested twice. The first time was almost thirty years ago, and the second time was a year after that.' I knew this bit already, but I let her continue. 'Both counts were for assault. When he used a knife the second time, he got six months in prison and that's where his life changed. He never went back to work after his release, but I found his profile lurking on an American biker forum. I think he spent some time there and might have moved around. The time after his stint in jail is a big black hole.'

'What was on the forum?' I asked.

'It was a dark web site called Sons of the False Sabbath. A lot of it was encrypted, but he uses his own name openly and talks about the big picture for biker gangs back home. I assume he means England. He doesn't say what his big picture is, but his comments left me with the impression he was there learning about how the bigger, more connected, American motorcycle clubs operate.'

What this gave me was an ambitious career criminal with a plan to lead. Now he was leading, and using terror tactics to scare people away. What was he scaring them away from?

'Thank you, Jane. Anything else?'

'Nothing of any worth. The lack of information on him is staggering. It makes me think he must have a pseudonym, a different name that he's created a false identity under. If you are able to get another name for him, I might find a lot more. He could have holdings, bank accounts, leased vehicles … you name it.' My brain flashed to the conversation with my mystery man an hour ago. He didn't know Evan Marlowe, but he was one of the Howlers, which meant the false name was quickly sounding likely. 'You also asked me to look for people suffering from shotgun wounds to the legs,' she prompted. 'Well, I didn't find any.'

I nodded and grimaced as another possible line of enquiry and opportunity for answers slipped away. It didn't surprise me all that much; it was possible that the injury was less horrific than I imagined. I needed to get off the phone and try to call my mystery Howler back. 'Okay, Jane. Brilliant as always. I'll see you in the office tomorrow.'

With our phone call ended, I tried the number mystery Howler used, but got no answer. He would call me back when he got the chance. Or maybe that should be if he got the chance. Maybe he already got caught, in which case I didn't fancy his chances.

'Got any bacon?' asked my father.

A tempting image appeared in my head. 'Fancy a fried breakfast?'

Chief Inspector Brite. Sunday, December 18th 1100hrs

WE HAD TO HURRY breakfast and hurry Big Ben to get his pants back on so he could collect us from my house. I called Chief Inspector Brite while the sausages sizzled, but while I wanted to see him and told him I had vital evidence to share, he acted reluctant and made it clear he didn't really have time today. It was sheer effort of will that forced him to give me a time when he could fit me in and typical that he chose one which meant we had to rush.

I couldn't decide whether to trust him or not. His actions were confusing, his results worrying, and his membership of KLoD disturbing. I would need the local police to perform the arrests when I got to the bottom of this case, and that meant I needed to work out whether I could trust him or not.

I had a glove to prove the werewolves were just men dressing up and I had a name for their leader. It was enough to convince any sane person to drop the supernatural theory and go with something more rational.

It therefore worried me when he refused to.

'What you are showing me is a glove, Mr Michaels,' he pointed out for the third time.

Forcing myself to be patient, I said, 'Yes, Chief Inspector. A glove which I ripped from the right hand of the Herne Bay Howlers' president.' We were at the small police station in Herne Bay where he unhappily agreed to meet me. 'If they wear gloves, they are just men. That's not really the issue though because their supernatural nature should never have been in question.'

Brite held up a hand to stop me. 'It is the only question, Mr Michaels. You think you have brought me unequivocal proof, but you haven't.'

Dad blurted, 'What?'

'It's quite simple,' the chief inspector replied, flicking his eyes to my father and then back to me. 'If they are werewolves, then I dare not send in ordinary, uniformed police officers against them. It would be a slaughter and I would be to blame. That is why I have kept this investigation quiet and will move on the Howlers when, and only when, I can be sure of victory. However, if what you are holding truly came from one of the Howlers, and they are indeed not werewolves, then I have no need to move against them at all.' He leaned back in his chair, satisfied to have made a winning point.

Whatever his point was, it had gone directly over my head. 'Are you insane, man?' I asked.

He'd been polite thus far, but I could see his demeanour beginning to change. 'You come here demanding I begin to investigate a man you claim to have identified as the Howlers' leader. I commend you for your efforts; the information will prove useful at some point. Yet in proving, as you claim, that they are not the werewolves I seek, surely you understand I must now look elsewhere. I have three bodies in the morgue that were killed by a pack of werewolves. That's the case I am focussed on. I'll deal with the naughty bikers another time.'

'Naughty bikers,' I repeated his phrase mockingly.

'Yes, Mr Michaels. I will have an officer record your statement if you wish to give one. However, I have to question why you did not report the alleged assault last night? I could have had officers at the scene in minutes. If they are not werewolves, as you so adamantly claim, then surely dealing with their misdemeanour right then might have seemed the obvious course, no?'

'Firstly, Chief Inspector, assault with a deadly weapon,' I held the clawed glove up to accentuate my point, 'is not a misdemeanour.' I got a disinterested face in return. 'Secondly, the Howlers ...' I stopped talking.

'The Howlers what?' he prompted.

Now I saw it. It wouldn't matter what evidence I presented, Brite was running his own campaign and it was all to do with the KLoD. I wanted to explore that, but it would have to wait. We were on our own so far as police support went. Normally, I would relish being left alone but the Howlers were a tough bunch and probably guilty of three murders that I knew of. A little back up might be comforting. Just as I thought that, a little seed of an idea popped into my head. It was an evil and twisted idea, but it possessed potential.

I tapped my pockets to make sure I had all my things, then got to my feet. Looking confused, my father started to get up as well. 'Thank you for you time, Chief Inspector. I shall take up no more of it.'

If he cared that we hadn't finished our conversation, he showed no sign. Mostly, he looked relieved that we were leaving. He left his chair to see us out.

Behind us, Big Ben, who hadn't bothered to take a seat, opened the door with one massive hand and stepped outside. I filed out after him, my interest in talking sense into the senior police officer now shelved.

'How about some brunch?' I asked, as if this were an ordinary Sunday and we were just leaving church. I wanted to convey a sense that we were giving up or moving on though whether the chief inspector bought it, I could not tell and did not care.

Once clear of the station, Big Ben said, 'He's a sandwich short of a picnic, isn't he?'

I thought it was worse than that. I believed CI Brite had a motive not linked to bringing the killers to justice and it was going to get someone killed. 'I think he gave us a bum tip the other day. Telling us the Howlers vanished by the pier was a lie to make us look in the wrong place. Maybe he doesn't know where the right place is yet, and maybe he does.'

Dad frowned. 'I'm not following you, son. What are you telling us?'

'He's a member of KLoD, possibly a senior member; I don't know how the League works, but his police investigation isn't getting very far and he told us why a few minutes ago: he's not going to send in officers to get killed. I think he plans to raid the Howlers with the KLoD.'

Big Ben saw the truth of it. 'We saw the weapons; they went to Frank.'

'And when we first met him, Brite bragged that the KLoD had banished were-wolves from this land once before,' my father reminded us.

Now it was my turn to frown. 'How do you remember that, dad? You were barely awake, didn't look like you were listening, and had half a pint of rum in your bloodstream.'

I got a grin from him. 'I was in the navy, kid. I drank rum before I started work most days of my career.'

'So what's next?' asked Big Ben.

Family Secrets. Sunday, December 18th 1152hrs

IT DIDN'T TAKE VERY long to get to the address I had for Evan Marlowe's parents, but they were not there.

'How old are they?' asked my father. He was looking at the car parked on their drive and most likely thinking the same thing as me.

'Unknown,' I replied honestly; it wasn't something I thought to find out. 'Their son is in his fifties though, so they will be in the early seventies at the very least.' On a Sunday morning, with their car on the drive, I expected them to be out because they went to church. Checking my watch, the service would have ended a short while ago. 'We'll hang around for a bit, if they went to church, they'll be home soon.'

'Unless they go somewhere else,' Big Ben pointed out.

He could be right; they could easily have planned lunch with friends after the service or even have a second car and be away for the weekend and not at church at all. We got lucky though, a couple in their eighties walking arm and arm toward us along the path because they chose to brave the cold rather than take the car. I reached into the back seat to fetch the dogs. They were both asleep, one atop the other to make one half-decent sized dog until I separated them again.

I got a grump of disapproval from Bull, who liked to make his opinion known, but I clipped them both to their leads and got out to plop them onto the pavement. Ruffling their fur, I whispered, 'You're up, boys.'

I'd found their cuteness to have almost universal appeal. It didn't work on everyone, but a dopey sausage dog can break down the hard exterior on most people. The old couple had no hard exterior to get through, and the dogs did the task of breaking the ice as if it were what God put them on the Earth for.

'Oh, look, Fred. Aren't they cute?' said Mrs Marlowe.

'Good morning,' I halloed them. I was less than six feet from Big Ben's car, not even pretending I was just out for a walk. 'You are Mr and Mrs Marlowe?'

My question caught them off guard, both appearing startled by the question from a stranger. They glanced at each other and then back at me.

'I'm sorry. My name is Tempest Michaels. I'm a private investigator. I was hired to look into a case,' I chose the word carefully; I didn't want to say murder and scare them, 'and it led me to your son, Evan.'

'We don't have a son,' argued the old man.

'You chose to disown him?' I knew they had a son.

Mrs Marlowe turned inward to her husband. 'I want to go inside, Fred.'

Mr Marlowe put a comforting arm around his wife's shoulders as he met my eyes. 'I'm afraid you've had a wasted trip, young man. We can't help you.'

When they turned to go inside, they found my father partially blocking their route. He'd exited the car and circled around to approach from behind them. Much closer to their age, he offered them a kindly expression. 'I can't imagine what it must be like to have a child who disappoints and hurts you. Tempest is my son, and I am very lucky to be included in his life. I cannot promise to be able to turn your son back to the right path, but I believe he is heading down a path that may end with his death.' Mrs Marlowe gasped, a whimpering sound of horror, as my father timed the awful word perfectly. 'If you will help us, we are trying to prevent further tragedy.'

Mr Marlowe stepped forward and my dad took a pace to his right to allow them passage, but Mrs Marlowe dragged her feet. 'Where is he?' she asked, her question filled with sorrowful hope.

Mr Marlowe didn't care. 'Leave it, Margaret. We've done this too many times. He's gone, love. He's never coming back.'

He was trying to guide her through the gate and down their garden path, but Mrs Marlowe stood firm. 'I just want to know if he is okay, Fred. He's still my little boy.'

Now getting angry, Fred snapped, 'He hasn't been your little boy for more than forty years, woman. Please, let's just go inside and have a cup of tea. We can forget all about this.'

'I don't want to forget,' she snapped back. 'That's your way of dealing with it.' Turning her whole body to look at me, she asked again. 'Is he here in England?'

I tried to return her hopeful look. 'He is. I saw him yesterday.'

She gasped again and glanced once more at her husband. When she looked back at me, she asked. 'How did he look?'

I didn't think bonkers and murderous were good adjectives to use, so I went with, 'Healthy and strong.' She was teetering on the edge of giving in and helping me; it didn't take much to push her over. 'He's in trouble. I need your help to help him.'

Slowly, she nodded her head. 'I think you had better come inside. Did you say your name is Tempest?'

'Yes. Tempest Michaels.'

She indicated her garden path. 'Please.'

'Thank you. I will join you I just one moment.' The dogs were already trying to follow her. They knew a friendly person when they saw one. Their heads were most likely already filled with images of custard cream biscuits as they tugged my arm. I handed them to dad and crossed the six feet of pavement to get to the car. 'You want to stay here?' I asked Big Ben.

'Yeah. I'm kinda tired. I'll get a nap if you are going to be a while.' He looked tired.

'Maybe you should have got some sleep instead of entertaining a lady when you finally got home,' I commented as I began to close the door.

'Stephanie? That's not what's making me tired, normal-sized person. It's the effort of being this good-looking. You've no idea how tough it is on a person.'

Wishing I had something blunt to throw at his head, I closed the door on his daft, mocking grin and jogged to catch up with the old people just as they were opening the door.

'I'll put the kettle on,' volunteered Fred once his coat was hanging up and he'd helped his wife from hers.

'Come through to the living room,' she beckoned, then paused to slip her shoes off and put house slippers on. It was an awkward process for her; age and frailty robbing her of the flexibility such a simple task required. It made me want to dash forward to help, though I held myself in check lest I highlight the daily difficulties old age presents.

Her living room was at the front of the house, her couch positioned to look over the front garden so a person would have to sit at an angle to watch the old box-square television sitting in the corner with a VCR beneath.

'He was such an angelic little boy,' Mrs Marlowe told me as she lowered herself slowly into an armchair. 'Growing up, I hardly ever had to tell him off. It all changed when he was sixteen.'

'What happened?' asked my father with a soft, caring voice.

We could all hear Frank clanking along the hallway outside as the spoons and cups rattled on the saucers. As I knew he would, he'd made a pot of tea using their best china teapot. The cups and saucers were all matching – a prized possession a different couple might want to pass down to a child or grandchild. Not so this couple.

The conversation paused while Fred did the honours, asking about sugar and handing out cups. I hissed at the dachshunds until they reluctantly came to heel. They would happily buzz around Fred's feet and trip him in the hope he might have a biscuit to drop. Once Margaret saw that everyone had theirs and Fred was reversing into the armchair next to hers, she picked up where she left off.

To answer dad's question, she said, 'He saw a movie. It was an old one, but it spoke to him because everything changed after that. He became so passionate and difficult to manage. He changed his clothes and refused to get a haircut.'

'What was the film, please?' I begged to know, curious to hear what kind of movie could incite such a change in personality.

It was Fred who replied with a bored sigh, '*Werewolves on Wheels.*'

If there was a winning score button in my head, then his answer hit it because my brain lit up like a fruit machine paying out the jackpot. Evan Marlowe, the leader of a biker gang pretending to be werewolves, once watched a biker movie where the bikers were werewolves. Talk about life reflecting art.

'It wasn't even a good movie,' Fred added with a huffiness to his tone. He felt it was all stupid rubbish and it made me wonder if his attitude then had pushed his headstrong teenage son to go even further with his fantasy.

Keeping my voice neutral, I asked, 'What was it about?'

I aimed my question at both parents, but it was Fred who answered once again. 'It was all nonsense. It barely even had a plot, but they were supposed to be a hard, criminal biker gang of outlaws. On the run from the police they hide in a church and become cursed for their sins. Something like that anyway. They all die in the end.'

'I tried to watch it once to better understand what got Evan so excited but there was too much nudity and swearing for me,' admitted Margaret. 'I guess both those things appeal to a sixteen-year-old boy.' Her expression was wistful when she said, 'We both expected him to grow out of it.'

Fred reached across to put his hand on hers. 'The next thing we knew, he's gone and bought a bike. He turned seventeen and suddenly was a big chrome thing on our drive that he could never have afforded to pay for. I asked where he got the money from, but he wouldn't tell us. I got mad,' admitted Fred, showing the first tinge of regret. 'I thought he must have been stealing. Or that maybe he stole the bike.'

My father asked, 'Did you find out?'

'He got a loan from the members of a motorcycle gang he joined,' Fred replied. 'He'd joined a local Hell's Angels club on the coast, and they let him borrow it. I think they were impressed to have someone so young wanting to join them.'

My brain made a leap, connecting two dots I hadn't known existed until that point. 'The Whitstable Riders.'

'Yes, that's right,' said Margaret. 'Is he back with them?'

'Not exactly.' I didn't expand on my cryptic reply, pushing forward with another question instead. 'Have you ever heard the name Davis Milnthorpe?'

I watched their faces but neither knew the name and neither was lying. 'How about Moose?' I tried but got the same reaction. Pressing on, I asked. 'What happened at the club? Do you know? I found evidence that suggests he was in America.' When I said it, my brain flashed to a memory from Moose's office. There were lots of photographs on the wall, and though it was completely circumstantial, some of them were in America when he was in his twenties. Moose and Evan had been in the same motorcycle club at the same time, they were around the same age and both were in America around the same time. I was willing to bet money they were there together.

In response to my suggestion about an American trip, Margaret nodded. 'He did go to the States. I got a few postcards from him. There was never an address to write back to. I don't know how long he was there for, just a few years in his early twenties, I think. The next time we heard from him was when he got in trouble with the police.'

'They just turned up at the door,' explained Fred. 'He'd been arrested and gave them our address as his place of residence.' Lost in the memory, Margaret looked forlorn. Fred gripped her hand all the tighter.

Things were staring to add up. I could make connections and one or two of them were worrying. The picture on the wall in Moose's office for a start. Their similarity in age would have drawn them together. My guess was that something happened between them and that was why Evan was here now and targeting the Riders. I would have to ask Moose what it was; I didn't think the Marlowes would know. That wasn't the whole picture though; the Howlers wouldn't form as a group and pretend to be werewolves because one man once watched a movie. There was something else driving them to employ the terror tactic and I still had no idea what it was.

'Do you still have any of his possessions?' I asked hopefully.

Fred snorted a despairing laugh. 'Any possessions?'

Margaret tutted and took back her hand grumpily. 'His room is still made up as it was when he left,' she told us.

'She cleans it every day,' Fred revealed, his words intended to belittle his wife.

Ignoring him, she pushed herself out of her chair. 'I'll show you.'

Margaret used a stair lift to get to the upper floor of their house, my dad and I trailing slowly behind her carrying a dog each. The house was a detached place in the heart of a small village and deceptively big. We had only seen the entrance hall and living room until we left to go upstairs but got to appreciate how nice it was now. Evan's bedroom was at the back of the house where it overlooked their large rear garden filled with fruit trees. They were denuded now but would burst into beautiful colour again in the spring. To one side I could see a forgotten greenhouse which once might have been the hub of garden activity but now lay forgotten as the residents accepted advancing limitations.

Inside his room, I could imagine a teenage boy fitting right in. In some ways, it looked a lot like mine had. There were still posters on the walls showing films and athletes. They were faded now, the eternal sunlight washing the sharp colours away. It was like looking at a moment frozen in time. That his mother still hoped he might come home saddened me greatly. He might live through what was to come, but the only place he would go would be a prison cell.

'May I?' I pointed to shelves containing books and photograph albums.

'Of course, please.'

With Mrs Marlowe's permission, I entered what felt like a shrine to person long dead, put Bull on the floor to join Dozer as he scampered about looking for forgotten snacks under the bed, and began to poke about. Dad joined me, neither knowing what we might be looking for and both hoping one of us might find it.

'How old was he when he left home?' I enquired over my shoulder.

'Eighteen,' she replied. 'It was May 18th. I'll never forget it. I came home from church angry with him because he'd refused to attend the service again. He used to be a choirboy, you know. He was outside the house wearing a large backpack. We could see he was leaving. He and Fred got into a fight. Nothing physical,' she added quickly. 'Fred would never hurt his son, but he screamed at us for stifling him and he rode off on that big dangerous bike. I've never seen him since.'

The pain in her words was heart-breaking.

Dad nudged my arm. 'Look at this, son.'

He had a photograph album in his hands; the third or fourth he'd looked through, but I knew instantly which picture he wanted me to look at. On the right-hand page was a shot of Evan leaning against his bike, but it wasn't the man or the machine which drew my eyes, it was the background behind him.

'Where was this taken?' I begged Margaret. Her son looked young in the shot, barely at an age where he would need to shave and if the picture were in an album in the house then it must have been taken before he left home.

Margaret left the doorway to come into the room, taking the album from my father's hands so she could bring it into focus. 'Oh, that's Potter's Hollow. It's down on the coast on the way to Reculver.'

I shot a questioning look at dad; I'd never heard of it. From the look on his face, he hadn't either. 'Is it well known?' he asked.

Margaret tilted her head, thinking. 'Only by the locals, I suppose. I've never thought about it. Might be that not that many locals know about it either.'

'How big is it?' I asked, moving around so I was next to her and looking at the photograph the right way up again. Evan and his bike were in a large cave. He had to be near the entrance because of the level of light in the picture; I could see it fading into the cave as it went deeper.

'I'm not sure, love. I've never been there myself. I remember kids playing there when I was a little girl. A long time ago that was,' she chuckled. 'They used it as a shelter during the war too. Not an official one, mind, but locals went there if they didn't feel safe in their houses.'

It was big enough to hide families in. We were going there next but what was I going to find?

We found Big Ben asleep in his car right where we left him. He'd chosen to swivel around in his seat so his gargantuan legs were across the transmission tunnel and on the passenger seat. He looked comfortable enough but leaving him to rest wasn't an option, so I opened the driver's door and caught him when he fell out backwards with a squeal of fright.

'You utter dick,' he growled as I chuckled. Then he slapped my hands away. 'Get off me, I can manage.' He performed a crunch to get upright again before drawing his legs back to his own side of the car. Rubbing his face with both hands, he asked, 'Was it worth the trip?'

A wry smile made its way to my lips. 'What if I told you his favourite movie is *Werewolves on Wheels*?'

He pursed his lips. 'That might explain a few things.'

'What if I then told you there's a large cave near Herne Bay that most people probably don't know about. I think that's where the Howlers have been vanishing to. The other night when they tried to run me off the road, the police chased them but lost them even with the use of a helicopter. CI Brite lied about them vanishing by the pier, it was somewhere else entirely.'

'So you were right about him too,' observed my father, settling into the back seat with the dogs who then chose to climb on his lap.

I couldn't argue. 'It's starting to look that way.'

Big Ben asked, 'Anything else?'

'He joined the Whitstable Riders when he was a teenager. He would have known Moose; they are about the same age, and I think Moose went to America with him. Moose has a picture on his wall with him on a bike and Mount Rushmore as the backdrop. He's in his twenties in the picture. If I make a leap to connect the dots, I think they fell out about something and Evan is back from the wilderness, so to speak, looking for revenge.'

My father and Big Ben were silent for a minute while they ran it through their heads. Dad was the first to shake his head. 'I get the bit about Evan wanting revenge. I can make that fit, but why would the rest of the Howlers join in?'

'Exactly,' echoed Big Ben. 'I could understand them being willing to help a buddy out but murdering three people is too much.'

'Which is why we need to check out Potter's Hollow.

Potter's Hollow. Sunday, December 18th 1241hrs

MARGARET SAID IT WAS on the way from Herne Bay to Reculver but in my excitement to get there; it didn't occur to me to ask how to find it. I knew from two nights ago that the police chased the Howlers into Herne Bay before losing them, so it couldn't be far from the town itself. However, I could imagine them turning off their lights and proceeding on dark lanes all but invisible to the helicopter above.

We had a rough idea where to find it, but there were no signposts for it that we could find. All three of us were looking out the windows, scanning around for anything that could contain a cave and be accessible on a bike.

When nothing presented itself, I found someone to ask, picking an old chap out walking his dog. His dog, a bull terrier with an attitude, tried to eat me as I approached, but I got lucky first time.

'Potter's Hollow, you say? I haven't heard anyone talk about that place in .... Ooh must be decades. I remember going there to avoid the doodlebugs in 1944. I were only a lad at the time, but mum used to pack a picnic during the day in readiness and the whole family would traipse down there before it got dark.'

I waited politely for him to finish reminiscing while silently wishing he would. Finally, I got to ask the most important question. 'How do I get to it, please?'

'Oh?' The man looked about, raising his arm uncertainly as he looked for a direction to send me. 'Oh, I'm not sure you can even get to it now. I think it was boarded up years ago for public safety. I believed him one hundred percent but that just made it even more likely the Howlers were using it as a base. 'Err, you get to it on foot via Bishopstone Lane. Now, you are already on Reculver Road, so all you need do is ...' The old man went into giving directions mode and yet again, I waited politely and patiently for him to give me a turning by turning break down of how to find the road I wanted. I was just going to use the GPS in Big Ben's car, but I didn't say that.

Finally, back in Big Ben's car, I got him to drive onward. We were already pointing in the right direction and it was less than half a mile before we found Bishopstone Lane. Big Ben spotted the street's name on the side of a house before I could even load it into the car's satnav.

'The gentleman said that once we are in Bishopstone Lane we will see the path leading over the headland,' I told them. There wasn't a path though. The path he remembered would have been well-beaten, but it was long forgotten and so completely grown over that we couldn't even find it. There were houses on the coastal side of the lane, but facing inland, nothing but green.

I took the dogs. 'Let's spread out and see what we can find. If the Howlers are riding their bikes to it, there has to be a path.'

Dad went left, I went right, and Big Ben jumped straight over the fence. An explosion of swearing followed. Backtracking ten yards to see what might have befallen my friend, his head popped back over the fence. 'Shopping trolley,' he explained. 'Kids must have thrown it over. There's several of them.'

The other side of the fence was a breeding ground for litter and people's waste. In one glance I saw old TV sets, vacuum cleaners, and rusty bicycles. It was a depressing sight. Using my hand for leverage, Big Ben managed to extricate himself. Then he set off, ploughing through the undergrowth, which thankfully in December, wasn't very high.

My father found the path about twenty minutes later. I'd worked my way around to the next street without finding anything and was on my way back when he called my phone. 'I've got a secret entrance,' he growled like a villain in a kid's play.

I saw what he meant when I got to him. By then, Big Ben had already arrived, and the pair were messing around with the fence panels. Bishopstone Lane is a long road right at the end of the seaside town. It links several roads with houses as it heads east and then ends some seventy yards beyond the last one. It was odd that the lane extended that far beyond the last road and it seemed to lead to nowhere. It did lead somewhere though, and we were about to find out where that was. The fence had been fitted with new hinges, so it acted like a gate but didn't look like one.

'I spotted the tyre marks,' dad pointed out. On the fence, at about knee height were tyre marks where the Howlers must have approached the gate at speed and used the tyres to knock it open. The hinges were sprung to always swing shut again. Running from the police, they escaped in the dark along a lane at the edge of the town and then across the unlit coastline. All around us the undergrowth was growing out of control but leading away across the land to the east was a path where multiple tyres over multiple trips had created a furrow.

We had found their lair.

'Take a look?' asked Big Ben.

'Carefully, yes. I have a feeling that whatever this is all about is hidden in the cave at the end of this path. We cannot afford to get caught now.'

Big Ben sucked air through his teeth as he looked about. 'There's not exactly a lot of hiding places here, Tempest.' He wasn't wrong. The land, while undulating, was featureless and open. On our bellies, wearing camouflaged clothes, we could hide easily enough. In office-wear selected for visiting little old people after church, we might as well be wearing neon.

My dad started walking, purposeful strides drawing him over the ground, spinning about to walk backwards, he waved us on. 'Let's get it done and hope there's no one home. I'm getting hungry.'

Following the track through the underbrush required no skill; the bikes had formed a path a meter wide and it was a straight line with no bisecting routes we might have to flip a coin about taking. We found dead ground after a few hundred yards, the land sweeping down and then back up as the coastline gradually rose from the sea. Three miles ahead of us, the cliffs at Reculver were visible, jutting from the sea like the white cliffs of Dover a few miles away.

At the crest of the next hill, I spied what looked like a wire-mesh fence in the distance, like the kind they put fake electrical shock signs on to keep people away. As we drew nearer, I could see the angled uprights. They would have barbed wired on them even though we were still too far away for me to be able to see it.

'Do we need to approach stealthily in case there's a sentry?' asked my dad.

Big Ben shook his head. 'If there is someone watching, then we are already in sight and they will have spotted us. If we start acting like we are doing anything other than going for a countryside walk, we will tip them off.'

I agreed. 'If we are really lucky, there is no one there and we can have a look around. If there is someone there, all we need to do is spot them. Then we come back later when it is dark, and we have prepared. We shouldn't even need to get too close this time.'

'You think that's it?' asked Big Ben. 'It looks like nothing.' He was right. There was a hump of rock behind the fence, but we could all see the same scrubby grass going up the slope facing us.

'Yeah, I think that's it. We'll know soon enough, but I don't see anything else around here that could be the entrance to a big cave.'

Dad squinted at the fence which was becoming clearer with every step. 'Where's the cave though? That small hillock doesn't look big enough for it to be in.'

He was right; the land ahead wasn't flat, but it wasn't very lumpy either. However, we were maybe a hundred and fifty feet or more above sea level, which gave plenty of room for there to be a cave going down.

Sure enough, drawing ever closer and still seeing no movement, we could all see the absence of ground beyond the fence.

Big Ben stopped to listen. Out here in the open, where there was no sound but the wind, chatter coming from behind the fence or any non-natural noise would be detectable. Dad and I stopped too, but only for a second.

'It's deserted,' Big Ben announced.

Hoping this hadn't been a red herring or that the Howlers had been using this as a base but had already moved on, we looked for a way in. Just like the fence back at the end of Bishopstone Lane, the Howlers had modified a portion of the fence to allow easy access. Finding it was easy too because all we had to do was follow the tyre marks. They went right up to the fence and then carried on, vanishing on the other side as the land dipped away.

Kent is a big ball of chalk.

I've heard it described like that many times and the statement held true. Everywhere you wish to dig in the county, you will find chalk. Bluebell Hill, right next to where I live, in fact visible from my garden, has lines of white running across it where the chalk shows through the foliage. The cave wasn't chalk though. There was chalk in it, but the cathedral-sized natural hole was formed out of ancient rock. Covering the entrance were sheets of corrugated steel erected on a frame, yet again, to keep people out. I guess the area was considered unsafe like the old man with the aggressive dog said.

Approaching cautiously, we followed the tyre marks right up to the sheets of wriggly steel. Where they continued on as if the wall was a hologram, Big Ben listened with his ear against a gap, gave a thumbs up, and pushed. The steel panel gave way, just like the two fences and we were inside their lair.

It was dark inside, and it stunk.

There were bunks for sleeping on, a portable generator sitting idle and quiet next to several jerry cans, and fold out chairs strewn around a pit they'd used for a fire. Beer cans were mounded in a corner where rubbish sacks held takeaway cartons and other food wrappers. Then I saw something that caught my eye.

Huffing out a breath, I opened the camera app on my phone and began to film. Pinned to the side of a bunk was a jacket. It was one of the Rider's jackets and I found another one and then yet another shortly afterwards. With the lights on, I would have spotted them instantly, but it was like Moose said; the Howlers took them as trophies. I filmed it all in silence but didn't touch them. They might have DNA that could be tied to the killers and I did not want to add mine to it.

'There are footprints here, Tempest,' Big Ben called across the cavern, his shout echoing loudly. There were lights above our heads to be powered by the portable generator. Without them on, it was dark inside, so we were using our phones for light. Dad didn't have a phone, so he was watching the door and keeping hold of the dogs.

I went over to see what Big Ben had found but he told me before I got there. 'These are women's footprints,' he pointed. 'Dainty feet in ballet pumps or that kind of shoe. But these,' he pointed again. 'Are kids.'

I joined him, adding the light from the torch on my phone to better illuminate the sight. The floor of the cave was a fine, dusty dirt, the footprints reminded me of those left on the moon.

'There are lots of them,' he told me. 'All different sizes and they go in a line through the cave heading back into the dark.'

'Do they come out again?'

'Yeah. There's a separate line just over there. I'm not Navajo or anything but this looks like families to me. Going into the cave in a controlled line and then coming back out again.'

He didn't ask why because we both suspected the same thing. Without exchanging words, we followed the footprints into the darkness. Fifty yards back, much further than light could penetrate and where the lights near the entrance would be little more than a dim glow, we found where the families had been. We also found the source of the smell – you can't have people without a toilet, and I hadn't spotted one on our way in.

'Boys!'

My father shouting got our attention quickly. Neither of us could see him from where we were, but we didn't bother calling out to ask what he wanted: he could only be calling for one reason and we soon heard it too. The rumbling roar of large-engined motorcycles, and it was coming close very quickly.

We weren't going to be able to get out.

Trapped. Sunday, December 18th 1432hrs

I SPRINTED BACK THE way we had come with Big Ben hard on my heels. Despite his size, he could move fast when he needed to. The thin shafts of light coming around and between the sheets of corrugated steel did nothing to illuminate the front end of the cavern, so we almost bumped into my dad as he came running toward us.

His voice an urgent whisper, he hissed, 'Too late. They're about to come through the gate. I just didn't get enough warning. Where were you?'

'No time, dad. Ben, kill your light. Let's see what they do. How many are there, dad?' I was hurrying deeper into the cavern again, using the natural darkness there to envelop us. If we stayed still, and quiet, and they didn't venture back there for any reason, we could expect to stay hidden. I was hoping they were back to collect something and would leave again soon.

That wasn't to be.

I counted us lucky when we saw that it was only four of them. They roared into the cavern, the front rider pushing the door open with his front wheel and then holding it open for the others to go around him. It was a practised manoeuvre that required no conversation.

In my arms, Bull was going nuts, growling and wriggling as he tried to get free. He wanted to bark at the new people the same way he would anywhere else.

Big Ben was having the same fight with Dozer, both of us trying to keep the dogs calm without smothering their faces.

The door swung shut and the engines turned off, blissful silence returning after the deafening sound in such a confined space. I held my breath and spoke quietly into Bull's ear, urging him to be calm. Mercifully, both he and his brother resorted to wagging their tails.

A moment later the portable generator sprang into life, casting light down onto the four men from the naked bulbs strung above. The lights were only in that area and the glow that illuminated them failed to penetrate the deeper sections of the cave.

'I should have stopped for lunch,' grumbled dad. 'If my stomach makes any more noise, they are going to hear it.'

I shushed him. The men were talking but the same generator noise that made it unlikely they would hear us, created the same issue for us as I tried to eavesdrop on their conversation.

Gritting my teeth, I handed Bull to my dad. 'I'm going to try to get close enough to hear what is being said,' I whispered, Big Ben and my dad crowding their heads together so they would hear me.

'There's only four of them,' dad pointed out. 'The three of us can take them with the element of surprise.'

Big Ben liked that idea. 'It's better than waiting for more to arrive and then finding we really are trapped.'

I blew out a frustrated breath. They were right, but once we had done that, the Howlers would know their secret lair was compromised. They could be gone in hours, dropping everything, and escaping. Then they would set up their operation elsewhere and begin a new reign of terror in a new town.

'Can you give me a few minutes?' I begged. 'I want to catch these guys. We are so close now.'

Big Ben put a hand on my shoulder. 'Alright, but ten minutes, dude. Ten minutes and then I'm busting out of here and stealing their bikes to get away.'

'Agreed.' I could do nothing but.

Trashing my clothes, I got on the dirt and started to crawl forward. I was going to have to get really close if I wanted to hear them. Sneaking up on people in the dark was a skill I learned not in the army but in the boy scouts. Playing games at night, I discovered a natural ability to be where people wouldn't look. Small movements, no noise, and using the natural shadows to remain invisible had seemed obvious back then even though none of my early teenage friends thought to employ the same tactics.

Over the next five minutes I got to within ten yards of them and by then I could hear every word they said. Knowing Big Ben would be itching to attack and counting down the ten minutes he allowed me, I stilled my breathing, heavy from the effort of crawling forty yards, and listened.

'You think they'll have more women this time?' said one voice. His timbre was that of a young man. I mentally labelled him as Dickhead Number One.

'There were loads of women last time,' argued another. He had a rough voice that sounded like he smoked too many cigars. In my head, he became Death Breath.

The first voice replied, 'No. I mean nice women. Young women. Not middle-aged mums. Who wants to bother themselves with middle-aged mums?'

I couldn't see their faces; they were below the lights but if I raised my head to look at them, I risked being seen myself. Of the four men I'd seen, only two were currently talking, but then a third spoke up.

'I'm hungry. What've we got to eat?' I called him Hungry Boy.

Dickhead Numero Uno snorted a laugh. 'Nothing much worthwhile. There's some biscuits and crisps and few cans of beer left. Lynx wanted the supplies run down so we're ready to move if we have to.'

'I'm hungry too,' said Death Breath. 'You want to run into town and get something?'

Hungry Boy whined, 'We've only just got back.'

'Are you hungry or not?' asked Death Breath, talking down to the other man as if he had position and right to do so. When he got no answer, he said, 'You're only going to get hungrier and we will be working half the night bringing in the new refugees.'

'Refugees!' laughed Dickhead. 'You make it sound like we are doing them a favour.'

'We are doing them a favour,' argued Death Breath. 'They would never get into this country without us. Admittedly, we lie to them that they will be free to go and sell them into sweat shops where they have to work off their debt. But we do get them into the UK. It's a sweet deal: they get what they want, and we get paid up front by them and then by the guys running the sweatshops.'

Dickhead laughed again. 'It sure is lucrative. That Lynx ... I tell you: He is the man. Do you know how many we have tonight?'

'No. Lynx will let us know when he gets back. All I know is they are coming at seven,' said Death Breath.

'I'm still hungry,' whined Hungry Boy again.

'Then go to the chip shop,' growled Death Breath. 'Make yourself popular and get enough for everyone. The rest of the gang will be back soon. We need to get ready for the next shipment.'

I lapped up all the information, wishing I were able to record it. My phone was in my pocket and I was too close to attempt to get it out now. It wouldn't matter, I could get out of here soon and bring the police down on them like a ton of bricks. The Howlers were trafficking people and making money doing it. They were not the first and wouldn't be the last, but they had to be stopped. England was such a hallowed ground for so many Europeans. In the last twenty years, millions had flooded in our direction from former Soviet Bloc countries. All eager to taste the freedoms and opportunities they believed our nation offered.

Most made it to France but found themselves stuck at one of the ports, unable to get any further because the natural water way was too wide to cross. Hundreds die each year attempting to do so, most vanishing without a trace and no one even knowing they were gone. It sounded like the Howlers were targeting any of them who had money and taking it from them in exchange for passage. What this had to do with the Whitstable Riders I could not yet fathom, but that was something I could work out later.

My time was almost up, and Big Ben was going to attack at any moment. If he just waited, he would have better odds because at least one of them was about to leave.

Hungry Boy stopped whining. 'Okay, yeah. I think I will. I'll get fish suppers for everyone.'

'I don't like fish,' moaned Dickhead. 'Get me a pie. Or maybe a battered sausage.'

'I want mushy peas,' grumbled Death Breath.

'This is getting too complicated,' said Hungry Boy, his whiny tone back.

Dickhead grunted, 'Good grief. I'll go with you. It'll be easier than listening to your pitiful complaints.'

'Hey,' whined Hungry Boy.

They continued to bicker like school children, but they were packing up and leaving. I hoped Big Ben could see them. Another minute passed and he still hadn't clobbered anyone so I guessed he must have chosen to wait. Then, as Dickhead and Hungry Boy left, a shaft of daylight flashing across the cavern as they took their bikes back outside, I heard the sound of snoring.

The fourth person, I guessed, the one who I hadn't heard speak, had gone to sleep on one of the bunks. That just left Death Breath to deal with. We couldn't dawdle; the gang were expected back, and we needed to be long gone by the time they got to Bishopstone Lane. As quickly as I could, I carefully began to slide my way back through the dirt.

Ten yards farther into the dark, I got off the ground, and hugging the wall of the cave, I hurried back to find Big Ben and my dad.

They saw me coming, as did the dogs, who wagged their tails like mad things. Mercifully, they didn't bark. 'There's only one left,' I whispered. 'Or two, rather, but one is asleep.'

'What did you hear?' asked dad.

I didn't think we had time for that. 'I'll tell you all about it once we are clear. You take the dogs and we'll clobber them.'

Big Ben nodded his head toward the cave entrance. 'That one's going outside.'

'Looks like he's going for a smoke,' said dad.

It meant there was only one left in the cavern, and he was asleep. Big Ben started toward the door.

I caught his arm. 'Wait, I've got an idea.'

Escape. Sunday, December 18th 1500hrs

WASTING NO TIME, WE hurried as quietly as we could to the door. The sleeping form was on his side facing away from us. Fully dressed, he could be on his feet and ready to fight in a heartbeat, so I left Big Ben standing over him in case he woke up.

Then dad peeked through a crack in the steel panels. He had a dog under each arm, holding them tight because they knew something was occurring and they wanted to be a part of it. Dad looked about, spotting the lone Howler outside and doing his best to point out his rough location.

I was going to rush the man and whack him on the head with a handy rock I liberated from the floor of the cave. The rock would then go next to the sleeping form with some obvious blood on it, so it looked like one had attacked the other. This plan relied upon Death Breath not seeing me as I snuck up on him. Dad was going to cue me in.

He couldn't do it with his hands full of dogs though. He didn't want to speak, not even at whisper volume, there was no sound here, so any noise was amplified by the shape of the cave. Getting frustrated he put Bull down so he could point.

I knew it was the wrong thing to do but couldn't get to him soon enough to stop it happening. Like a wind-up toy with its wheels already spinning, Bull's paws hit the dirt and he was already running, zipping through a gap between the panels to get to the man outside.

Swearing inside my head, I abandoned my neat plan to get him from behind and burst through the door to attack blindly.

Death Breath's eyes were on the tiny dog now barking like mad as he flew across the ground in his direction. 'What the hell?' It was all the Howler had time for because Bull was upon him. Getting ravaged by a Dachshund isn't that bothersome though. They mean well, and they are tough little buggers, but for a large man wearing biker boots, it was little more than the buzzing of flies.

However, with all his focus on the dog bothering his boot-clad ankle, he didn't see me until the last moment and by then it was too late for him to stop me. I could have used the rock, but I couldn't be sure it wouldn't accidentally kill him and felt sure the sleeping man inside had to now be awake. I leapt.

His arms came up to ward off the surprise as I flew toward his head, but I already had hold of his neck by then. Wrapping an arm around his throat so his Adam's apple nestled in the elbow, I swung around his body to land on his back. My weight and inertia pulled him over backward to land on his back with me beneath him. My legs hooked over his waist and he was pinned. The sleeper hold, when performed correctly only takes fifteen to twenty seconds to rob the victim of consciousness.

Death Breath was no different, but with all my limbs employed to keep him down, I couldn't do anything about the over-excited Dachshund who climbed onto my face to lick my nose repeatedly. He was then joined by Dozer as my father came out behind me.

I held on a few seconds more until completely content that the Howler wasn't about to get up again. Only then did I get to deal with my stupid dogs.

'Sorry, kid,' whispered dad. 'I couldn't keep hold of him. He went nuts once his brother was down.'

Big Ben poked his head out from between the steel panels. 'I don't now how, but sleeping beauty is still asleep. You made enough noise to wake the dead.'

Clambering to my feet, I considered our latest problem. 'We need to take this one with us.'

Dad gave me a look. 'Won't that be suspicious?'

'Not as suspicious as leaving him here to tell all his friends I attacked them and know where their base is.'

'Then we need to take his bike as well,' said Big Ben, going back inside.

I got the dogs clipped back to their lead and got ready to go. Big Ben could ride the bike with the Howler on it. The rest of the Howlers would assume he went for a ride or absconded. It didn't matter so long as they didn't assume he'd been kidnapped.

Big Ben re-emerged. 'Small problem,' he grimaced. 'I don't know which bike is his.'

Good point. I patted down Death Breath's pockets, finding keys in his front right trouser pocket where I would keep mine. I tossed them to Big Ben who vanished back inside to appear once more thirty seconds later pushing a large motorcycle.

'You want me to take him?' he asked.

I nodded, grabbing the biker around his shoulder to heft his dead weight off the ground. 'Yeah. Let's get back to your car and hope we can get clear before any of them return. Dad and I will have to take the long way around; there's too great a risk the Howlers might catch us crossing the open ground if we go that way.'

'You're going down to the beach?' Big Ben double checked.

'That's the plan.'

Between the three of us, we wheeled Death Breath's motorcycle away from the cavern, got Big Ben on it and then laid the unconscious Howler over it.

Death Breath chose that moment to come around. 'What the hell?' he asked, lifting his head, and tensing his muscles to get up.

'Hello,' said Big Ben and punched him hard in the side of his skull. Death Breath went floppy again.

I slapped Big Ben on the arm. 'Get going, buddy. We'll meet you back at your car. Stay out of sight.'

He roared off along the path that led back to Bishopstone Lane and into civilisation. On a bike, it would take him only a minute or so to cover the distance. Dad and I were going the long route, setting off at ninety degrees to the direction we wanted to go. This would eat up more time than I wanted it to, but I wasn't going to force my father to run the whole way. We walked quickly and I told him what I had learned. The biggest piece of it was the time. Their next shipment of refugees would arrive at 1900hrs. Knowing that meant I could bring the police, intercept the Howlers, and catch them in the act. It didn't solve the case, not the one I started with anyway. They could all go to jail, but I was supposed to be finding out who killed the Whitstable Riders and why. Everything pointed to Evan Marlowe but suspecting him got me nowhere. I needed to find proof.

Well, I was going to have to hope it all washed out once we took them down and I knew just the man to call to help me achieve that. We were coming through a cutting in the shoreline. Following the land as it contoured downward, we had to look for a safe path, but got lucky and found a signposted coastal walk. It ran along the edge of the cliff, which was only a few yards high at this point, but then a natural gap had been widened to provide a path down to the beach. This would keep us well out of sight until we reached Herne Bay.

Looking down at my phone, I flicked through my recently-called list to find the one I wanted. It started to ring, but before the call was answered, my dad nudged my arm. 'Um, Tempest. We have a small problem.'

I looked up to find a dozen Howlers staring at me.

Small Problem. Sunday, December 18th 1515hrs

As I TWITCHED WITH an instant jolt of adrenalin, I already knew our situation was hopeless. I could turn and run. Against the odds, I might even get away, but my father was in his late sixties and would be caught. I was going nowhere. Fighting didn't seem a good option either. Two against twelve? Terrible odds. We were a mile from anywhere with no hope of backup arriving.

'I think perhaps you should hang up that call,' suggested Evan. None of the Howlers had bothered with their fake glowing contact lenses, clawed gloves, or facial prosthetics, so we were getting to see their faces for the first time. That they were relaxed and happy for that to happen didn't bode well for our future.

I didn't get to hang up the call, the phone was swiped from my hand by a Howler moving in from my right. I expected him to crush it under his boot and was surprised when he chose to lock the screen and pocket it instead.

'What's the plan, Evan?' I asked, doing my best to keep my voice even.

He paced around a little as the Howlers fanned out to surround us. 'They do not know me by that name. I stopped being Evan a long time ago. To my brothers I am Lynx. None of this matters to you now.' He moved his eyes to look at my father. 'I assume this is your dad? I can see a family resemblance. How nice that you are so close. My own father rejected me as soon as I was old enough to think for myself.'

Sensing a glimmer of an opening, I said, 'I know. I spoke with him just a few hours ago. Your mother misses you. I ...'

I didn't get to finish my sentence because Evan darted forward. I saw him tense and move and knew he was going to hit me: mentioning his mother was the wrong way to go. I could have parried the blow, or even turned his attack against him, but in our present company, I doubted that would work out for me.

Instead, I let the punch come and took it on my jaw, riding it to take out most of the power. It gave him the satisfaction he craved, and he stopped at one punch as I prayed he would. Around him, the Howlers bayed for more, but he nodded his head, his eyes focused on something behind me and suddenly all my nerves caught fire as I was tasered from behind.

Twitching spasmodically, I fell to the pebbles on the beach. I couldn't control my muscles and just before I passed out, I saw hands grabbing my dogs. They went into a hessian sack; Bull then Dozer as if they were litter being collected. Beyond them I could see dad twitching on the ground just the same as me.

Then it went dark.

Sing for your Supper. Sunday, December 18th 1645hrs

WHEN I AWOKE, IT was because a bucket of water had been thrown over me. The shock of cold brought me back to a conscious state in the most unpleasant way and now I was freezing cold to boot.

The sound of spluttering a few feet away turned out to be dad who was coughing and choking on the water which must have hit his face as he took a breath. He was half sitting and trying to get his bearings but looking bedraggled and confused.

My hand on his shoulder startled him, but I needed to get him on his feet to face whatever was about to come. 'Get up, dad.'

We were outside somewhere in the countryside. There were trees in every direction, but we were also surrounded, once again, by the Howlers. Using me for support, dad clambered to his feet. I wanted to know where my dogs were, but I doubted they would tell me, and I didn't bother to ask.

'How you doing?' I asked dad once he was upright. I did so at normal volume, ignoring the faces around me.

'He'll be doing much worse soon,' a voice answered for him. It was Evan/Lynx, the name didn't matter; he was the leader of the Howlers and a scumbag I

185

needed to deal with. 'You shouldn't have taken the case, Mr Michaels, and you certainly shouldn't have involved your father. It is an odd thing, is it not, to investigate the paranormal?'

Dad no longer needed me to keep him upright. He'd caught his breath and, like me, was looking about to get his bearings. It was full dark though I had no way of knowing the time. The moon was above us and a cloudless sky made it cold. We'd been stripped of our outer layers leaving just shirt, shoes, and trousers, which were all soaked and offering no protection from the cold. If we were out here long enough, hypothermia might be a problem, but I suspected the Howlers had something more immediate planned.

To answer my captor, I said, 'No stranger than pretending to be a werewolf. Still stuck on a movie you saw as a child?'

'Ah, yes,' Lynx replied calmly. 'You met my parents. Yes, they never did understand. The movie was utter rubbish, of course. The point was the potential it represented. I don't think I'll bother to reveal my master plan; what would be the point? I suppose you could claim that you solved the case, Mr Michaels. You did find our base, and you do know what we are up to. Of course, now you must die, which will help to strengthen our grip of terror.'

Stalling for time as I looked around, I asked, 'Why are you killing the Whitstable Riders. Is it all to do with Moose?'

'That would be a question he should answer, Mr Michaels. Let's just say, he deserved it. He did something no one can ever be forgiven for doing, but my revenge is almost complete. Soon the truth will out, and he will fall under the hands of his own men.'

I didn't have the faintest idea what he was talking about, but there would be no more questions, because a truck was coming.

'Ah, here they are,' shouted Lynx over the noise of its engine.

I had a nasty feeling about what was in the truck, but before my fears could be confirmed, one of the Howlers stabbed my dad.

He'd taken two purpose-filled paces and jabbed him in the arm. As dad yelled out in pain, I got the same treatment from the other side.

Still shouting to be heard, Lynx explained. 'They cannot resist the scent of blood. They've been trained to follow it. I keep them hungry, you see. That way, they are always looking for their next meal.' The truck driver shut the engine off and killed the lights.

I sucked on my lips and tried to still my breathing. My left deltoid hurt like hell where the blade had penetrated the flesh. Dad had the same wound on his right side.

'This is just a little sport,' Lynx announced. 'Something for the guys to bet on. There's a road about two miles from here. It's in that direction,' he pointed directly behind us. 'That's not a clever bluff to give you hope. There really is a road. I just don't think you can make it there.'

The truck driver opened the back door of the truck. We couldn't see what was inside from where we were, but a long, mournful howl chilled my blood. It was joined by another and then more as the pack of wolves inside the van sang for their supper. We were going to have to run and run fast, but it wasn't a tactic that could work. I was willing to bet that the others; Vole, Salmon, and Rattlesnake had all tried to run. Lynx most likely depended on it. Instead, I wanted weapons to fight them off. My pockets, not that there had been much in them, were picked clean. I felt certain dad's would be too, so there were no pocketknives or zippo lighters to hand.

We were in trouble and no mistake.

Lynx wasn't done talking. 'I'm afraid we cannot hang around to watch as we usually do. The kill is always so spectacular. Tonight, we have a fresh shipment coming in; the rest of our brothers will arrive imminently, so we must dash. I will give you both the standard five minutes head start, of course. We'll arrange for your bodies to be found in the morning and the papers will have a field day this time: five victims in little more than a week. There's nothing like having the state do the publicity for you,' he beamed a smile of joy. 'The werewolf thing has been a dream of mine for many years, but to see it work so well ... The illegal immigrants are cowed anyway, but when they see us as supernatural predators, they are so terrified, they will do anything.' Then he chuckled. 'Listen to me. I've gone and done the big reveal anyway.'

'Time, Lynx,' said one of the Howlers standing close to him.

He nodded in understanding. 'Yes, enough chatter. Bring out the traitor.'

I hadn't noticed it, but what I thought was a log just behind where Lynx stood chose that moment to move. Two of the Howlers moved in with knifes, cutting away to reveal a man inside a large canvass sack. They didn't need to stab him; he was already bleeding from multiple wounds.

He fell to his knees. 'Lynx, I'm begging you, just shoot me, man,' the man cried pitifully in a gruff voice. 'Don't feed me to the wolves.' It was the man who called me earlier wanting to escape from the Howlers but unwilling to go to the police.

Lynx looked down at him with a bored expression and then back up at me. 'I believe this is the point where you should all start running.'

I had no idea if he would give us the five minutes or not, but we needed to put distance between us and them, and I wasted no time thinking about it. With my good arm gripping dad's, I spun us around and ran, pulling him along behind me.

As we passed through the Howlers, they all started howling, each man doing his best impression of a wolf. Their eerie wails mixed with the real ones and followed us into the blackness as we ran onward.

Even though I knew it was hopeless, I tried to keep on the same course. With no markers, no reliable view of the stars through the canopy above, and no compass, I knew I was running blind and could easily go around in a circle. The trees were densely packed, spiteful low branches whipping into our faces as we ploughed and stumbled as fast as we could.

The other man, whose name I never got, didn't follow us. I turned to shout to him, but he had already fled in a different direction. Too late now, I pushed his plight from my mind and callously wondered if the wolves might chase him down first and give us more time.

'Tempest!' my father called, grabbing my arm to slow me. 'Tempest, you go, son. I'll climb something here and they will surround me. Maybe that way you can get away and come back with help.'

'Not an option,' I growled and pulled him along after me. I could sense that he was getting tired and slowing already, and when he spoke, his words came out around heaving breaths where I'd forced him to run faster than he was used to.

The sound of howling died away as we forged through the underbrush and over fallen branches. Thorns tore at my clothes, spiking my skin and drawing blood, yet I pushed harder to get away. I wanted to find some ground we could use. I wanted something we could get our backs to. A fallen tree might do it if the trunk were big enough. Backed against the exposed root, we would be able to shut off at least a hundred and eighty degrees of potential attack. Maybe more. That would give us a chance to defend ourselves at least. We would still need something to use as a club, and now that we had some distance between us, it was time to start looking.

'Rocks, dad!' I yelled in desperation. 'We need rocks and sharp sticks and branches we might be able to use as clubs. We are going to get our backs up against something and fight the wolves on one front. We might have to hold them off all night, but I'm not getting eaten and having Frank Decaux lament that I was killed by a werewolf because I wouldn't listen to him.'

I was angry. My situation, and that my father was stuck here with me, was causing rage to rise to the surface. And they had my dogs. Last seen being dumped into a sack, they could have been thrown into a river still inside the sack for all I knew. If the wolves were going to get me, they were going to pay a price first.

Spurred on by my determination, dad was scrambling around on the ground. He yanked something free of the matted weeds and grass and held it up to the light. 'That'll work,' he proclaimed, holding an old wine bottle up to the night sky.

He was right. It could be used as a club or broken to form a stabbing weapon. I found numerous branches that I could heft like a bat or club. But we were short on time and when the distant sound of the truck starting up again, reached my ears, I knew it would be less than a minute before the wolves found us.

'Quick, dad! We need to find something to cut off one angle of attack.' I shouted the words; it wouldn't matter if the wolves heard me, they would be able to smell the blood from miles away. Knowing we might have only seconds to spare, I picked a direction and ran, towing dad along behind me with my good arm, while I clutched a collection of sticks to my side with the other.

A scream of terrible pain away to our left told me the other man had already been caught. Then, as I looked in that direction and not where I was going, the ground went away from beneath my feet and I fell. I had to let go of the sticks and my dad to protect my face as I pitched forward. I hit the ground about eight feet later, dad tumbling after me to land with an outrush of air as he winded himself.

The excited barking/whining of the wolves drove me off the ground. My weapons were lost in the dark, but just as I thought all might be lost, salvation gave me a lifeline. A fallen tree, an oak by the look of it, lay a few yards away. I saw it only because the moon shone through a small gap in the trees at precisely the right moment.

With my jaw set and my teeth clenched, I shouted at myself as much as my father when I grabbed him and started to run again. I had to pull him along, exhaustion, blood loss, injury, lack of food, and more besides all combining to defeat my elder, but we weren't done yet and I could lend him my strength until his returned.

The tree trunk had to be almost ten feet high. Too high for the wolves to jump, and the branches now lying across the ground made climbing easy. 'Go, dad.' I gave him a shove to get him started and glanced back just in time to see a blur whip past where I had fallen.

Dad slipped, lost his grip, and fell backward. I heard his yelp and shot both hands above my head to arrest his downward movement. 'My fingers are half-frozen,' he told me. His feet were still on a branch, and he started climbing again instantly, but I was out of time.

I caught a flash of something as moonlight caught on the eyes of a wolf and I jumped. Nothing else was going to save me, so I leapt as high as I could, grabbed a branch above my head and pulled my feet up. My biggest fear, that dad might fall again, was now out of my ability to prevent as the pack slammed into the tree trunk a few feet below me. With them snarling, growling, and snapping their teeth inches beneath my feet, I clung to the branch and swung to get myself on top of it.

'Good view up here,' joked my dad. He was still out of breath, but he was doing well enough that he could find something funny to say. Finally out of danger, for a moment at least, I took my time climbing up to join him on top of the fallen trunk.

He was right about the view.

The trunk was just high enough that we could see above the undergrowth for the first time. Even in winter, the low-lying bushes that covered the ground beneath the trees were greater than six feet tall and most retained their leaves to create an impenetrable wall of black. Now standing above them, I could see a good distance in each direction. Seeing how cold he looked and the dark stain on his arm where the Howler stabbed him, I did my best to make sure he was okay. I was about as cold as I could get, or so it seemed. Dad had more body fat than me, but the extra thirty years he carried would make the harsh conditions harder to resist.

'How are you holding up, dad?' I asked, grabbing his hands, and rubbing them to keep the blood circulating.

Suddenly animated, dad grabbed my arm – my freshly stabbed one – which drew a yelp of pain as I turned to see what had got him so excited.

'Sorry, kiddo. I just saw headlights.'

'Really?' Lynx said he wasn't lying about the road, but I figured he was lying about not lying. Dad made an arrow with his arm so I could track where he was looking.

Silent for a few seconds while we both squinted into the darkness, he said, 'I'm sure I saw headlights.'

The wolves continued to growl and snarl and look for a way to get to us. So far, they weren't having any luck, but they continued to circle and whether they found a way to climb the tree or not, we were stuck up here with no means of attracting a rescue. The Howlers could go about their business tonight and come to look for our bodies in the morning. When they found us still alive, they weren't going to congratulate us and call it quits.

No matter what, we still needed to escape.

It was an annoying fact that became an urgent requirement a second later, when a scrambling noise coming from the much narrower top end of the fallen tree turned into a wolf climbing onto the upper surface of the trunk.

I gulped involuntarily as another joined it. 'Dad.'

'I see them.'

They were stalking slowly toward us, being careful because the tree was narrower where they were and more rounded to make their footing feel less sure. They growled as they came closer, still thirty yards away but getting more confident as they advanced.

I looked over the side, back down at where we had climbed up. There were no wolves left there now, the message had been passed and they were all coming onto the trunk to corner us.

'Are you ready to run again?' I asked.

Dad shook his head. 'Do I have a choice?'

The wolf at the front chose that moment to start running. The trunk had widened to a width it felt comfortable with and it was in attack mode once more.

Shouting, 'Go!' to my dad, I pulled him over the side with me as the wolves charged. When they reached this end of the trunk, they wouldn't be able to follow; the drop was too great, and they would have to backtrack. At least that was what I told myself as I dropped from branch to branch, bruising myself in my haste to get down to the ground again.

There was a snap of teeth by my head and it came close enough that I felt the heat of its breath. I was close enough to the ground to drop the rest of the way so that was what I did, hoping I wouldn't turn an ankle when I hit the invisible ground below.

Dad lost his footing again and fell the last few feet. I didn't know if he was okay, and there was no time to find out. However, he felt the same urgency as me, getting up and starting to run before I had a chance to say anything.

The wolves wouldn't take long to get back down; they would find a spot and jump so we had to pray dad really had seen headlights and try to stay ahead of the deadly canines chasing us. We weren't dead; that was something, and maybe we would find another fallen tree to climb.

A snarl, all too close to still be on the tree, brought me to a stop. I wheeled around to face the oncoming threat, intending to take it head on and do what I could. It was closer than I expected, and the large blur of movement leapt into the air to get to my face almost before I could get my hands up.

I heard dad shout something as I fell backwards instinctively. The wolf's front paws hit my shoulders just as my rising hands caught its ribs. It snapped at my face, but my backwards motion carried it over my head.

Knowing there would be another on me in a heartbeat, I tried to flip myself up, but something stepped over me and growled. The guttural noise spiked fear into my heart as my panicked brain asked what new level of hell I would have to deal with now.

Then the growling above me stopped. 'Bad dogs!'

I blinked.

Still lying on my back, I scooched to one side so I could look up at the thing standing over me. 'Ben?'

'Did you miss me?' he asked, looking down with his usual daft grin.

One of the wolves must have moved because Big Ben started growling again, a fearsome noise that was enough to make the wolves question their motivation. Still standing over me, he moved one foot and offered a hand down to help me up. Dad was standing right next to us, keeping within Big Ben's circle of protection.

'How are you doing that?' dad asked.

Big Ben stopped growling. 'Easy,' he grinned. 'I am the alpha male. They know better than to mess with me.'

I rolled my eyes, the motion lost in the dark, so I groaned instead. 'You are such an insufferable dick.'

'I can always just leave you to deal with the naughty doggies yourself if you prefer.'

Dad patted Big Ben's enormously muscular shoulder. 'No, that's alright, Ben. I think I'd like to leave here now if it's all the same to you.'

Big Ben reached around to a backpack I hadn't noticed he was wearing. As he pulled it off and flipped the top open, I realised I could smell food. Lunch never happened, nor dinner for that matter, so it was no surprise when my stomach rumbled deeply.

'Come on, pooches,' he called to the wolves. 'Follow Big Ben to his truck for some nice supper. Yes, good doggies.' He was cooing at them and walking backwards so they would follow. Dad and I went ahead of him, not that we knew where we were going. When I asked, he pulled out his keys to make his truck's lights flash.

Now that I had a direction to head in and felt a degree of safety. I had to ask a burning question. 'How in the world did you find us?'

He continued to coo encouragingly to the wolves for a few more seconds before answering, 'Graham was surprisingly informative.'

'Graham?'

'Yes. I believe you called him Death Breath. You do remember that you sent me off on a stolen bike with a Howler folded over the fuel tank? Well, that was Graham. Full name Graham Mark Benson, he had plenty to say once I got him talking and he gave me this piece of woodland as the likely location to find you. When I got here all I had to do was listen for the noise.'

Dad had seen headlights; they were Big Ben's. He'd tracked us down and saved us and now I was never going to hear the end of it.

'Where is Graham now?' I enquired cautiously.

'In the car.' He was, too. Big Ben's giant off road Ford truck had a utility load bed on the back with a solid canopy over the top. Lying on the floor of the load bed, hogtied and looking miserable, was the Howler I'd knocked out earlier this afternoon. The fingers of his right hand were set at unusual angles. I didn't ask, but I felt sure they were the result of refusing to answer Big Ben's questions.

Big Ben opened the load bed, folded down the tail gate, and then yanked Graham out by his feet. 'You'll get to ride on the back seat now,' Big Ben told him. 'Unless you would rather stay in the back with the wolves.' Graham's eyes flared in horror when he saw the pack of wolves emerging from the wood line. Big Ben had been throwing them titbits of kebab meat to draw them onwards. Now, with Graham out of the way he threw the rest of the meat and backpack itself into the load bed and whistled for the wolves to help themselves.

To my great surprise, when we backed out of the way, the pack jumped in. One by one, but quick as a flash, their hunger pushing their natural fear of people to one side as they fell upon the offered feast. Big Ben closed the tailgate as gently as he could and folded down the glass lid to seal the wolves inside.

I counted eight of them. They were responsible for at least three deaths, but that wasn't their fault. They were secure inside Big Ben's truck from which we could deliver them to an appropriate animal welfare organisation or zoo. The police would be able to deal with it.

They were neutralised as a threat and that meant I could focus on the Howlers again. Lynx left me to die and condemned my father alongside me. He also had my dogs and that meant the gloves were off. I was going to take the fight to him, and he really wasn't going to like the way I chose to do that.

The Big Reveal.
Sunday, December
18th 1837hrs

WE LOST A LOT of time getting tasered and chased through the woods. I saw the time on the dashboard clock of Big Ben's car as I leaned through from the back. I'd switched places with dad, putting him in the front with Big Ben so I could be in the back with Graham. I didn't think the Howler would try anything, but I wasn't leaving my dad back there to deal with it if he did.

Graham was tied up with duct tape, Big Ben explaining that he keeps rolls of it everywhere because it fixes everything. Whatever other uses it might have, it was doing a good job of keeping our captured Hell's angel in place. I wanted to gag him as well, but the risk of someone pulling alongside and seeing him was too great.

'Did you search him?' I asked, hoping Big Ben would have found the items I wanted.

He reached across and flipped open a cubby hole between the seats. As we both peered in, he said, 'Is this what you were hoping to see?'

I reached in and took out the items.

Big Ben guessed where I wanted to go next; he and I had been operating side by side for enough years that we were in tune, so all it took was a look and he set off.

It was time to close the case.

Graham had the good sense to stay quiet though he winced occasionally as the car shifted his weight and he squashed the broken fingers he was sitting on. His silence broke when he saw where we were going. 'No, no, no, no, no. You can't take me in there. That's the same as killing me.'

'Nothing will happen,' I assured him.

He shook his head vigorously, his eyes wide as Big Ben stopped the car. We were at the Whitstable Riders clubhouse, waiting outside the gate for Gopher to appear. Big Ben honked his horn to get the attention of those inside.

Faces appeared at the windows in the roller door, hands cupping around their faces to see outside. A rectangle of light appeared to the left as the door opened and it was indeed Gopher, the club's probationary member who came out to let us in. I reached forward to pat dad on his shoulder; even with the heater on full whack, I couldn't stop shivering from the cold which had penetrated my body. Still soaking wet, I needed a complete change of clothes, a hot drink, and something to eat if I could get it. All of that had to happen in a very short space of time and dad had to need it more badly than me.

Gopher came to the driver's window. 'Hey, guys. Back again?' then he caught sight of the Howler on the back seat behind Big Ben and thrust an arm through the gap to get to him. Graham dodged to get away and I slapped Gopher's arm before he could grab him, but the reaction had been instant and instinctual.

'You see!' wailed Graham. 'If you take me in there, they will kill me!'

I understood his concern, but I wasn't going to let anything happen to him, any more than I would have allowed the torture of an enemy combatant in my army days. 'You'll be turned over to the police. Rest assured.'

He didn't believe me, but I could use that to get more out of him.

Big Ben pushed Gopher away with one giant hand. 'Back up, kid.' Then he drove down to his usual spot and parked.

The Riders were coming outside, drawn by Gopher gesticulating and yelling. They wanted to see what the fuss was about and soon spotted Graham trying to shrink away to nothing on the back seat.

As they rushed forward, Big Ben got out and stood in front of Graham's door with his arms folded. The Riders ground to a halt, unwilling to challenge the giant man but all eager to get to the Howler they could see. Then the wolves started snarling and snapping at the Riders through the glass, and the men backed away, the ones nearest the car bumping into those behind who hadn't quite got the message yet.

Moose pushed his way through the Riders, his men parting to let him through. He looked like he was about to demand Big Ben step aside but got me in his face instead.

I held the pair of claw gloves in one hand and the facial prosthetic in the other. Big ben took them from Graham when he searched him. 'Here's your were-wolf!' I shouted so everyone would hear me. 'Nothing but a fancy costume.'

The Riders' faces stared at the items I held with incredulous eyes and no one spoke until a familiar voice cried out in dismay, 'Oh, no! Not again!'

I turned my face just as someone too small to be visible shoved their way through the press of men looking my way. He was too short to see over the heads of the larger men, but when he got to the front, he burst through to gawp at the gloves and mask in disbelief.

Surprised to see him, I asked, 'What are you doing here, Frank?'

His expression switched, his more commonly seen smile returning. 'Looking for you lot. I called Amanda a couple of hours ago to check how you were getting on and she said she hadn't heard from you. We tried calling, but your phone is permanently engaged, so I came looking and this is the first place I tried.' My memory flashed to the call I made earlier. The Howler took my phone and blanked the screen, but he must have omitted to end the call – perhaps he hadn't noticed it – but whatever the case, the person I called was yet to hang up.

That might be a good thing.

Frank's appearance had stalled proceedings. 'We need to get inside,' I wasn't asking anyone for permission. 'My father is hurt. We both need medical supplies, fresh clothes, and a hot drink.'

'Hot toddy?' my father asked hopefully.

Moose didn't move. 'You have one of the Howlers there, Brother Weasel,' Big Ben sniggered at my club name again. 'You need to hand him over and disappear. If they are not werewolves, we'll deal with them ourselves. This is club business now.'

I stepped forward and right into his face, my chest all but touching his as we met eye to eye. The Riders crowded around threateningly but I wasn't backing down. 'You made me an honorary member, Moose. Remember that? I know about the illegal import of flowers,' his eyes twitched with surprise and a ripple of whispers radiated outwards through the press of men. 'The Howlers are into something much worse. They are trafficking people: men, women, and children and a new shipment of them is going to arrive any minute. This gang,' I chose the word deliberately and looked around to make eye contact with as many of the Riders as I could, 'is going to help me stop them. Tonight, you ride for decency and humanity. Tonight, you save lives and rescue innocents. You will help me defeat them and I will hand them over to the police.' The unspoken threat that I would reveal what I knew hung heavy in the air.

No one said anything for what felt like an eternity as I stared at Moose and he stared back.

I waited for him to open his mouth to start speaking and cut him off swiftly the moment he did. 'The leader of the Howlers is a man called Evan Marlowe.' I got another ripple of whispers, this one was mostly questions, though, as most of the Riders had no idea who Evan Marlowe was, and it was then that I worked it out.

Moose panicked. Just for a second, he looked like he wanted to bolt, and the answer came to me. When I first saw the name Evan Marlowe, it rang a bell deep inside my head and I hadn't been able to work out where I knew it from until now.

Without breaking eye contact with Moose, I nodded my head. I was nodding at myself, agreeing with the image I held there. Around me, some of the older Riders, those around Moose's age or older were telling the younger men who Evan Marlowe was.

When I next spoke, I had the full attention of the entire gang. 'He also goes by the name Lynx, which he was given when he joined the Riders. Isn't that right, Moose?'

Moose swallowed. 'This is all old history,' he argued, finding some gumption at last. 'If it is Lynx leading the Howlers as you claim, then he's about to get a taste of his own medicine.'

'He's the name on the wall, isn't he?' I stated. 'The one that's been mostly burnt out. He was the president of the club before you. What happened to him? What happened between the two of you?'

'It's all in the past,' Moose tried to push past the question.

It was Bear who spoke next, 'No it isn't Moose. It's right here with us now. Three of our brothers have died. I want to know why.'

Moose roared. 'I said it's in the past!'

Bear folded his arms and stood his ground, forcing Moose to deal with him. 'When this is done, Moose, the club are going to take a vote and we shall see who leads the Riders then.'

It was an open challenge and it started a lot of argument, as advocates of Moose shouted their support for him, and others got behind Bear. As the two men got into each other's faces, Big Ben opened the driver's door of his car and leaned on the horn.

The loud blaring noise cut through the night, drowning out everyone's voice. When they fell silent, unable to make themselves heard, he released it. In a loud voice, he growled, 'Alright, cupcakes. You can debate leadership later. Right now, you have two injured men who require your attention, and an enemy fortress to storm. Are you going to ride like Hell's Angels? Or fanny about debating club politics?'

His words were like a slap to the face to all the Riders, but it was Moose who recovered the swiftest, grasping the opportunity to snap out some orders. 'Bear, Elk, Muskox, make sure the bikes are all fully fuelled. Gator, Puma, get that Howler inside. Don't hurt him, okay? I mean it. We'll do this Brother Weasel's way. Cuff him to the pipes in the boiler room and leave him there.' Moose looked about for someone else to point his finger at. 'Chicken Hawk, take Viper and Catfish, grab the first aid kit and find these men some dry clothes to wear. And Turkey,' Big Ben punched the air in a silent cheer, 'get the kettle on.'

Everyone started moving instantly. Whichever side of the divide they fell on, tonight was a chance to be a Hell's Angel and ride into battle alongside their brothers. They were putting their differences aside to focus on what needed to be done. I didn't know how tonight would go, but I had a fair idea about how it might all end.

Then, just as I got inside and finally felt some warmth on my face, Frank threw me a curve ball.

'I think the League are going to raid the wolf pack tonight, Tempest,' he whispered quietly. 'I lost contact with them a while ago; I think they went into radio silence which they would do if they were planning something big.'

I drew in a sharp breath as I considered the ramifications of the KLoD turning up with live guns. 'Are they being led by that idiot Brite?'

Frank nodded glumly. 'Are you sure they're not werewolves?' he begged.

I put my hand on his shoulder. 'Frank, I love that you want to believe in all this paranormal nonsense, but I have one of them in Big Ben's car and there's a moon outside shining down on him.' Frank jinked his head to look out of the window to the car outside. Graham's still-bound form was on the backseat where we left it. He looked scared still, but he didn't look like a werewolf.

'He might be able to control the change?' Frank tried feebly.

'Come on, Frank.' I put an arm around his shoulders and walked him across to the Riders' bar area where dad was already getting changed and did indeed have a hot toddy on the go. Catching a whiff of the warm whisky honey and lemon juice concoction, I snagged one myself from Brother Turkey as he handed them out.

'How do I look?' asked dad, looking around for a mirror.

The Riders had dug around to find spare clothes, boots, and gloves so now my dad looked like one of them. On his legs were a pair of faded, dark denim jeans and a set of leather chaps with frills down the outer leg seam. He had a white t-shirt with some black oil marks on it and a denim jacket with a second leather jacket over the top.

I wanted to say that he looked damned ridiculous, but I wasn't in the right company to have such an opinion. Also, they had a complete set of clothing for me to change into and I was about to look just the same as him.

'You look great,' said Moose. 'But if you are going to look like us and ride like us, you need to be one of us. Your son is already an honorary member, what do you say, Brother Grey Fox?'

'Grey Fox?' echoed dad, cutting his eyes upward to catch a glimpse of his almost white hair. 'I kinda like that.' It was a lot better than weasel, that was for sure.

'What about me?' asked Frank. 'I'm coming too.'

I grabbed Frank's arm and pulled him to one side out of the Riders' earshot. 'What are you doing, Frank? I have to go. I must see this madness ends, plus there are people to rescue. Without Big Ben and me there, the two gangs might kill each other but it's the innocents I am worried about. Brite is preventing the local police from coming to the rescue and the KLoD might turn up with the weapons you gave them.'

'That's why I must come, Tempest. If the Howlers really aren't werewolves, someone has to stop the League from attacking them. They won't listen to you, but they know me. They see me as legitimate.'

I grimaced because I knew he was right. With an exasperated breath, I shook my head; Frank was as brave as he was crazy. 'Okay, Frank. Go and get re-christened with whatever daft name they have for you.'

Expecting Moose to name him Mouse or Rat or something equally suited to his small stature, I almost spat out my teeth when Moose introduced the club to Brother Grizzly.

I blurted, 'What? He gets to be Grizzly, my father is Grey Fox, but I get to be a weasel? What the hell man?'

Dad took a glug of his hot toddy with a satisfied smirk.

'Me next,' volunteered Big Ben. 'I'm coming too. You all know I can fight.'

Moose narrowed his eyes in thought, sizing Big Ben up as he considered what name might suit him. I waited and held my breath, praying Moose would go with Chipmunk or Blue Jay.

I got robbed again.

'Brother Sasquatch!' Moose announced triumphantly to a roar of respect from the Riders.

Big Ben raised one of his enormous fists into the air as he accepted the glorious new title. I face palmed.

Then it was time to go and all trace of mirth or silliness evaporated as the Riders mounted their bikes. Two dozen engines roared to life.

Elk handed me two sets of keys. 'Here. These belonged to Rattlesnake and Vole. It's the two bikes in the corner. You can use them tonight.'

It was that or we had to ride pillion behind someone else. I tossed a set to Big Ben who caught them one handed. 'Thanks, Weasel,' he goaded. He had a spare set of his black combat gear and Kevlar vest in his car for occasions such as these and had changed at the same time as dad and me. When he straddled the bike, he made it look tiny and he looked right at home as he kicked it into life and stroked the throttle to make the bike growl.

I clambered onto mine, dad getting on behind me and Frank slid in behind Big Ben. 'Alright there, Weasel?' Big Ben shouted above the noise of the bikes. I was going to have to come up with something ingenious to make him pay. As the Riders began to peel out of the club house, he had one final thing to say. 'Now you know what daily life is like for me.'

I knew it was a mistake, but I said, 'Huh?'

With a cocky grin, he said, 'You've finally got something huge and throbbing between your legs.'

Then he gunned his accelerator and took off before I could respond. I was going to get him. Oh, boy, was I.

Gang Versus Gang. Sunday, December 18th 1953hrs

I PURPOSEFULLY REFUSED TO tell Moose or any of the Riders the location of the Howlers base. There was too much chance they would go hell for leather without a plan. The only instruction they got was to go to Bishopstone Lane.

In spite of myself, I had to admit that riding the bike through the cold night air was exhilarating. I didn't want to enjoy it, I'd never been one for motorbikes and considered them to be little more than two-wheel death traps, but now that I was out on one with the roar of engines around me, an unwanted grin crept onto my face.

The Riders powered through Whitstable and along the coast road to Herne Bay. There were very few people out on the roads, but those who were out stood and gawped at the procession of bikes going by.

In Bishopstone Lane, they slowed to a stop, leaving a gap at the side for me to weave my bike around to the front. Moose was there with Bear, the two of them maintaining an uneasy alliance for the time being.

Moose pulled off his helmet. 'So, come on, Brother Weasel. This clearly isn't it. Where are we going? Where is this lair you promised us?'

I put down the bike's stand and unclipped my helmet. Killing the engine, I said, 'We go the rest of the way on foot.'

With the way things went today, I hadn't had a lot of time to devise a spectacular strategy. We needed to attack a position which had narrow fields of approach and a superior view over the ground it dominated. With more time, I might want to approach from the sea, climb over the top of the hillock on the seaward side of the cave and rappel down into the entrance from above. That wasn't an option, but my concerns about approaching the Howlers' stronghold were based on experience of attacking enemy positions. The Howlers would not have sentries armed with bipod mounted machine guns waiting to lay down suppressing fire. They might not have sentries at all. They also wouldn't have planned and practised drills for repelling an attacking force. If considered like that, a person might just walk up to them, but prudence dictated I assume they would be bright enough to post a look out and that they might very well be armed. My strategy attempted to take advantage of those assumptions.

Since it would be Moose who gave the orders, I convinced him to follow my tactics and had him divide his force into three unequal parts.

The main bulk, with Big Ben, Frank, me, and dad in it, skirted around to the coast so we could approach Potter's Hollow from a direction that could not be seen from the Hollow itself. We could sneak right up to the edge of the fence and only then would we be visible.

A second, smaller force were going to approach from the front. Giving us a ten-minute head start because we had further to go, four of the Riders would walk along the beaten path to approach the Howlers head on. If the Howlers were watching, which I felt confident they would be, it would draw more of them outside of the cave to see who was coming their way. It might even draw them outside of the fence line. Sending just four, the Howlers wouldn't see it as a threat, so while they might grab something to threaten the intruders with, in the dark they wouldn't be able to see who it was until the last moment.

That left the third segment of the club, who were already pushing their heavy bikes across the dark scrubland as fast as they could go. On Moose's signal, they would ride their bikes directly at the Howlers from the other side of the cave. It would draw them out, creating a panic we could use to cover our attack because by then we would be positioned right next to the fence.

It was genius, even if I did say so myself.

Yeah. None of that happened.

Half an hour went by as we hurried along the edge of the coast to get up next to the cave. The four Riders walking directly toward the cavern were invisible to us: black figures on a black night against a black backdrop. The moon shone down but it wasn't enough to illuminate the dark scrubland. So, too, the team pushing their bikes.

If the Howlers spotted the direct approach along the path, there was no sign of it. No one left the cave to challenge them, nothing happened at all until we were in position and ready.

I tapped Moose on the arm, a silent instruction that he should give the order in ten seconds, then I turned to the man next to me, who happened to be my dad, and had him pass word down the line that it was go time.

We were about to attack.

That was when the lights came on.

Instantly blind, I threw my arm up to shield my eyes against a harsh white light so intense I could feel it warming my skin. The Howlers had spotlights on us.

They'd been waiting in ambush!

They knew we were coming!

The sound of shouts and a cry of pain came out of the dark as the Howlers ambushed the team with the bikes. Similar sounds from in front of the cave told me the four Riders approaching head on got the same.

Not only did the Howlers know we were coming, they knew our exact plan. The mole had struck once more and this time they had won completely.

The blinding searchlight went out, leaving a glowing corona in my eyes as I tried to get them to focus. Dark shapes came toward us, but with no night vision, I could see nothing more than indistinct shapes.

Had I wanted to scream a banshee war cry and attack, the ratchetting of multiple weapons being cocked was enough to put me off. All the Riders with me had the good sense to freeze. They were armed but the Howlers had the drop on us.

'Well, well, well, if it isn't Brother Moose,' said Lynx surprising me once again because the facial mask did so little to impede speech. As my eyesight began to adjust, I could see the Howlers were all wearing their facial prosthetics and contact lenses and the effect was as horrifying as ever. Even though I knew it was all fake, my body tensed with terror at the line-up of gun toting werewolves.

Lynx stood a few feet in front of the line of Howlers, a general leading his men. He cast his eyes along the line, stopping when he recognised me. A snort of laughter escaped his nose. 'I thought you to be dead, Tempest Michaels. That you are not is most impressive. Had you shown enough sense to keep running, I would have honoured my offer to let you go. Since you have returned ... well, your fate will be the same as your new friends.'

Big Ben touched my arm. He was crouching behind me to conceal his true size and he was ready. Quite what he or I or anyone could do, I had no idea. We had an almost sheer cliff to our rear and a firing squad to our front. He was ready, though, and that was comforting.

Lynx dragged his attention back to Moose. 'I wondered how I was going to lure you from your hideout. I was beginning to think I would have to set fire to the place. Thank you for saving me the effort. Now perhaps you would be so kind as to die.' The sound of Lynx firing his gun was shockingly sudden and deadly accurate. One moment Moose was standing next to me, the next he was sprawled on the floor by my feet.

He wasn't dead though; Lynx had chosen a gut shot to put the large man down. From the floor, and clearly in pain, he croaked, 'Why?'

To respond to his question, Lynx said, 'Alex, won't you join me?'

With stunned eyes, I watched the probationary member, Gopher, leave the ranks of the Riders and walk to stand beside Lynx. I'd been right from the start and now I knew why the shotgun wound hadn't turned up in the hospital; he was never injured. It was probably a real cartridge Gopher shot, but all he had to do that night was aim wide and have the man pretend to be hurt. We'd been played from the very start and now I was about to find out why.

'You lied to me, Moose,' the young man spat. 'You're not my dad!'

Even with guns on them, a ripple of whispers shot through the Riders.

'I raised you, son. I loved you,' Moose croaked from his position on the ground.

'But he was never yours and you knew it,' argued Lynx calmly. 'Even though she was with you, Cathy loved me, and when you found out she was pregnant you knew it wasn't yours.' Lynx turned his head and raised his voice to address the Riders. 'I was the president of the club, but he killed his wife and framed me for her murder. The club senior council bought the lie and came for me. I had to run for my life. For nineteen years I've been plotting my revenge, Moose, and now you get to watch your whole club be slaughtered while I reclaim my son.' His voice was a crazed rant as he raised his gun again.

The line-up of Howlers all leaned into their guns too, ready to fire on their leader's command.

'We go straight for Lynx,' whispered Big Ben. It was a hopeless tactic but the only one we had.

The first shot hit Lynx high on his right shoulder, a spray of blood shooting from the wound as the bullet exited to the front. It was followed by a trumpet from a traditional hunting horn as if the hounds were on the fox, and the crack of more shots as an attack began.

Seeing a chance, Big Ben exploded into action. He bumped me to get me moving too, but I needed no such nudge. The Howlers were paused in confusion as their leader tumbled forward, dropping his weapon, and yelping in pain. If we were going to get a shot at surviving, this was it.

Big Ben bellowed, 'Riders forever!' as if he were a lifetime member, but it did the trick, girding the bikers into action.

I got to the line of Howlers as they were still trying to work out who they needed to fight. Some of them were shooting into the dark, picking up muzzle flashes from those shooting at them and returning fire. Others had seen us move and were shouting to get their gang members attention. Caught in that split second of indecision, they lost the initiative and that was all we needed.

I launched myself high off the ground. Conscious that bullets were flying around which meant nowhere was safe, I ignored the danger they represented and took out a Howler. He was shooting at something unseen in the dark until both my knees struck his neck. I came down on him like a wrecking ball, riding him to the ground where he stayed unmoving as I rolled off to find another target.

Before I could regain my feet, a body flew over my head - Big Ben had picked a man up and hurled him like a child's toy. As I bounced upright into a crouch, I saw him throw a haymaker that shunted a Howler's head back six feet.

He wasn't someone I needed to worry about; somewhere in the dark were my father and Frank, neither were particularly well-equipped for this.

Frank found me before I found him. 'It's the League!' he yelled excitedly. 'I knew they were planning an attack, but I didn't know they'd found the hideout too. They don't know the werewolves aren't real! I must get word to them.' Then he stood up. In the middle of a firefight, he stood up and cupped his hands to his mouth. 'League of Demonologists, this is Frank Decaux. Call off the attack.'

I kicked his legs out from under him just as a hail of bullets came his way. 'Are you nuts, Frank!' Keeping low, I crawled on my belly to get away. The wide, sweeping scrubland in front of Potter's Hollow had become a kill-box. Bullets were flying in every direction as three different forces all tried to dominate the open ground.

I checked behind to make sure Frank was coming with me, but he was already gone, the crazy little man choosing to go a different way. To my left, perhaps forty or fifty yards away, someone was shouting orders. It sounded like Chief

Inspector Brite which I decided it probably was. He was leading the KLoD in an illegal attack using illegal firearms because he believed in all the supernatural rubbish.

I needed the real police and I needed them now.

Now that I had covered a few yards, the fighting was mostly to my right, which meant I could get off my belly and run in a low crouch. I got about two yards before I found the body of a Rider. It was Elk and he'd been shot in the chest. I checked his pulse, finding it weakened but steady and moved on. Until the fighting stopped, there would be nothing anyone could do to help him.

I was heading for the cavern, expecting to find terrified people there, but as I drew close, two more Howlers appeared, running out of the cave and into the darkness. Both were carrying weapons and wearing their full werewolf gear, but they'd just left the artificially lit area beyond the doors and their night sight wasn't up to scratch yet. As they ran out the gate, I stuck my foot out to trip the first and watched as the man behind tripped over him.

They didn't get time to react or right themselves as I fell upon them with a hard elbow. It hit the neck of the man on top who I then kicked roughly to the side as his companion tried to get up. I don't think he even knew he was being attacked until I punched him in the throat. He gagged and I hit him again. Then a shadow fell over me as the third Howler I hadn't seen came at me with a knife.

Instinctively, I rolled to get my arms and legs facing toward him, but he vanished beneath a blur of motion when someone hit him hard from the side in a perfect rugby tackle.

I didn't wait to see who'd come to my rescue; I rolled again to get to the man still partially trapped beneath my saviour, kicked his knife away, and smacked his head off the ground until he stopped fighting.

'I think I broke my arm,' said my dad, gingerly pulling it out from under the fallen Howler's legs.

The firefight was no more than two minutes old but seeing my dad in one piece and moaning about an insignificant arm injury filled me with joy. I wrapped him in a fast hug as I scanned around for the next threat.

Shouts drew my attention across the open ground and away from the cave as the shooting petered out. One side had won, it seemed. I listened for a moment and heard CI Brite's voice booming loud and clear.

'We must burn all the bodies. Each werewolf can return if the body is not destroyed. Search the area and find any that remain. We cannot afford to let any live.'

I heard shouts of understanding as his team of KLoD idiots fanned out, and more shouts as several men, who might have been Howlers or Riders, tried to protest their non-supernatural nature.

Swearing, I grabbed my dad and headed towards the voices. With the firefight over, a momentary lull in any other background noise allowed me to hear a low buzzing noise. It was coming from out to sea. I turned my head and squinted into the dark. When I could find nothing there to see, I let it go and broke into a jog: there were people to save.

'But I'm not a werewolf!' shouted a man. 'I'm not even one of the Howlers. Check my jacket. I'm a Rider.'

'How hard would it be to switch jackets, eh?' sneered Brite. 'Do you think quickly transforming back to your human form will fool me, or any of us. We are the Kent League of Demonologists and we are charged with a most glorious task.'

Marching into the little clearing where he had four men at gun point, I snarled, 'You're crazier than a cat on LSD,' and punched him right on the nose. As he reeled from the blow and took a stumbling step, I shouted, 'They're just men! You absolute moron. How many men have you killed tonight?'

The four men on their knees wanted to get up but were held in place by other members of the KLoD whose guns were twitching between their prisoners and me.

Brite got his footing. 'Well done, Mr Michaels. You can consider yourself under arrest. You just punched a police officer.'

'You're not a police officer,' I snarled again, advancing on him as my anger drove me forward.

He put his gun right in my face. 'Oh, yes I am, Mr Michaels. I am a police officer and a hero to the League. The beasts we kill tonight will ensure the safety of this county and beyond.'

'They're just men,' I growled, refusing to take my eyes off him or look at the gun.

He chuckled at my foolishness. 'How is it then, that they die when I shoot them with silver, Mr Michaels? Can you explain that?'

'It's a bullet, you brainless idiot! It doesn't matter what it's made of, it will still kill a person if you shoot them with it.' I was raging at him, the only thing stopping me from pushing in his face was the gun he had in mine.

'He's right!' Frank shouted, the bookshop owner finding us in the dark. He was out of breath and bleeding from a cut to his head, but he gulped in a deep lungful of air to blurt, 'He's right, Angus. I've seen it. They're not werewolves. The whole thing is a scam. It's all about smuggling immigrants in from Europe.'

CI Brite frowned and shook his head. 'You must not be thinking right, Frank. That blow to your head has robbed you of your senses.'

The low buzzing noise I'd first heard a minute ago, suddenly became a pair of helicopters as they swooped up and over the cliff. Bright searchlights burst to life, bathing the ground in broad swathes of light.

'Lay down your weapons!' ordered a voice from above.

My head spun in reaction to yet more new sounds as headlights appeared from five different directions. The sound of vehicle engines racing announced the arrival of the cavalry just as much as the voice from above.

'This is the police,' Chief Inspector Quinn's voice boomed from above. 'You are all under arrest, lay down you weapons, or I will give the order to open fire.'

'But I am the police,' screamed Brite as he rejected the order. I was glad because it gave me just what I wanted: an excuse to hit him again. With his attention on the helicopter above, he didn't see me take a meaningful step forward. My knuckles connected with the tip of his upturned chin and he went over backwards like a puppet with its strings cut.

To my right, dad knocked the gun from the unprotesting hand of another KLoD idiot and his remaining colleagues dropped theirs.

I didn't know how he'd managed to find me, but this was one of those very rare occasions when I would be glad to see Chief Inspector Quinn. As his helicopter slowly descended with the intention of landing, the headlights converged on our location.

I was risking things by not staying put: the police wouldn't know one combatant from another, but I needed to check the cave.

I called, 'Come on, dad,' as I set off.

'Really,' he shouted as he started to jog after me. 'We haven't done with running yet?'

'Just one more task,' I promised him.

Frank came too, the three of us arriving at the gates of the cave together. We didn't need to go inside to rescue people though, they were already coming out. The Howlers had left them, running out into the fight, and hadn't returned, so the bravest of those inside plucked up the courage to see if they could escape.

Upon seeing us, they cowered back, looking to get back inside the cave where they were no doubt told to stay. 'It's alright,' I called, then realised they might not speak English and tried French and then German.

Before I could get to the tiny bit of Spanish I knew, one of them said, 'You are not the werewolves?' It was a woman who spoke, a thin child of about three years of age clung to her leg. Her accent was Eastern European though I could be no more accurate than that. She spoke English clearly and confidently.

I held out my hands to show her they were not only just hands and not werewolf paws, but also devoid of any weapons. 'No, we are not with the werewolves. We are here with the police. I believe you are safe now.'

They would most likely be deported, but that would be better than what the Howlers had planned, and they would all be given a chance to state their case. Maybe some would be granted asylum.

The police had plenty of other people to deal with but must have spotted the three of us running away because there were four armed officers heading toward us with their assault rifles up and ready.

I raised my hands. 'Hi, guys,' I called out. I knew they were going to arrest us and make sure we were unarmed but I had a go at reducing the roughness with which they might tackle the task. I got to my knees before they got close enough to give that order. Frank and my father copied me. 'If you could be gentle, chaps. We're the good guys, believe it or not.'

'Don't move,' shouted, the lead cop.

'Already not moving,' I replied jovially.

A shout stopped the four men just before they reached our position. They kept their weapons trained on us even though we couldn't have offered less threat if we tried.

The familiar form of Chief Inspector Quinn emerged from the dark. I smiled at him and lowered my arms back to my sides. 'Good evening, Ian.'

'Mr Michaels,' he replied. 'You have surpassed yourself this time. A firefight in Kent? However do you manage to create these situations?'

I pointed into the darkness beyond the fence. 'You need to get more officers, Ian. You have a lot more people to deal with than you thought.'

The armed officers trained their weapons in the direction I pointed; the torches mounted on them illuminating the sea of faces behind the wire.

It was enough to make Chief Inspector Quinn utter an obscenity, but he recovered quickly, grabbing his lapel microphone to relay messages as he came forward for a better look.

Finally, I could hand this stupid case over to the police.

'Ian, what's the meaning of this?' CI Brite stormed toward me with several of Quinn's officers on his heels. 'Your men have just ruined a delicate sting operation.' He'd recovered from the punch I gave him and was back to his usual indignant self.

'Sorry, sir,' apologised one of Quinn's officers. 'He produced his police identi-fication. Says he's the chief inspector here.'

'And that man just assaulted me,' shouted Brite, jabbing a finger at me.

Quinn cut his eyes at me. 'Is that true? Did you just assault a senior police officer?'

I folded my arms. 'You're damned right I did. In fact, I'm thinking about doing it again right now.' I didn't tell him it might not be Brite that I punched depending on what Quinn's next words were.

Quinn nodded thoughtfully. 'Place him under arrest.'

One of the armed cops took a pace toward me.

'Now hold on a second,' protested my father.

Quinn held up a hand. 'Not him.' He pointed at Brite. 'Him.'

'What?' snapped Brite, his voice incredulous.

Quinn turned around to look at the illegal immigrants again. 'Now, Mr Michaels, how about you do me a favour and tell me what the hell is going on?'

Supper. Sunday, December 18th 2104hrs

As one might expect, we were not allowed to go anywhere. The police did their best to shut off the whole area and round up all the injured. The Howlers, Riders, and KLoD were all arrested. Those who managed to escape serious injury were loaded into police vans and carted away. Paramedics were on hand to deal with those who were injured but their treatment only served as a delay to their incarceration.

The Riders protested their innocence, Bear acting as spokesman for the club when the chief inspector came for him. 'We came here as concerned citizens,' he insisted. He was talking to Chief Inspector Quinn, but not knowing him, Bear didn't know how futile his words would prove. 'We heard about the immigrants being trafficked into the country by the Howlers and tried to stop them. Brother Weasel,' CI Quinn jinked his eyes at me and got a shrug in response, 'said the police here were compromised. I knew it was our civic duty to risk our lives to rescue those people.'

CI Quinn nodded along as Bear demanded his club members be released, saying nothing until the president-in-waiting finished. Then he pounced. 'Illegal importing of taxable goods.'

Bear's eyes flared. 'What?'

'That is what I am arresting you for, Isambard Clover. That is your given name, yes?'

Meekly, Bear nodded his head. 'I'm afraid a piece of evidence came into my possession earlier today which implicates you in the trade of illegally imported goods.' Listening to the chief inspector, I had to wonder how that might have happened. 'It implicates every member of your club, in fact. I have already dispatched officers to search your clubhouse for additional evidence.'

Bear had nothing else to say as they took him away.

The police found Moose when I gave them a direction to look in and they found Lynx too.

Both were dead, their wounds too great to survive.

There were seven other bodies, five of them Howlers, but one was Brother Turkey, depleting the Riders numbers even further. It was now five they'd lost in a week. The other body belonged to a KLoD member who also turned out to be a police officer. Brite had got one of his own killed but I suspected he was going to be charged with multiple counts of murder for leading the attack. This just added to the list of his crimes.

They wouldn't let me go into the compound where the police chose to keep the immigrants because they could be controlled there. I wanted to search for my dogs. The best I could do was beg the officers now inside the compound to have a look for them.

Sick to my stomach with worry, the first bark echoing out from the cave brought a tear to my eye. Moments later a cop emerged holding a crate in both arms. It gleamed like it was brand new, which it was I discovered when they handed it over.

My fear that the Howlers might drop them in a river still in their sack or abandon them in the woods where they dumped my dad and me, was all for naught. They'd done the complete opposite and my dogs had a pair of bowls in the crate along with a new soft bed and they were both wearing little faux leather jackets which had *bad to the bone* made out in little metal studs on the back.

'Found them then?' said Big Ben appearing from the dark.

I hadn't seen him since the police first showed up. 'Where have you been?'

'Handing out cards,' he explained. 'There are girl cops here. Your dad's back at the command tent with some supper for you.' Big Ben carried business cards with him most places he went. Not that they were actually business cards. They advertised his sexual prowess and gave the recipient methods by which to contact him. I doubted anyone else on the planet could get away with it, but for him they worked like a charm.

My stomach gurgled at the mere mention of food. 'Really?'

'He moaned at them until they gave up and went to get him some. Also, your mum knows.'

I hung my head. 'How?'

'Apparently, she got home, and your dad wasn't there so she phoned you.'

'And she couldn't get me,' I surmised, remembering that I still hadn't found my phone.

'That's right. So she phoned the police, the fire brigade, and everyone else and I guess they have up to date data stuff in their mobile command centres because someone told her that you are both here. She's on her way. Your dad looks a little terrified.'

I snorted a tired and desperate laugh. My father and I were in for a butt-kicking. He had bruised abs and a stab wound to his shoulder. He was fine with his injuries. In fact, he would probably totter down to the veterans club and show off his wounds when the local newspapers got hold of the story, but by then he would also have a black eye to show off courtesy of my mother.

Big Ben came with me when I went to look for him. He really did have supper waiting for me. It was only sandwiches from an all-night petrol station, but I fell upon them ravenously.

A paramedic had given him a proper check over and dressed the stab wound to his shoulder more properly than the sticking plaster he got at the Riders clubhouse. Dad was tired but he was okay, and he'd had an incredible weekend; that was how he saw it.

'I'm Grey Fox,' he bragged. 'Just look at my fine clothes.'

Taking a moment from coordinating the efforts of half the planet, Chief Inspector Quinn wandered over to where the three of us were stood. 'I thought you might like your phone back.' He held out his hand which had my phone in it.

I stared down at it. 'How did you end up with it?'

With a tone tinged with boredom, he said, 'An hour ago you asked me how I found you. You called me earlier today, but when I answered, you were not there. I almost hung up, but something about the timing of your call made me wait. So, I waited, and I waited, but there was still no one there and that struck me as unusual for you, Mr Michaels. Unusual enough, in fact, that I decided to track the phone's signal. When I discovered its location and saw that it was in the middle of nowhere, I called Chief Inspector Brite.'

'You couldn't raise him, could you?' I asked, but I said it as a statement.

'I could not,' he admitted. 'I heard rumours that he had a hobby on the side. I didn't realise he was a fanatic.' He had a faraway look for a second but caught himself quickly and flipped his eyebrows. 'Anyway, that was when I chose to believe that I had a problem to attend to. It is a relatively simple equation I have developed you see. There are variables within it, but the fixed integer each time is you. You are my impossible, Mr Michaels. You are the intangible non-linear variable around which the equation functions. In essence, where you go, trouble follows.'

I felt he was being a little harsh, but his tone wasn't resentful or accusing; for the first time ever, it was gentle and caring. CI Quinn was giving me respect.

Honestly, it felt a little weird.

Chief Inspector Quinn's benevolent mood passed in a heartbeat. We both knew he was going to come out of this smelling like roses, but he wasn't about to give me any real credit. 'You've created a terrible mess, Mr Michaels. Whether intentionally or not, I stand by my claim that you should leave this to the professionals. My work is hard enough without amateurs like you getting involved.'

All I could do was laugh and shake my head; I was simply too tired for anything else. 'Ian,' I used his first name because he hated that I even knew it. 'Ian, I hope you never cease to surprise me. This is how you got the evidence on the Riders, isn't it? You got your hands on my phone, looked through it, or more likely, had one of your officers do it for you, and found the video I took last night. Is that even legal?'

He shot me a look, then turned and went back to the things he felt more comfortable doing. A short while later, we had given statements and were free to go. Somehow, despite all the bullets traded tonight, none of us had more than a few bruises and scrapes. Dad and I both had stab wounds from earlier, but all our injuries would heal. Two motorcycle gangs were on their way to jail, one for murder and human trafficking, the other for dealing in illegal flowers. I had to wonder which of them would fare better behind bars – dealing dodgy blooms wouldn't get the Riders much respect. Dad elected to wait for mum to arrive, he would travel home with her and though we joked about how scary she was, it would be the scared and worried version he got tonight. Big Ben, Frank and I caught a lift back to the Riders' clubhouse where we found his car to be devoid of wolves: Quinn dispatched animal control to deal with them the moment we told him about them.

Frank shook my hand before he left in his car; he was despondent about the KLoD. Tonight's arrests would impact the ancient order terribly, he felt. I couldn't care less, but I didn't say that, instead suggesting a new organisation of crazy people would replace them soon enough.

With nothing left that we had to do, I thanked Frank for his help and let Big Ben take me home.

Amanda. Monday, December 19th 1152hrs

SHE'D BEEN DISTANT FOR the last few days. More distant than at any point since I'd met her just a few months ago. I was in love with her, although I knew, somehow, I wasn't supposed to tell her yet. Amanda Harper is beautiful and incredible. She also has big boobies and I knew I wasn't supposed to factor that into the equation, but it just kept popping up in my head whether I wanted it to or not.

I'm a guy. Sue me.

When I got my phone back last night, I had a text message from her to let me know she was taking a personal day. She sent it before the events at Potter's Hollow took place so she knew nothing about the battle last night and I left it that way.

That she didn't want to come to work today was a non-issue; everyone is entitled to a day off and since we regularly work evenings, nights and weekends, the office doesn't have any kind of working hours. However, with the case closed, her message prompted me to investigate why she had been so weird about my taking it.

All it took was a call to Patience and I had my answer. The truth surprised me, not because Amanda chose to hide it from me, but because she felt the need to.

After a lie in to recover from the rigours of the last few days, a slow breakfast, and a leisurely dog walk, I went to the office. There was work waiting on my desk which consisted of several new cases for me to consider. At the top of the pile was the pyromancer Jane felt she didn't have time for. I was intrigued enough to look at it but there was no client yet. All I had was an email address and name provided by Jane for the person who alerted the business to the case. All of it was going to have to wait because I was leaving the office to visit my girlfriend.

I bought flowers and took the fat white envelope full of cash with me. I would need both. Following Patience's advice, I found Amanda at St Matthew's hospital in Borough Green. She was in the Intensive Care Unit, sitting next to a bed where she was reading a book to a man in a coma. The man was in his early thirties and might once have been handsome and muscular but looked gaunt and withered now. I already knew that he had been in his current state for five years.

Waiting in the doorway, I spoke gently as I interrupted her. 'Amanda.'

She looked up, the story trailing off as she stopped reading. 'Patience?'

I nodded. 'Yes. Am I intruding?'

I thought for a moment that she might ask me to leave, but she gave a gentle shake of her head. 'No. Come in, Tempest. I would like you to meet Peter. He's my fiancé.'

The news that Amanda was engaged to be married to another man might have come as a shock if I'd heard it under different circumstances. As it was, any surprise had already been eliminated by Patience. I pulled a chair up next to her and sat down, taking her hand as we both watched the machines monitoring the man's condition.

I knew the story but encouraged her to tell me anyway: we needed to talk. Peter Dutton had been a detective; that was how he and Amanda met. They dated for two years in her mid-twenties, culminating in his proposal at the foot of the Eiffel Tower in Paris. Three days later he was involved in an incident in the line of duty. It left him with damage to his brain, the extent of which could only be determined when he awoke. After five years, it was unlikely he ever would.

The incident took place in Whitstable and though nothing was proven, two members of the Whitstable Riders were arrested and questioned due to their proximity. Peter had been investigating them.

'That's why I got so upset when you took the case,' she admitted quietly. 'I couldn't handle it happening again. All the old memories came flooding back,' she paused, looking at the floor and then at me. 'He doesn't know that I have moved on. For him, if he wakes up, it's still three days after he proposed. It makes me feel terrible whenever I think about it. I waited three years. Three years of loneliness and heartache. I would have waited forever. It was his doctors that convinced me not to. They say he's never coming back. He's in a vegetative state but he's not on life support, other than the feeding tube, and he might go on for years yet.'

I stayed quiet, letting her talk, and hoping there was something cathartic in doing so. She fell silent and neither of us spoke for several minutes. I couldn't think of anything to say, but she rescued me by asking, 'Why don't you tell me about the case?'

Over the next fifteen minutes I took her through the whole adventure, leaving nothing out and giving all the grizzly details. She wanted to see the stab wound on my left shoulder. It was dressed, of course, but I took off my shirt anyway and let her see the rest of me to prove I was still in one piece.

'I heard that you put them all behind bars, but I don't like that you took their money, Tempest.'

I took the envelope from my jacket pocket. 'There must be a charity supporting his treatment,' I said, handing it over. 'There's ten grand in there. I think we should donate it.'

She gave my hand a squeeze. 'You're a good man, Tempest Michaels.' Then she laid her head on my shoulder and we were quiet again.

Back from the Dead. Monday, December 19th 1346hrs

AMANDA WOULD COME TO my house tonight so we could have dinner and talk some more. She still had the outfit from Anne Summers to show me, she'd said with a smile. I could look forward to that.

When I left the hospital, I went home for some lunch and collected the dogs on my way to the office. With Amanda off for the day, and Jane out investigating a case, the office was closed. We don't get many drop-ins so the locked office didn't bother me from a business perspective, and though there was no particular need for me to go there, it was a comforting place to work without the distractions I find at home.

I went in through the back door, flicking the lights on as I went. The dogs scurried and scampered, running with joyful abandon and chasing each other as they followed my feet to the front door where I spotted a shadow outside.

I said, 'Hello,' as I opened the door from the inside. 'Sorry you found the office shut.' The lady outside looked ready to bolt, her eyes wide as if terrified to now be faced by me. I gave her a kindly smile. 'Would you like to come inside? We can just chat if you like.'

'You're the paranormal investigator, aren't you?' she said.

I figured she already knew the answer to that question, but I smiled and said, 'Yes,' backing up a pace and holding the door open so she could come inside. The tactic worked, the prospective client's legs reacting to my body language as they carried her through the doorway and into the office.

'Would you like a coffee?' I asked, heading to the machine. 'I'm getting one.'

She murmured her thanks, but it was clear to me she had something she wanted to discuss and not talking about it was driving her nuts. As there was no one else in the office and we were unlikely to be disturbed, I sat on one of the chairs next to the coffee machine and encouraged her to join me.

'What is it that brings you here today, Mrs ...'

'Moore,' she supplied. 'Monica Moore.' Mrs Moore was in her early forties and wearing it well. Only the crow's feet appearing at the edge of her eyes and few thin lines around her mouth gave any indication of her age. She was short at less than five and a half feet tall, with curly dark brown hair tamed with clips and pulled into a ponytail that hung over her left shoulder to rest at nipple-height.

I waited for her to answer my question, letting my silence prompt her into talking. After fifteen seconds of watching her chew her bottom lip and stare at the carpet tiles, she finally said, 'I think my husband is back from the dead.'

The End

Author Note:

IT'S LATE ON A Monday as I write this author note. I have Avengers: End Game playing on the television, two dachshunds asleep on the couch next to me, and a choice of about six books to write next.

I have been wanting to get back to the Blue Moon series for a while and find myself constantly torn regarding what book to write next. I devised the concept of the Whitstable werewolf pack about eighteen months ago. It was on a day when I was still in full-time employment and had to drive all over the country as part of my job. The hours on the road gave me time to dream up story lines. Originally this was to be Amanda's fourth or fifth book, with her as the lead, but Tempest was long overdue a return as the central character.

You will have seen me cue up the next story, or actually, if you were paying attention, perhaps you saw the start of several stories. The pyromancer is coming, I still need to wrap up Jane's storyline with the Sandman, and I have a dozen other ideas floating around which I need to get onto paper. The next story will be ***Undead Incorporated***. I started it already and plan to supply you with several Blue Moon adventures over the next few months.

In the book I mention glowing contact lenses, which Tempest researches and finds he can buy on the internet. They are a real product if you wanted to get yourself a pair. The film I reference, *Werewolves on Wheels*, is also real. It came out in 1971, though I must admit I have not watched it.

The idea of the president's board came to me because we had them in the army. The guy running the shop got his name on a board in the central area of the building for all to see. With a typical tenure lasting just a couple of years, the boards for a century of leadership often had fifty or more names on them.

Much like my characters, I never seem to get enough sleep, a situation not helped currently by the six-week-old child sleeping next to my wife. I won't complain though; I know how lucky I am. With two small children to keep me entertained and a wife who appears to be content to be stuck with me, I have everything I could ask for in life. Now if this silly virus would go away and the pub the other side of my garden wall would reopen, life would be perfect.

I'll be back with another book soon.

Take care.

Steve Higgs

June 2020

More Books By Steve Higgs

Blue Moon Investigations

Paranormal Nonsense
The Phantom of Barker Mill
Amanda Harper Paranormal Detective
The Klowns of Kent
Dead Pirates of Cawsand
In the Doodoo With Voodoo
The Witches of East Malling
Crop Circles, Cows and Crazy Aliens
Whispers in the Rigging
Bloodlust Blonde – a short story
Paws of the Yeti
Under a Blue Moon – A Paranormal
Detective Origin Story
Night Work
Lord Hale's Monster
The Herne Bay Howlers
Undead Incorporated
The Ghoul of Christmas Past
The Sandman
Jailhouse Golem
Shadow in the Mine
Ghost Writer

Felicity Philips Investigates

To Love and to Perish
Tying the Noose
Aisle Kill Him
A Dress to Die For
Wedding Ceremony Woes

Patricia Fisher Cruise Mysteries

The Missing Sapphire of Zangrabar
The Kidnapped Bride
The Director's Cut
The Couple in Cabin 2124
Doctor Death
Murder on the Dancefloor
Mission for the Maharaja
A Sleuth and her Dachshund in Athens
The Maltese Parrot
No Place Like Home

Patricia Fisher Mystery Adventures

What Sam Knew
Solstice Goat
Recipe for Murder
A Banshee and a Bookshop
Diamonds, Dinner Jackets, and Death
Frozen Vengeance
Mug Shot
The Godmother
Murder is an Artform
Wonderful Weddings and Deadly
Divorces
Dangerous Creatures

Patricia Fisher: Ship's Detective Series

The Ship's Detective
Fitness Can Kill
Death by Pirates
First Dig Two Graves

Albert Smith Culinary Capers

Pork Pie Pandemonium
Bakewell Tart Bludgeoning
Stilton Slaughter
Bedfordshire Clanger Calamity
Death of a Yorkshire Pudding
Cumberland Sausage Shocker
Arbroath Smokie Slaying
Dundee Cake Dispatch
Lancashire Hotpot Peril
Blackpool Rock Bloodshed
Kent Coast Oyster Obliteration
Eton Mess Massacre
Cornish Pasty Conspiracy

Realm of False Gods

Untethered magic
Unleashed Magic
Early Shift
Damaged but Powerful
Demon Bound
Familiar Territory
The Armour of God
Live and Die by Magic
Terrible Secrets

About the Author

At school, the author was mostly disinterested in every subject except creative writing, for which, at age ten, he won his first award. However, calling it his first award suggests that there have been more, which there have not. Accolades may come but, in the meantime, he is having a ball writing mystery stories and crime thrillers and claims to have more than a hundred books forming an unruly queue in his head as they clamour to get out. He lives in the south-east corner of England with a duo of lazy sausage dogs. Surrounded by rolling hills, brooding castles, and vineyards, he doubts he will ever leave, the beer is just too good.

If you are a social media fan, you should copy the link below into your browser to join my very active Facebook group. You'll find a host of friends waiting there, some of whom have been with me from the very start.

My Facebook group get first notification when I publish anything new, plus cover reveals and free short stories, but more than that, they all interact with each other, sharing inside jokes, and answering question.

 facebook.com/stevehiggsauthor

You can also keep updated with my books via my website:

g https://stevehiggsbooks.com/

Printed in Great Britain
by Amazon

35845237R00138